"If all we have to do is sit and wait, why can't we have sex?"

He nearly choked on the banana he'd been munching. "Did you just say what I think I heard?"

She hadn't expected to have to say it again. But she'd made up her mind and she wasn't going to back down. "I want to have sex with you, Michael."

He shifted away from her—clearly establishing both a physical distance and an emotional withdrawal.

"I'm not asking for a relationship or a commitment," she told him. "I just want to forget, for a while, that every minute on this island could be my last. I want to forget that we could both end up dead.

"And the only thing I can think of that would possibly drive those thoughts from my mind is sex. With no strings attached."

Dear Reader,

November is full of excitement—vengeance, murder, international espionage and exploding yachts. Not in real life, of course, but in those stories you love to read from Silhouette Intimate Moments. This month's romantic selections will be the perfect break from those unexpected snowstorms or, if you're like me, overeating at Thanksgiving (my mother challenges me to eat at least half my body weight). Oh, and what better way to forget about how many shopping days are left until the holidays?

Popular author Marilyn Pappano returns to the line with *The Bluest Eyes in Texas* (#1391), in which an embittered hero wants revenge against his parents' murder and only a beautiful private investigator can help him. *In Third Sight* (#1392), the second story in Suzanne McMinn's PAX miniseries, a D.C. cop with a special gift must save an anthropologist from danger and the world from a deadly threat.

You'll love Frances Housden's *Honeymoon with a Stranger* (#1393), the next book in her INTERNATIONAL AFFAIRS miniseries. Here, a design apprentice mistakenly walks into a biological-weapons deal, and as a result, she and a secret agent must pose as a couple. Can they contain their real-life passion as they stop a global menace? Brenda Harlen will excite readers with *Dangerous Passions* (#1394), in which a woman falls in love with her private investigator guardian. When an impostor posing as her protector is sent to kidnap her, she has to trust that her true love will keep her safe.

Have a joyous November and be sure to return next month to Silhouette Intimate Moments, where your thirst for suspense and romance is sure to be satisfied. Happy reading!

Sincerely,

Patience Smith
Associate Senior Editor

Please address questions and book requests to:
Silhouette Reader Service
U.S.: 3010 Walden Ave., P.O. Box 1325, Buffalo, NY 14269
Canadian: P.O. Box 609, Fort Erie, Ont. L2A 5X3

BRENDA HARLEN

Dangerous Passions

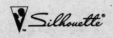

INTIMATE MOMENTS™

Published by Silhouette Books

America's Publisher of Contemporary Romance

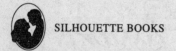 **SILHOUETTE BOOKS**

ISBN 0-373-27464-5

DANGEROUS PASSIONS

Copyright © 2005 by Brenda Harlen

This edition published by arrangement with Harlequin Books S.A.

® and TM are trademarks of Harlequin Books S.A., used under license.
Trademarks indicated with ® are registered in the United States Patent
and Trademark Office, the Canadian Trade Marks Office and in other
countries.

Visit Silhouette Books at www.eHarlequin.com

Printed in U.S.A.

Books by Brenda Harlen

Silhouette Intimate Moments

McIver's Mission #1224
Some Kind of Hero #1246
Extreme Measures #1282
Bulletproof Hearts #1313
Dangerous Passions #1394

Silhouette Special Edition

Once and Again #1714

BRENDA HARLEN

grew up in a small town surrounded by books and imaginary friends. Although she always dreamed of being a writer, she chose to follow a more traditional career path first. After two years of practicing as an attorney (including an appearance in front of the Supreme Court of Canada), she gave up her "real" job to be a mom and to try her hand at writing books. Three years, five manuscripts and another baby later, she sold her first book—an RWA Golden Heart Winner—to Silhouette.

Brenda lives in southern Ontario with her real-life husband/hero, two heroes-in-training and two neurotic dogs. She is still surrounded by books ("too many books," according to her children) and imaginary friends, but she also enjoys communicating with "real" people. Readers can contact Brenda by e-mail at brendaharlen@yahoo.com or by snail mail c/o Silhouette Books, 233 Broadway, Suite 1001, New York, NY 10279.

To Leslie Wainger—
For making me strive harder and write better.

To Susan Litman—
For continuing to guide me on that journey.

To Anna Perrin—
For everything.
I'll always be grateful to the fate that crossed our paths,
and to you for your incomparable friendship.

Prologue

Zane Conroy was dead—shot and killed by police in Fair-weather, Pennsylvania.

Michael Courtland wasn't surprised by the news or the method of his demise.

Conroy had been investigated frequently over the years, but no prosecutor had ever had the guts—or the evidence—to make him stand trial until Assistant District Attorney Natalie Vaughn made it her mission to build a case against him. In a desperate effort to avoid imprisonment, Conroy had taken her hostage to bargain for his freedom. It was in that final confrontation that he was killed.

The news caused shock waves to ripple throughout the entire criminal organization he'd controlled. From Pennsylvania to Florida and all points in between, Mike knew that the balance of power was now in flux. Already alliances were being forged and broken, loyalties tested, rivalries resurrected.

There was no way to predict the outcome of this violent

struggle or anticipate the victor's agenda. No way to know what it meant for Shannon Vaughn, Natalie's sister and Mike's current assignment.

He zeroed in on her position on the white sand beach, the vague sense of familiarity nagging at him. He was sure they'd never met before, and yet he couldn't shake the feeling that he recognized her. His gaze skimmed appreciatively over the creamy skin that showed hints of a golden tan, the fiery hair that glinted like copper in the afternoon sun and the long, lean figure clad in a two-piece bathing suit the same emerald color of her eyes.

There was one thing he knew for certain: he was going to enjoy keeping a very close eye on Shannon Vaughn.

Chapter 1

What was she thinking?

It wasn't really a question so much as a reprimand from her shocked conscience—a reprimand Shannon was finding all too easy to ignore. With Michael's hands and lips on her, she could barely think, never mind attempt to rationalize her behavior.

Yes, she was acting impulsively. Maybe even recklessly. But she didn't care. Since the failure of her marriage nine years earlier, she'd focused exclusively on her career. She hadn't let anything—or anyone—distract her.

Then she'd met Michael Courtland on the beach.

One look in his warm gray eyes, and her knees had gone weak. Then his lips had curved upward in a smile filled with charm and self-confidence, and she'd practically melted like a sno-cone in the Florida sun.

They'd strolled barefoot in the sand, eaten dinner at a little café by the water and lingered over coffee as the sun bled crimson into the ocean. Then they'd kissed under the light of the moon, and she'd invited him back to her room.

She knew his name and very little else about him. Most important, she knew that she'd never need to see him again after this night. That meant she could indulge desires too long forgotten and walk away in the morning, back to her carefully structured life, with no one but herself to ever know about the reckless indiscretion.

She'd always thought of holiday flings as tawdry and clichéd. Casual sex wasn't something she indulged in—ever. But all her values and beliefs had been thrown into turmoil when her sister was nearly killed.

The close call had reminded Shannon to live for today, because there were no guaranteed tomorrows. So for once, for tonight, she was determined to follow her heart instead of her head.

Of course, what she was feeling right now had more to do with hormones than emotions, but that didn't make the need any less compelling. She was a scientist. It was her job to accumulate and analyze data, to establish conclusions only after careful and thorough research. But from the first moment she'd set eyes on Michael Courtland, she'd wanted him. Nothing else seemed to matter.

His hands slid up her back, his touch burning even through the cotton barrier of her T-shirt. She wanted those hands on her bare skin; she wanted her hands on him. She wanted to feel his skin against hers, the slide of naked flesh against naked flesh as their bodies moved together in the primitive rhythm of mating.

The need pulsing through her veins was foreign to her, this kind of behavior completely out of character. She knew that regrets and recriminations would follow, but hopefully not until much, much later.

When the elevator dinged to announce their arrival on the eighth floor, Shannon was trembling with a desire unlike anything she'd ever experienced before. She led the way down the hall, her fingers shaking as she removed the keycard from her purse. She turned to the door, fumbled when Michael's teeth closed gently over her earlobe.

Somehow she managed to jam the card into the slot and push the door open. She didn't bother with the lights but drew him into the dark room, not stopping until the backs of her legs came into contact with the mattress, then pulled him down onto the bed with her.

His hands slid under her shirt, deftly finding and unfastening the clasp at the front of her bra. He pushed the satin aside and cupped her breasts in his palms, a low groan of satisfaction rumbling deep in his throat. His thumbs stroked over the aching tips, shooting spears of fiery heat from the peaks to the very center of her being. A soft whimper sounded from somewhere deep inside.

He dragged his lips from hers to rain kisses along her jaw, down her throat. His teeth nipped, his tongue soothed, and all the while his hands continued their delicious torment. Then he pushed the shirt up and found one throbbing nipple with his mouth. He suckled, hotly, hungrily, until she nearly screamed out with pleasure in response to his ardent caress.

She wanted him inside her. She wanted to feel him pressing into her, filling her, fulfilling her. This was desire in its most primitive form—raw, powerful, inescapable. But she didn't want to escape. She only wanted.

She was hot, burning with hunger for him, and grateful for the air-conditioning that offered respite from the sultry heat flowing into the room. The warm breeze wafted across her skin again and a chill skittered down her spine, raising goose bumps on her flesh and turning the heat that coursed through her blood to ice.

Sensing her abrupt withdrawal, Michael raised his head. "What's the matter?"

Shannon pushed herself into sitting position, crossed her arms over her naked breasts, her gaze fixed on the patio door.

The *open* patio door.

"Someone's been in my room."

Those few words, spoken with quiet conviction and an edge of panic, effectively shattered the moment.

Mike slid off the bed, away from Shannon, and took a deep breath—as if distance and oxygen might somehow manage to control the hormones raging in his blood. Not likely, when just looking at her made him hot, when he'd been subconsciously dreaming of this night since he'd first set eyes on her. But he disregarded the unfulfilled needs of his body to focus on the implications of her statement. "Did you say that someone's been in your room?"

She nodded, refastening her bra and tugging her shirt back into position before leaning over to switch on the bedside lamp.

He frowned as he glanced around at the tidy space that was almost a carbon-copy of his own. "How do you know?"

"The door's open." She raised a hand, gestured to the curtain that fluttered gently in the summer breeze.

"Housekeeping probably just forgot to close it when they made up your room."

"No." She slid farther back on the bed to lean against the headboard, crossing her arms over her chest. "Someone else was here."

"How do you know?"

"My room was already made up when I came in to change before dinner. I pulled the curtains myself."

"Maybe the maid brought fresh towels or something."

"Maybe." But she sounded doubtful.

"Why don't you call the manager?" he suggested. "He

might know if housekeeping or maintenance had any reason to be in here."

"Oh. Okay." She exhaled a shaky breath and reached for the phone.

As she dialed, he crossed the room to examine the door and its frame. He inspected both the inside and out, relieved to find no proof of tampering.

Outside on the balcony there was a plastic table flanked by two loungers. A beach towel was draped over one of the chairs, an empty Dr Pepper can on the ground beside it.

He glanced over the railing, down to the swimming pool eight floors below. He considered the distance, shook his head. It was unlikely—if not impossible—for someone to gain entry by climbing up to the balcony.

Remembering some of the tasks he'd been required to perform in Ranger training, he revised his opinion. But while scaling the building might be possible, it couldn't be done without someone noticing. Even at this time of night, there were dozens of guests in and around the water.

He turned back to the open door and glanced up.

It would be much easier to access the eighth floor of a ten-story building by climbing down. But the absence of any evidence of forced entry convinced Mike that scenario was equally unlikely.

Shannon was ending her call when he stepped back inside. He closed the door tight and flipped the lock into place.

"He said he has no record of the hotel staff accessing my room during the time I was out," she told him. "But he thinks that's probably what happened."

Mike could tell by her tone that she remained unconvinced.

She wandered through the room looking around, into the bathroom and back again.

"Something isn't right," she insisted.

He wasn't prepared to ignore her instincts. Not when her

safety was the reason he'd come down to Florida in the first place. But he needed facts to back up those instincts. "Is anything missing?"

"Not that I can tell. But…"

"But what?"

She looked away, her cheeks flushing with color. "My sister likes to joke about my organization," she admitted. "I have a specific way of doing things, a structure to my life that I never deviate from."

Her blush deepened, and he knew she was thinking about her behavior with him tonight—which was something he was trying *not* to think about.

"Almost never," she amended. "And that's how I know someone's been here. Someone moved my book—it was on the other side of the table when I left. And I always align the cap of the toothpaste with the bristles of the toothbrush, but the toothpaste is upside down now."

She shook her head. "You probably think I'm a nutcase."

On the contrary, he was starting to believe she was right. Someone *had* been in her room, looking around, searching for something.

But what?

And why was the patio door left open?

Unless whoever was in her room wanted her to know he'd been there. That was a far more sinister possibility than a random burglary attempt.

"I thought I heard you ask the manager about moving to another room."

"I did, but there aren't any vacancies in the hotel."

"You could stay with me."

She eyed him warily.

He smiled, trying to put her at ease. "As much as I'd like to pick up where we left off, it's not an offer with any strings attached. There are two beds in my room, too."

But she shook her head, rejecting the offer. "I'm sorry for the way things ended. I didn't mean to mislead you, but I really just want to be alone right now."

"I don't think that's a good idea."

"I'll be fine."

She sounded as if she believed it, but she didn't know the truth about who he was and why he was in Florida. She didn't know that she might be in real danger.

Would she believe him if he told her now? Would she be willing to accept his help and his protection? Or would she feel betrayed by his deception?

Not that he'd intended to deceive her. He'd never intended to make contact with her at all. His instructions had been simply to watch out for her, but from a distance. Lieutenant Dylan Creighton—now Shannon's sister's fiancé—had instructed Mike to be discreet in his surveillance so as not to alarm Shannon unnecessarily.

Mike believed the break-in justified sounding the alarm. But as much as he wanted to share his suspicions with her, to make sure she understood how serious the situation could be, he had to talk to his client first.

"Please," she said. "I'd like you to go."

"Okay." He relented to her request only because he had no intention of going any farther than the hall and he wanted to call Dylan without Shannon overhearing the conversation.

"Thank you," she said stiffly.

He wanted to reach out to her, to offer her comfort and reassurance. But her spine was rigid, her arms crossed over her chest in a defensive and distinctively hands-off posture. He turned away. "Lock up behind me."

He stood outside the door, waited to hear the lock click into place, then reached for his cell phone. He powered it up, only to have it beep once and shut down again.

Damn.

The battery was dead and the spare was in his room upstairs. He tucked the useless phone back into his pocket and leaned back against the wall. The door directly across the hall was clearly marked Stairs. He could run up to his room to retrieve the extra battery and be back within five minutes.

But still he hesitated, his instincts warning him not to leave her, not even for five minutes. Was it worry about Shannon's safety that made him so reluctant to step away from her? Or were his instincts off-kilter because of the desire still pulsing in his veins?

He mentally cursed again.

This was exactly the reason he'd tried so hard to keep his distance from her. Because personal involvement interfered with objectivity, and emotional responses led to mistakes. It was a lesson he'd learned in Righaria, when his mistake had cost his best friend's life, and when his guilt over Brent's death cost him the woman he loved.

He pushed aside the past to concentrate on the present. He was here now to protect Shannon—everything else was secondary.

But he'd be better able to protect her if he could tell her the truth, and he couldn't do that until he'd spoken to Dylan Creighton. And he couldn't talk to Dylan without returning to his room for the spare battery.

He glanced back at her door, hesitated.

He'd checked the locks on the windows himself, heard her flip the security bar into place. She was safe inside, probably already in bed—

He shoved that thought aside and headed for the stairwell, taking the steps two at a time.

Only five minutes.

Shannon stared at the back of the door for a long moment after Michael had gone, wishing she'd let him stay. She already missed his comforting presence, his reassuring strength, but she wasn't used to relying on anyone else or asking for help. Despite his offer, she was determined to stand on her own.

But somehow that conviction was harder to find when she was alone.

She made a quick tour of the room again, confirmed there was nothing missing. That fact bothered her more than if she'd come back to her room and found all her personal items gone. Not that she had much, and certainly nothing of significant value, but she couldn't believe a thief wouldn't have at least scooped up the loose change on the dresser.

Maybe Michael was right. Maybe no one had been in her room except a member of the hotel staff. She wanted to believe this explanation, but she still couldn't shake the unease as she moved into the bathroom to get ready for bed.

Looking into the mirror, she was startled by the reflection that stared back. Her hair was tousled from Michael's fingers running through it, her mouth red and swollen from his kisses.

She pressed her fingers to her lips, hard, trying to erase the feel of his mouth against hers. She looked like a wanton woman—hardly surprising considering the fact that she'd acted like one. And although she knew she should be embarrassed by her behavior, she only regretted the way the evening had ended.

But despite her resolution to live for the moment and regardless of how much she wanted him, she knew that having sex with Michael would have been a mistake.

The knowledge was little comfort when she continued to ache with wanting, when something inside her cried out against the injustice of a promise unfulfilled. Shannon shook off the feeling and moved back into the bedroom. Hopefully everything would be back to normal in the morning.

She opened the drawer to retrieve her nightshirt, her heart rising in her throat as her fingers tightened around the silk garment.

It was inside out.

Again, it was a small thing, but she knew without a doubt that when she'd put it away, it had been right-side out. Someone had definitely been here, gone through the dresser, pawed through her things.

Another shiver snaked up her spine.

Why?

She shoved the silk back into the drawer, trying not to think about the possible answers to that question. She would sleep in her clothes tonight. If she slept at all.

The knock at her door made her jump.

She pressed a hand to her heart as she glanced at the clock on the bedside table. It was almost midnight.

The knock sounded again.

Michael?

An unexpected and comforting warmth spread through her as she considered the possibility that he'd come back. This time she promised herself as she walked on unsteady legs to the door, she would swallow her pride and ask him to stay. Not to have sex, but just to keep her company—just so she wouldn't need to be alone.

Disappointment replaced anticipation when she looked through the peephole.

It wasn't Michael.

In fact, she was sure this man wasn't anyone she'd ever seen before. She hesitated, reluctant to respond to the summons of a stranger at this time of night.

He knocked again, impatience evident in the rap of his knuckles against the wood.

She swallowed. "Yes?"

"Ms. Vaughn?"

"Yes," she said again.

"My name is Michael Courtland," he told her. "I'm a private investigator from Fairweather, Pennsylvania. Can I talk to you for a minute?"

Michael Courtland? A private investigator?

She shook her head to clear away the questions that came at her from all directions.

"It's late," she said.

"I apologize for that," he said easily. "But this really can't wait."

She hesitated again. "Can I see some identification?"

"Of course." He pulled a wallet out of his pocket and withdrew something the size and shape of a credit card. "I'll slide this under the door so you can take a look at it."

She bent down to retrieve the laminated rectangle. It was a private investigator's license bearing the name Michael Andrew Courtland.

She'd never seen this kind of identification before and wondered if it was legitimate. Or was she being paranoid to even suspect it might be fake? Since her unfortunate experience with her ex-husband, she found it difficult to trust anyone.

"I also have a driver's license and several credit cards if you need further proof," he said.

His offer, and a glance at the photo, reassured her that he was who he claimed to be. The picture bore a distinct likeness to the man standing outside her door and none at all to the man who'd been in her room with her earlier. A man who'd also claimed to be Michael Courtland.

Nausea rolled in her stomach. If *this* man was really Michael Courtland, who was the man she'd met on the beach?

It was possible, of course, that two different men had the same name. In fact, it was possible there were several Michael Courtlands in the world. But what were the odds that she would meet two such men on the same day and in the same city?

Someone had lied to her, and as this man hadn't hesitated to prove his identity, she had to believe it was the *other* Michael Courtland. The one who'd kissed her until her head was spinning, who'd touched her boldly, intimately, stoking the flames of her desire until she'd been sure they would consume her. The man with whom she'd almost had wild, passionate sex.

Her stomach churned again. Why had he lied?

What reason could he have had to pretend to be someone else? And why hadn't she thought to ask him to prove his identity?

The answer to the last question was obvious—because she didn't want to know. Because she'd wanted only mind-numbing, bone-melting sex without any complications.

"Ms. Vaughn?"

The question from outside the door broke through her self-recrimination. She felt the heat of shame flood her cheeks and pushed aside all thoughts of the other man as she opened the door—but only a few inches.

"I'm sorry," she apologized, handing back his identification through the narrow opening.

"There's no need to apologize for being cautious."

He smiled at her, and she realized he was more attractive when viewed directly. Close to six feet tall, she guessed, with sandy-blond hair, blue eyes, and a square jaw with just the hint of a dimple in the middle.

"Mr. Courtland—"

"Call me Drew."

She frowned. "I thought your name was Michael."

"It's also my dad's name," he said. "Andrew's my middle name. My mom started calling me Drew when I was a kid— it made things less confusing around the house."

"Oh." She relaxed again at the easy explanation. "Okay, now I know who you are, but I still don't know why you're here."

"Lieutenant Creighton didn't call you?"

"No." Bony fingers of fear slid along her skin. "Has something else happened to my sister?"

"No," he responded quickly to her obvious panic. "Natalie's fine. I'm here because of you."

"Why?"

"Because Creighton is concerned that Zane Conroy's associates may have followed you to Florida."

She remembered the strange feeling that had persisted over the past couple of days, the uncomfortable sensation of being watched. She'd finally discarded the idea as paranoia, but now she wondered.

"In fact, you may have been tracked to this hotel."

She swallowed. "I think someone was in my room tonight. Earlier. While I was out."

His gaze sharpened. "Then we need to get you out of here as soon as possible. If they've already been here, confirmed you're staying here, they'll be back."

The chill went through to her bones. "Why?"

"Because they'll be seeking revenge for his murder."

"But I had nothing to do with anything," she protested. "I didn't even know Conroy."

"Your sister did," he reminded her. "And that puts you at risk."

His warning shook her to the core. Shannon had thought Conroy's death was a blessing, but if what this man said was true, not only could she be in danger, but Natalie and Jack might be, as well.

"I didn't mean to scare you," he said. "But you need to understand why Creighton wants you out of this hotel."

"Where—" she swallowed "—where am I supposed to go?"

"I have a safe house ready."

It was all too much for her to comprehend, but she wasn't quite ready to run off with a total stranger just because he'd flashed his ID. "I want to call my sister before I go anywhere."

"Of course."

Somewhat reassured by his response, she closed the door

again, leaving him outside in the hall. She moved across the room to the phone, her hand trembling as she picked up the receiver. She took a deep breath before dialing.

Natalie answered on the second ring, sounding groggy and slightly panicked. "Hello?"

She cringed. "I forgot what time it was."

"Shannon?"

"Yeah. I'm sorry I woke you."

"What's the matter?"

"I, uh, is Dylan there?"

"Dylan?" Natalie was obviously awake now. "No. He was paged about an hour ago. What's going on?"

Shannon hesitated. Her sister had been through so much in the past two days and she didn't want to cause her any more concern. But she also didn't want to go off with Michael Courtland without confirming the information he'd given her.

"Did Dylan mention anything to you about sending a private investigator to Florida?"

"Oh, yeah. I meant to tell you about that when I spoke to you earlier."

"Tell me what?" Shannon prompted.

"Just that Dylan asked Michael Courtland to keep an eye on you while you were on vacation because of Conroy's connections down there. But I'm sure there's nothing to worry about now."

"The P.I. seems to think otherwise."

"Why?" Natalie asked.

She didn't want to worry her sister further by telling her about the break-in of her room, so she only said, "I'm not sure, but he's suggesting that I go to a safe house with him."

"Oh, Shan. I'm so sorry. I never expected any of this to affect you."

"It's not your fault." As shaken as she was by recent events, Shannon didn't want her sister to feel responsible for something over which she had no control. "I just wanted to know what you thought of his plan before I agreed to it."

"Dylan didn't say anything to me about this," her sister admitted. "But maybe he didn't have a chance."

"What do you think I should do?"

Natalie didn't hesitate. "Go with him. If Dylan trusted him enough to send him, you can trust that he'll take care of you."

Shannon wasn't comfortable with the thought of anyone taking care of her, but after the recent attempt on her sister's life, she was willing to make some concessions. At least until she had more details about what was going on.

"Okay," she agreed. But because her suspicions weren't completely alleviated, she asked, "What does Michael Courtland look like?"

"Why are you asking? I thought you'd already met him."

"No, um, he called me," she hedged. "I just want to make sure I don't run off with the wrong man."

"If this situation wasn't so serious, I might be able to laugh at the thought of you running off with *any* man," Natalie said. "But under the circumstances, I'm glad you're being careful."

"I'm always careful."

"I know," her sister agreed. "As for Michael, I've only met him once or twice, but I remember that he was tall—around six feet, maybe a little taller—brown hair, blue eyes."

Her sister's response didn't alleviate Shannon's uncertainty. Both of the men who had identified themselves as Michael Courtland had been at least six feet. The first one had brown hair, but his smoky-gray eyes would never be described as blue. The second one—the one waiting in the hallway outside her room—had blue eyes, but his hair was dark blond. She didn't think it was dark enough to be mistaken for brown, but Natalie admitted she'd only met him twice. It was possible her sister was mistaken.

"I know that description's vague enough to fit almost anyone," she continued. "But he stands out from a crowd. Very good-looking. Very sexy."

Sexy.

It was definitely the thought that had come to mind when she'd met the first man, but as attraction was always subjective, she didn't consider that conclusive evidence.

"The more I think about it," Natalie said. "The more I'm thinking that you and he trapped in close quarters together might not be such a bad idea."

"You wouldn't," Shannon said dryly. Her sister had always been a romantic at heart.

"Give me a call when you get a chance," Natalie said. "But if I don't hear from you for a few days, I'll assume you're—" she paused dramatically "—otherwise occupied."

"I'll call you."

Natalie laughed and said goodbye.

Shannon hung up the phone but didn't move off of the bed.

Go with him, Natalie had said.

But despite her sister's assurance, there was something about the man standing outside in the hall that made her uneasy.

As she heard a soft click, like that of a door latching, another chill snaked up her spine. She turned her head to see that he was now *inside* her room.

She jumped up from the bed, her heart hammering furiously as she took an instinctive step backward.

"I didn't mean to startle you," Drew said. "But we really need to hurry."

"H-how did you get in here?"

He held up a keycard. "I borrowed it from the maid."

His voice was gentle, almost soothing, as if his explanation was perfectly reasonable.

But the smile—

She watched the way his lips curved with slow satisfaction.

She saw the predatory gleam in his eyes. And she instinctively knew that despite what he'd said earlier, despite what Natalie had told her, this man wasn't here to protect her.

She rubbed sweaty palms down the front of her skirt as her brain desperately scrambled for a response to the situation. But her usually rational mind had gone blank, fear and panic escalating until there was room for nothing else, no way to compute anything beyond the obvious threat. She drew in a deep breath, battled back the fear.

But what could she do?

She eyed the phone, but Drew was moving steadily closer and she knew she wouldn't have a chance to press a single button before he reached her.

"I, uh, just need a few minutes to pack my things."

He frowned, evidently surprised—and maybe a little disappointed—by her compliance. "Be quick."

She threw her suitcase onto the bed, then began opening drawers and pulling out articles of clothing.

He was standing between her and the hotel phone, but maybe she could use her cell. If she could somehow slip into the bathroom for a minute…

Her gaze slid back to the corner of the dresser, to her purse with the phone inside it.

She continued shoving clothes into the case, as if she was as anxious as he to get out of this room, away from this hotel. The knots in her stomach tightened painfully, but she couldn't let him see her fear, couldn't let him suspect that she knew.

"Ready?" he asked.

She realized the last drawer was empty.

"I need some things…from the bathroom."

His gaze narrowed.

Could he hear the tremor in her voice?

"And…I should go…before we go."

It would give her a reason to close the door, to implement her plan. She scooped up her purse, turned toward the small room that was her last hope of escape.

She hadn't gone two steps when he caught her arm.

"We can't afford to waste any more time."

"But I really need—"

It was all she managed before she felt the prick of the needle in her arm.

Chapter 2

Where the hell was she?

Mike banged on the door again, more than loud enough to wake her if she was sleeping.

There was still no response.

He'd been gone twenty minutes—fifteen minutes longer than he'd intended. But his phone had been ringing when he'd stepped into the room and he'd automatically picked it up. It had been Romeo Garcia, a detective with the Miami P.D. and a friend of Dylan Creighton, calling to update him on the situation with respect to Conroy's connections in Florida.

According to Garcia, word on the street was that certain key players in Conroy's organization had a new quest: to avenge their leader's death. Although Natalie was the most obvious target for retaliation, her relationship with Lieutenant Creighton made another attempt on her life risky. As a result, Garcia believed Shannon could be in danger for no reason other than that her sister had been involved in the altercation that had cost Conroy his life.

Armed with his new information, the back-up battery in his cell phone, and his Glock, Mike had returned to Shannon's room. But in the twenty minutes he was gone, something had happened.

He turned back to the stairwell, racing away from the memories that haunted him as much as he was racing to find her.

He was on his way toward the manager on duty at the registration desk, to demand to be let into Shannon's room, when he spotted her. She was outside the front doors of the hotel, being helped into the passenger side of a late-model silver-colored Mercedes sedan.

He started to run.

The car was pulling away from the curb before he'd even made it outside.

Damn. He'd been an idiot to expect that she'd stay put in her room until morning. Now, everything was FUBAR.

He considered getting his own vehicle, but it was parked at the back of the hotel. By the time he got to it, Shannon would be long gone. Instead, he jumped into the back of a taxi parked beside the hotel and directed the driver to follow the Mercedes.

He tried to convince himself that there was no reason for the humming of his nerves, no rational foundation for the escalating feeling of dread. But he knew better. After Brent was killed in Righaria, Mike had stopped fighting his instincts, and he was cursing himself now for ignoring the intuition that had warned him against leaving her alone—for even a few minutes.

But he'd been so caught up in wanting her, he'd been unable to separate his personal desires from his professional instincts. Mistakes were made when impulse was allowed to overrule reason, and mistakes could cost lives. Brent's death had taught him that more effectively than any training exercise ever could.

He pushed the memory to the back of his mind. He didn't have time to deal with the ghosts of the past; he couldn't let himself be paralyzed by grief and guilt—not if he was going to protect Shannon.

Protect her from what?

The question nagged at him, unanswered, as he pulled out his cell phone and dialed the number Garcia had given him. From what he could see, Shannon had gotten into the vehicle willingly. She certainly hadn't appeared to be in any danger.

But Mike knew that things weren't always what they seemed, and what Garcia told him confirmed this suspicion. The registered owner of the Mercedes was Andrew Peart, a suspected illegal arms dealer and member of Conroy's organization.

Again his instincts hummed. The information had been too readily available. If Peart was abducting Shannon, why wouldn't he have taken more care to cover his tracks? Why would he have used his own vehicle? What kind of game was he playing?

The taxi driver signaled to turn onto the private drive leading to the exclusive Tradewinds Marina. Mike ordered him to stop. If Peart caught sight of another vehicle on this road at this hour, he'd know he was being followed. He shoved a fistful of money at the driver, then slipped out of the vehicle and into the shadows to continue his pursuit on foot.

He followed the taillights of the Mercedes, conscious of the growing distance between himself and the vehicle. Again he thought of Brent, about the obstacles he'd failed to overcome to save his friend. He couldn't fail again. He ran harder, refusing to believe that he would be too late.

He had to save Shannon.

* * *

Shannon shifted in her seat, turning to press her cheek against the cool leather. She blinked, but her vision remained fuzzy. She tried to think, but her mind was even fuzzier.

She was conscious of only two things. The first she accepted with overwhelming relief: she wasn't dead.

At least, not yet.

The second caused trepidation rather than relief: she was going to vomit.

Whether it was fear of imminent death that had churned up her insides to the point of nausea or a reaction to whatever drug had been injected into her system, she only knew that she was going to throw up.

Drew braked abruptly, threw the gearshift into Park.

It was the final straw for her heaving stomach. She felt the bile rise up in her throat, groped frantically for the door handle. Her fingers finally closed around the metal but seemed unable to interpret the command from her brain to pull.

Then the door opened from the other side.

She fell out of the car, the rough concrete abrading her palms and her knees. She tried to swallow, gagged.

"What the—?" Drew started to reach for her.

She clamped a desperate hand over her mouth and tried to will away the nausea.

He finally seemed to recognize the reason for her position and carefully stepped back, out of range, just before her stomach spasmed and emptied its contents.

"Are you okay?" he asked, almost courteously.

She would have laughed at the absurdity of the question if she wasn't too groggy and weak to do anything but nod.

"Come on, then." He took her arm to help her to her feet.

The world tilted and swayed.

He tightened his grip and hurried her along.

Where were they going? And why was he in such a hurry?

She tried to focus, but everything remained a blur.

"Shannon, wait!"

The distant call, the vaguely familiar voice, startled Shannon and spurred Drew into action. He picked her up and lifted her onto the deck of a boat.

A few seconds later she heard the rumble of engines and felt a cool breeze against her cheeks. She could smell salt in the air now, confirming that they were on the ocean.

But where was he taking her?

Why?

She had so many questions but her brain was still too muddled to attempt to come up with any answers.

Instead she closed her eyes and drifted into sleep.

From as far back as he could remember, Mike had been groomed to take over the family business. For almost the same amount of time, he'd balked at being fitted for that mold. He wanted to make his own way, without reliance on the family fortune or social connections. He'd done so, first by joining the army and later—and quite successfully— through his partnership in Courtland & Logan Investigations.

Still, Mike's father never passed up an opportunity to express disappointment that his only son had abandoned his legacy. And his mother never failed to point to his single status as proof of the unsuitability of his career for someone of their social standing.

Only his sister, Rachel, supported his choice. Partly because she coveted the job he'd been offered at Courtland Enterprises, but mostly because she understood him—what he wanted and what he needed—better than anyone else ever had.

So when he found himself at the end of the dock, watching Peart's boat disappear into the darkness, he didn't think twice about what he was going to do. He didn't wonder whether it was luck or coincidence that Peart had chosen to moor his yacht at the same marina where Rachel docked *Pure Pleasure*. His only concern was getting to Shannon.

Not that his sister's boat was any match for the powerful engines on Peart's luxury yacht, but if he couldn't catch up immediately, Mike was confident he could at least keep track of it while he radioed back to the Coast Guard for help.

He wasn't too proud to ask for backup, not when Shannon's life could be in danger.

He picked up the handset, saw that it had been forcibly disconnected from the receiver/transmitter. He stared at the broken radio, suddenly sure Peart's choice of location had been deliberate—an intentional act to bait him into following.

Which meant that his cover had been blown. Somehow Peart had figured out that he was in Miami to protect Shannon, and he was counting on Mike to go after her.

Even knowing it was a setup, he considered no other option.

He flipped open his cell phone, glanced at the signal indicator. It was weak but steady. He kept his eyes focused on the dwindling shape of Peart's boat as he steered through the choppy water and pressed redial.

She was still on the boat.

It was Shannon's first thought when she woke up, substantiated by the gentle rolling motion of the vessel moving through the water.

She glanced around the room, at surroundings illuminated by the gentle glow of light from a shaded lamp on the bedside table. Dark walnut furniture polished to a high gloss and trimmed with gleaming brass hardware. A wide bed with fluffy pillows and a cream-colored satin comforter.

She sat up cautiously, leaned back against the headboard and exhaled a slow sigh of relief that the world remained upright and relatively stable.

Her vision was clear but her throat was tight and dry and the inside of her mouth tasted sour. She slid her legs over the side of the bed, found the floor.

Her legs trembled when she stood, but she carefully made her way toward the door only a few feet away.

A bathroom.

Head, she automatically corrected herself. On a boat it was called a head.

She nearly whimpered with relief as she opened the taps and cool, clear water poured out.

She splashed her face, rinsed her mouth, then drank, deeply, greedily. As she drank, her trembling eased and her mind cleared, and the events of the past several hours came flooding back to her.

A spiral of events that had all started with the man on the beach.

She thought she'd learned from the mistakes of her disastrous relationship with Doug. The impulsive marriage had been followed by a carefully planned divorce and a determination to never again succumb to impetuous desires that could easily lead her astray.

Then she'd met Michael—or whatever his real name was—and invited him back to her hotel room.

It was humiliating to admit that she could be so weak, embarrassing to accept that her more-basic instincts could overrule her common sense.

She turned off the water, dried her hands.

She felt no compunction about rummaging through the cupboards, and when she found an unopened toothbrush, she didn't hesitate to use it. She hadn't had a chance to retrieve her own toiletries and she was desperate to clean her teeth.

After she'd done so, she went back to the stateroom to search for her suitcase. She remembered packing it, but she couldn't remember carrying it out of her room. She didn't even remember leaving the hotel, and she still wasn't entirely sure why she was here.

All she knew was that she was on a yacht in the Atlantic Ocean on the way to God-and-Drew-only-knew-where. She frowned, desperately trying to get a handle on the direction in which they were headed. They'd been moving eastward when they'd left the marina, her senses hadn't been so disoriented she'd failed to register that fact, but she didn't know if they'd changed direction since then.

Maybe she'd take a walk around and try to get her bearings.

It wasn't until she was tiptoeing down the narrow, dimly lit corridor of the boat that she found herself wondering why she hadn't been locked in the stateroom. Why wasn't Drew concerned about her wandering around the boat?

She made her way up onto the deck and stared out at the endless expanse of ocean, the answer to her questions suddenly and painfully obvious: Drew wasn't concerned about her going anywhere because there wasn't anywhere to go. Everywhere she looked was water—eerily dark and ominously deep.

She looked up at the sky, at the thin crescent moon and the brilliant array of stars sparkling in the black velvet darkness. She could see the outline of an island in the distance, faint but discernible. The Bahamas?

If she knew anything about astronomy, she could use the stars to ascertain their direction, maybe figure out where they were going. Unfortunately, she knew nothing about the subject.

She sighed as despair threatened to overwhelm her. She shook off the sense of impending doom. Maybe she'd be able to see something more from the other side of the boat.

Silently she made her way around the stern, biting back a yelp of pain when she rapped her shin on a large wooden crate. As she bent to rub her injured leg, she saw that the lid had been knocked askew by her collision with it. Curious, she pushed it aside farther and stared in a combination of shock and dis-belief at the contents.

Weapons packed in a bed of straw. Lethal-looking military hardware she'd only ever seen on news reports about wars or terrorism in faraway countries.

Then she heard voices, softly at first, distant, then grow-ing louder as they drew nearer.

Her breath caught in her throat; her pulse hammered.

She glanced around frantically. There was a pile of scuba gear in the corner: wetsuits and tanks and masks and fins. She moved in that direction, crouching down to melt into the shadow of the equipment.

"…she wasn't part of the plan," an unfamiliar voice pro-tested.

"The plan changed." It was Drew who answered, unapol-ogetically.

"I didn't sign on for this," the other man grumbled.

"When you signed on with the organization, Rico, you signed on to do whatever needed to be done."

"Not murder."

She'd known what Drew was planning, had seen the blood-lust in his eyes before he'd jabbed the needle in her arm, but it still shocked her to hear the word spoken and know they were talking about her.

"I'll do it," a third man offered.

"No one is being asked to do anything…*yet*," Drew said. "But I appreciate your enthusiasm, Jazz, and will be sure to communicate your offer to A.J.—along with any concerns I may have about employee loyalty."

It was obviously a threat, and it hung heavy in the air be-tween the three men.

The one referred to as Rico cleared his throat. "My loyalty is, and always has been, to the organization."

"Good." Drew obviously wasn't concerned by the lack of

enthusiasm in his cohort's statement. "Because I'm leaving the two of you in charge while I return to Pennsylvania to attend Mr. Conroy's funeral."

"For how long?"

"Until I get back."

"But the shipment—"

"Will be made tomorrow afternoon as scheduled."

"What about the woman?" It was Jazz who asked this question, obviously relishing the prospect of her demise.

"She will pay for the role her sister played in killing Conroy," Drew said. "But A.J. will determine when and how she dies. No one is to do anything until then."

They moved farther along the deck to continue their conversation, their voices fading into the distance. Shannon had overheard more than enough and she had no intention of sticking around to find out the when and the how. She had to get off this boat before "when" became "now."

But they were in the middle of the ocean. How could she possibly escape?

She rose to her feet unsteadily, put a hand out for balance. Her fingers braced against the cool metal of an oxygen tank, and the first seeds of an idea were planted in her mind.

No—it was crazy.

She couldn't just strap on a tank and flippers and swim back to Miami. Even if the night wasn't dark and the distance prohibitive, she hadn't been diving in more than two years.

Although she'd planned to book an excursion while she was on vacation, she'd changed her mind when she'd heard a group of returning tourists raving about the incredible pair of hammerhead sharks they'd encountered on their dive. Shannon had walked away from the tour desk with no regrets, because if there was one thing she hated, it was sharks. Well, sharks *and* snakes, actually.

Even if she knew where she was going and was willing to

swim with the fish, there was the fact that she'd been injected
with some kind of drug only a few hours earlier. She didn't
know what substance she'd been given or whether traces of
it might still be lingering in her system, but she knew it would
be dangerous to dive under such conditions.

Despite the obvious and numerous risks of such an escape
attempt, Shannon didn't see that there was any other choice.

If she stayed on this boat, she would die.

She felt the tremor of fear ripple through her. She wasn't
ready to die. There was too much she hadn't seen and done,
too much living she still needed to do. There was no way she
was going to give up without a fight.

She'd have to take her chances in the water.

Impatient fingers drummed on the scarred oak desktop as
the second ring echoed through the handset. Each unanswered
ring represented yet another delay, and there had been too
many of those already.

The organization could afford no more.

A.J. would tolerate no more.

Conroy's death—so sudden and unexpected—had shaken
everyone. The powerful, fearless leader taken down in a simple sting operation he should have been able to smell from a
mile away. It was an unnecessary tragedy, but not really a surprising one.

Because Conroy had been weak.

His affection for a woman had interfered with his reason,
allowed him to get caught. Or maybe it was the fault of his
ego as much as his fondness for the woman, because he'd truly
believed he was invincible.

And he had been—until three bullets snuffed out his life.

There had been widespread shock and some tears, subtle
shifts of power and bold demands for vengeance. Through it
all, A.J. had risen to the top and was determined to stay there.

At last there was a click as the connection was made, then he answered. "Peart."

"Why are you on the boat?" The demand was made without preamble. There was neither the time nor the need to exchange pleasantries—a hierarchy was being reconstructed and the only purpose of this call was to enforce the new order.

"A.J., I was just going to call you." There was surprise, and maybe just a hint of fear, in his response.

"You shouldn't be calling. You should be on your way back here by now."

"I know. But I've got her." There was pride in his voice now, bold and unapologetic.

Both his confidence and his pride would need to be squashed. He was a tool—a valuable and necessary instrument on occasion, but still just a tool—and he needed to be reminded of that fact.

"I didn't tell you to get her. In fact, I didn't tell you to go anywhere near her."

"But I know you wanted—"

"You don't know *anything* about what I want unless and until it is expressed in terms of a direct order."

He didn't respond. He knew better than to speak out of turn again.

A.J. let the silence grow, felt his tension mount, before asking, "What about Courtland?"

"He's in pursuit. We're waiting for him to get close enough to—I mean, we, uh, we're waiting for orders to, uh, eliminate him."

It was satisfying to hear the stammer, to know he already recognized his mistake.

"You're going to wait a while longer," A.J. said. "What I want now is for you to get on the next plane to Pennsylvania."

There was a pause as Peart fought to swallow the silent "but" that hummed across the line as loudly as if it had been spoken.

To his credit he managed to conceal his dissent and respond, "I've already made plans. I'll be there as soon as I can."

"He will be buried tomorrow." A.J.'s voice had lowered, thickened with just the slightest hint of what might have been grief. In reality, it was excitement—the anticipation of opportunity overshadowing any remnants of sorrow. Tomorrow, finally, all the key players would be in place. "And we have some serious planning to do."

"What—" he hesitated, aware that he was treading on dangerous ground. "What about the woman?"

There was a pause, long enough to make him sweat, before the response. "I'm not going to commend you for overstepping your bounds, but I recognize the value of the offering and I will decide how to deal with her."

"Of course."

A.J. smiled at the submissive response and disconnected the call.

Peart was falling in line, as so many others had already done, recognizing the rightful heir to the throne of power.

Zane Conroy's authority had been absolute, his name spoken with reverence; his orders obeyed without question. He'd been unforgiving of mistakes, intolerant of fools and ruthless in dealing with any hint of disloyalty.

He'd been a truly great leader.

A.J. would be greater.

Chapter 3

Shannon didn't know how long she'd been underwater when the level of air in her tank forced her to surface. She was grateful when she did so to find that the first rays of light were starting to lighten the sky.

She had no idea how far she'd come, she could only hope it was far enough. But when she looked toward the island she'd focused on as she'd gone into the water, the hope slipped through her fingers.

The land mass was closer now, but still so far away. What had been an admittedly foolish and reckless impulse at the time seemed even more so now. She was a strong swimmer, but the ocean had far more breadth and endurance.

No, she couldn't think like that. She'd come too far to give up. She would push forward, ignoring the fact that her muscles were already screaming with the pain of exertion. She would embrace the pain, knowing that as long as it hurt, she was still alive, she still had a chance.

But how much of a chance? How could she ever have expected to succeed in this battle against nature? Maybe she couldn't. Yet she couldn't bring herself to give in, either.

She would persevere—in a minute.

For now, she just wanted to float. She used the last of the air to reinflate the life vest, then dumped the empty tank. Her limbs felt heavy and weak. She was exhausted, physically and mentally, and shivering uncontrollably. She was tempted to give in to the fatigue and the cold, to close her burning eyes and let herself drift into the blissful oblivion of sleep.

Logically, she knew she had to keep moving, she was still a long way from the island. How many more strokes would it take to reach the shore? One hundred? Two hundred? More? How was she ever going to find the strength when her arms and legs were already numb?

The questions shook her already-faltering confidence. Weariness weighed down her limbs; despair filled her heart. She couldn't believe this was happening. She was supposed to be on vacation—a much-deserved holiday before she accepted the promotion she'd been offered and moved to Paris.

She'd always wanted to visit France—stroll the Champs Elysées, cruise the River Seine, climb the Eiffel Tower. There was so much to look forward to; so much she might never get a chance to do.

No, she refused to succumb to negative thoughts. She would swim and swim until she couldn't lift her arms or kick her legs anymore. She would make it to the island. She would.

But for now she tipped her head back and let her eyelids drift shut—just for a second.

More than two hours had passed since Mike had watched Shannon slip over the side of the *Femme Fatale* and into the ocean. Two hours during which he'd tried to anticipate and match her path through the dark water. Two hours without a single glimpse of her.

He'd seen her climbing overboard, but he'd been too far away to reach her before she submerged. And he couldn't signal to catch her attention because doing so would alert Peart's men to her movements and his presence. So he'd watched, silently, helplessly, as she'd disappeared into the sea.

She had to be very brave or completely desperate to think she could survive such an escape attempt. He guessed she was a little of both.

He squinted against the brightness of the rising sun as he scanned the water again. During the night, the ocean had seemed black and treacherous. In the light of day, it was gloriously blue and temptingly inviting. It wasn't, however, any less deadly. And with every minute that passed, the likelihood of Shannon's survival decreased and his feeling of failure intensified.

He refused to give in to it; refused to give up. He refused to fail again.

But the memories hovered at the back of his mind, haunting him, taunting him. Memories so real he could almost smell the heavy scent of the Righarian jungle, feel the drip of moisture from the sodden leaves down his back, taste the fear that had risen like bile in his throat. And he could see—all too clearly—the picture of his friend as he lay dying: his helmet knocked askew, his blond hair matted with crimson blood, his dark eyes wide as they stared unseeingly at the man who'd let him down.

They'd been through so much together, seen so much death and destruction. But nothing they'd seen had prepared Mike for the shocking horror of Brent's usually smiling visage hideously twisted with pain.

He blinked in an effort to dispel the gruesome image. The picture didn't disappear, it only changed. The blond hair grew longer, darker, until it was brilliant auburn, the dark eyes softened to the color of green moss, the lips became wider, fuller, yet remained twisted in an expression of unbearable agony.

No—he refused to believe he was too late.

He started the engine again, steered slowly through the choppy water.

Shannon jolted, blinked into the bright sun.

She was tired and cold and so incredibly thirsty. She licked her parched lips, tasted the sharp tang of the ocean's salt.

So thirsty.

She shivered.

So cold.

Her eyelids drifted downward again.

So tired.

Then she heard it, the low drone of a motor across the water. Fatigue was chased away by fear, her heart sinking like the empty tank she'd discarded as tears of frustration and despair filled her eyes.

Dammit.

She didn't have the energy to swear aloud, but the oath echoed in her mind. She hadn't come this far only to let Drew find her, and she sank lower in the water now, hoping the boat would pass by without noticing her.

But as the vessel drew nearer she realized it was too small to be the *Femme Fatale.*

Relief surged through her as she forgot about the island and started praying for a rescue. A tourist charter, a fishing boat— she really didn't care.

She waved her arms over her head, hope expanding in her chest as the boat turned toward her. She continued to tread water as the vessel slowed and drew nearer.

Then she recognized the man at the helm.

Her jaw dropped, and she choked on a mouthful of seawater.

It was the man she'd met on the beach.

The one she'd invited back to her hotel room, almost made love to, and had last seen racing after her at the marina.

What was he doing out here?

Mike had never been as happy as he was when he recognized the spot of neon orange bobbing in the water as Shannon's life vest.

He slowed the boat so she wouldn't have to fight the waves churned up by the motor, then cut the engine completely as he came nearer. She was here. She was alive.

He hurried toward the ladder at the back of the boat to help her board. He was grinning like an idiot, but he couldn't seem to help himself. He wasn't too late. He hadn't failed her.

The realization, the relief, almost overwhelmed him.

Until he got closer to her.

Her deep-green eyes were shadowed and glassy with fatigue, her skin was pale and waxy, and she was shivering. He recognized the visible symptoms of impending hypothermia and knew she'd been in the water too long.

"I was beginning to wonder if I'd ever find you," he said, deliberately casual. He didn't want to alarm her by remarking on her physical condition. He just wanted to get her out of the water.

Shannon, apparently, wasn't so eager. She made no move toward the ladder and her only response to his comment was, "Why were you l-looking for m-me?"

"It's a long story," he admitted. "Why don't we talk about this on our way back to Miami?"

"B-because I'm not g-going anywhere with you until I know who you are and what you're d-doing here."

Who he was?

Mike's concern escalated. Maybe it wasn't just hypothermia. Maybe she'd suffered some kind of trauma or head injury and had amnesia.

"You know who I am," he reminded her. "Michael Court-land."

"I know that's who you *s-said* you were," she admitted.

Okay, so she didn't have amnesia, just a sudden case of distrust. He felt ridiculous carrying on this conversation over the side of a boat while she was shivering in the water, but he could understand that she needed some reassurance. He didn't know what had happened on that yacht to make Shannon jump overboard, but he knew it had to have been significant for her to take such drastic action.

"I don't know what Peart told you, but I'm exactly who I said I was."

She frowned. "Who's P-Peart?"

"Andrew Peart. The guy you left the hotel with."

"He said…" she trailed off, as if reluctant to confide anything the other man had told her.

As anxious as Mike was to finish this conversation, he was more anxious to get her out of the cold water. The bluish tinge of her skin worried him. "Would you please climb onboard so we can continue this conversation on our way back to Miami?"

"He said he was M-Michael Courtland. And he showed m-me identification."

He couldn't blame her for her doubts. During the time they'd spent together the previous evening, they'd talked about little of a personal nature. He'd certainly never told her about his reasons for being in Florida, his work or his indirect connection to her sister. And keeping that information from her—even if it had been his client's decision—had been a mistake.

"That's how he convinced you to leave the hotel with him," he guessed.

"He got m-me to leave by d-drugging m-me."

"If he drugged you, then it shouldn't surprise you to know he lied to you, too."

"It d-doesn't," she agreed. "B-but I want to know if you lied to m-me, too."

He met her gaze evenly, knowing that his assignment would be a lot more difficult—if not impossible—to carry out without her trust. "I didn't," he told her. "I might not have been completely honest about some things, but I never lied to you."

Still she hesitated.

He realized she was stubborn enough to freeze to death before she'd admit it was happening. But he refused to continue playing twenty questions while she was shivering. Not to mention that Peart's men were likely looking for her—for both of them. "Are you going to come aboard now or do I have to come in and get you?"

Her eyes widened. "You w-wouldn't—"

It was the chattering of her teeth more than the challenge of her words that mobilized him. He kicked off his shoes and dove into the water.

Shannon was sputtering when he surfaced beside her. "Are you crazy?"

His only response was to band an arm around her waist, then he started towing her back to the boat.

"I'm not getting on that boat with you." She struggled to free herself from his hold but was too tired to put much effort into her resistance.

"You don't have any other options."

As he reached the ladder, he lifted her onto his shoulder in a one-armed fireman's hold. He was suddenly aware of the softness of her breasts pressed against his back, the firmness of her buttocks beneath his splayed fingers. With every step, his breathing grew more labored—not from exertion but awareness.

He'd been too busy over the past few months to worry about his own physical needs—an oversight that his body had been protesting since he'd accepted this assignment and first set eyes on Shannon. He concentrated on the final rung, accepting that he would have to endure the protests a while longer.

Once on the bridge, he dumped her unceremoniously onto a padded leather seat. He knew there were towels belowdeck, but he didn't want to leave her for a minute. He didn't trust her not to disappear into the water again while his back was turned. Instead, he grabbed a blanket and wrapped it around her shoulders.

"You can ask all the questions you want on the way back," he promised her. "If at any point you don't like my answers—you're free to jump overboard again."

Shannon drew her knees toward her chest, tucking the ends of the blanket around her bare legs.

"Th-thanks." The shiver in her voice didn't quite conceal the sarcasm.

She was still so cold, so tired, so thirsty. But at least now she could close her eyes and not worry about drowning. Unfortunately, until all her questions had been answered, she wasn't going to take her eyes off this man who continued to claim he was Michael Courtland.

She shivered again, pulled the blanket tighter.

He held a plastic bottle of water toward her. "Drink."

She nearly wept with gratitude as she reached a hand out from beneath the cover to accept the offering.

"Th-thanks," she said again, minus the sarcasm this time.

But her fingers were numb, clumsy, and she couldn't seem to twist the lid. He placed his hand on top of hers, the warmth of his skin seeping into hers, and easily removed the top.

She felt her cheeks flush with humiliation. There was nothing she hated more than being helpless, and there was no denying how completely weak and helpless she was now.

Or maybe, a little voice inside her head taunted, the warmth

seeping through her limbs had nothing to do with embarrassment and everything to do with a more primal response to this
man. There was nothing personal in the way he touched her,
but she couldn't deny that the strength of his hand, the heat from
his skin, brought to mind very personal memories of last night.

She tipped the bottle to her lips and drank deeply, desperately.

"Slowly," he admonished.

She forced herself to take smaller sips.

He crouched beside her chair and rubbed his hands briskly
over her arms, the friction generating welcome heat. "Are
you okay?"

His eyes reflected the genuine compassion and concern she
heard in his voice.

Genuine?

She nearly laughed aloud at the thought. As if she would
recognize genuine. In the past several hours, she'd been
conned by two different men, including this one—and she was
determined not to let him con her again.

"F-fine," she finally responded to his question.

To her surprise he smiled. "You're one hell of a swimmer,
Shannon Vaughn."

The hint of admiration in his voice was as unexpected as
the smile. She didn't know how to respond to such a comment,
or even if she wanted to.

"I saw you go into the water when you left the *Femme Fatale*," he admitted. "Of course, I lost you when you submerged, but I figured you'd have to surface again eventually."

"You were l-looking for m-me? The whole t-time?"

He shrugged, stood up.

"Why?"

Instead of answering her question, he said, "Maybe that
should wait until we get back to Miami—in case you decide
you want to throw *me* overboard."

She shook her head. "You said I c-could ask whatever

questions I wanted. I n-need to know what's going on. Why Drew wants to k-kill me. And how you f-figure into this."

Michael slipped his shoes back on before moving toward the bridge to restart the engines and set them on course for Florida.

"I can't say for certain why he wants you dead," he said. "Except that it's probably retribution for Conroy's death."

"I didn't even know the m-man," Shannon protested.

"But your sister did."

She pulled the ends of the blanket more tightly around her. Warmth was slowly seeping into her limbs, numbness gradually giving way to a dull ache, but she still couldn't stop shivering. "How d-do you know that?"

"Because I'm a private investigator hired by Dylan Creighton to watch out for you while you were on vacation."

She remained silent.

"Let me guess, that's the same story Peart told you?"

She nodded.

Michael swore. "He obviously planned this whole thing through carefully, starting with the break-in of your hotel room."

"What do you m-mean?"

"It occurred to me that nothing was taken because he only wanted to scare you, so you'd be more susceptible to his story and more eager for his protection when he appeared at your door."

"But why? If he really wants m-me dead, why didn't he just shoot m-me then? Not that I'm not grateful he didn't, b-but why?"

He shrugged. "Zane Conroy was a master manipulator, and it's possible, if Peart's goal is to avenge Conroy's death, he plans to do so as Conroy would have done."

She remembered the way Natalie, as the new A.D.A. in Fairweather, had been set up to find a dead body and later to prosecute the murderer, who had also been set up by Conroy, and realized his explanation made sense.

"Or it could simply be that Peart isn't high enough in the organization to do the deed himself," he suggested as another possibility.

"He m-mentioned someone named A.J.," she admitted. "Said he would decide how and when I was to be m-made an example of."

"Then I'd say you're lucky you didn't stick around long enough to meet him."

She remained silent, but nodded her agreement.

"I know you're scared, but you can trust me, Shannon."

She wanted to trust him. She wanted to believe there was someone really on her side, that she wasn't alone in this. But how could she? How could she know for certain that this man was any better than Drew?

Okay, he had very likely saved her from drowning, and she had to admit that was a big point in his favor. But her doubts and uncertainties were too numerous to be so easily overcome, and they multiplied further when she realized Michael was turning the boat around again.

"Isn't Miami the other way?"

"It is," he agreed, his tone grim. "And so is the *Femme Fatale.*"

She squinted. She could see something in the distance—a dark blip on the horizon. But she couldn't tell if it was even a boat, never mind Peart's yacht.

"How d-do you know?"

He tossed her a pair of binoculars.

She held them to her eyes, adjusted the focus. Her breath caught in her throat as the boat seemed to jump toward her. It was the *Femme Fatale,* and it was moving fast, slicing easily through the choppy water as it sped toward them.

She lowered the binoculars, exhaling a shaky sigh when the vessel magically retreated into the distance again. "B-but there's no way they can know I'm with you, on this b-boat."

Michael didn't say anything.

"C-can they?"

"Peart used my name to get to you," he reminded her. "Which means he knows who I am and why I was in Miami. It's logical that he'd try to find me to find you again."

"M-maybe we should radio for help," she suggested, wondering that she hadn't thought of it sooner.

"The radio doesn't work."

"Oh."

He nodded grimly. "It's just you and me."

She shivered as she stared out at the blue sky and even bluer water—less from cold than apprehension this time. "What are we g-going to do now?"

"We're going to duck in behind that island," he said, nodding toward a small landmass directly ahead of them. "And hope like hell they go right past."

She fell silent, staring at the island that still looked so far away, not daring to watch Drew's yacht draw steadily nearer.

"Have you ever piloted a boat?"

The abruptness of the question startled her, and it took a moment for her to respond. "No."

"Well, let's hope you're a quick learner."

"Why?"

"Because I need you to take over here, just for a couple of minutes."

When she hesitated, Mike put his hands on her waist, guiding her into position at the helm. There was nothing of the passionate lover in his touch, yet somehow it evoked a flood of memories of those same hands on her skin the night before.

"Why?" she asked again.

But he'd already disappeared below deck.

Shannon blew out a breath and tightened her fingers around the wheel. She hoped he didn't have any particular course he expected her to follow, because she had no idea what she was doing. She simply fought to hold the craft steady as it bounced along on top of the rolling waves, lurching and swaying.

The blanket fell from her shoulders, but she didn't dare let go to retrieve it.

A couple of minutes, he'd said.

It was the longest two minutes of her life—except maybe those last two minutes she was in the water. Two endless minutes in which she couldn't help but wonder how her life had turned down this path, how everything had spun so completely out of her control.

Michael's return put an end to her ineffectual ruminations.

He carried a backpack slung over one shoulder, which he dropped at his feet before nudging her away from the wheel. "I'll take over now."

She stepped back gratefully, her gaze once again drawn reluctantly to the pursuing boat.

It was closer now. Too close.

Michael was right—there was no way they could outrun Drew's yacht. And although she still wasn't sure she trusted him, she couldn't deny that she needed him right now. Which meant that he needed to know the full extent of the threat they were facing.

She swallowed, forcing down the fear that was clawing its way up her throat, then said, "They have weapons on the yacht."

The information didn't surprise Mike; the fact that Shannon knew about the illegal arsenal did.

"What kind of weapons?" he asked.

"I don't know. They were packed in straw inside a wooden crate. Guns of some kind, and some tube-shaped things."

Her description, vague though it was, confirmed what Garcia had told him. "Could be AK-47s," he told her. "And shoulder-mounted rockets and RPGs."

He maneuvered the boat around the tip of the island, cutting the *Femme Fatale* from view—at least for the moment.

She worried her bottom lip with her teeth. "What does all that mean?"

He could give her any number of specs on each of those weapons: caliber, velocity, effective range. But he figured all she really needed to know could be summed up in a single word. "Trouble."

"I'm starting to wish I'd never left Chicago," she admitted.

"If Peart had already made up his mind that you were his target, you wouldn't have been any safer there."

She fell silent again.

He wished there was something he could say or do to reassure her, some way he could comfort her. But his priority right now was to keep her safe, and to do that he needed to stay focused. If last night had taught him nothing else, it had at least proven that touching Shannon Vaughn blew his focus all to hell.

He concentrated on steering the boat. They were getting into shallower water now, closer to the island. Close enough he could see through the turquoise water to the rocks on the bottom, and he didn't want to risk damaging the hull.

He heard Shannon's quick intake of breath and turned to see the bow of the *Femme Fatale* appear around the bend.

"We need to get to the island," he said. "It will be easier to evade them on land."

"Do you think we can evade them?"

"I *know* we can." He didn't believe in making empty promises, but he was confident the skills he'd learned and honed with the U.S. Army Rangers would ensure their survival—*if* they made it to shore.

He didn't know if she believed him, but she didn't argue the point. After a minute of tense silence, she spoke again. "They're not following anymore."

He turned to see that the *Femme Fatale* had, in fact, stopped pursuing them.

"That's good, isn't it?" Her voice was filled with cautious optimism.

"I wouldn't count on it." Even if the water was too shallow for the yacht to come farther, he didn't believe for a minute that Peart would give up.

Mike squinted against the sun, focused on the tall, dark-haired man on deck. Or, more specifically, on the weapon he was settling on his bulky shoulder.

He cut the engines and turned to Shannon. "We're going to have to swim."

She balked. "What? Why?"

He understood her resistance. She'd already spent too much time in the water, and now he was asking her to dive right back in. He understood, but he didn't have time to argue with her or explain.

Instead, he snagged the backpack with one arm, Shannon with the other, and jumped.

They hit the water only a heartbeat before the boat exploded.

Chapter 4

Shannon kicked her way toward the surface, sputtering and gasping as she broke through the water. She sucked in a lungful of air and blinked to clear her vision. The acrid smoke stung her eyes, burned her lungs. Broken pieces of fiberglass and twisted shards of metal—all that remained of the boat—slowly sank to their watery grave.

She twisted around, searching frantically through the debris for any sign of Michael, breathing an audible sigh of relief when he surfaced next to her.

She'd been shocked, even angry, at the way he'd thrown her overboard—until, even under the water, she'd felt the shock waves from the explosion.

He reached for her, squeezed her hand. "Are you okay?"

She nodded.

"Good. Because now we definitely have to swim."

This time, she didn't ask any questions. He'd saved her life, and that, she decided, entitled him to a certain level of trust.

Her muscles screamed in agony, but she swam. She found reserves of strength she hadn't known she possessed and followed Michael as he cut through the water. But her strokes weren't as strong or as smooth as his, and she quickly found herself falling behind.

Or she would have, if he hadn't taken her in a rescue hold and towed her.

She felt guilty for being such a burden, but she had no reserves of strength to draw on. He didn't release her until they were only in hip-deep water. "Can you run?"

She nodded, determined to at least make the effort.

And it was an effort, the drag of the water and the slickness of the rocks conspiring to impede their progress toward the beach. Her already overtaxed muscles threatened to give up entirely, and she knew it was only the solid grip of Michael's hand on hers that kept her moving.

She heard the sound of an outboard motor and knew that Rico and Jazz were in pursuit. She didn't turn to look. She didn't want to know how close they were.

The water was at her thighs, her knees, her ankles.

They were moving faster now, but the sound of the approaching engine was almost deafening. Or maybe that was the sound of her heart pounding in her ears.

The rocks gave way to sand, heavy and wet at first, then soft and hot beneath her bare feet. She was running as fast as she could, breathing hard with the effort of trying to keep up with him.

"I can't—"

"You can," Michael interrupted. "Into those trees."

Over the drone of the motor, she heard the staccato burst of gunfire. She recognized the sound because she'd heard it so often in movies, but it was louder and sharper in real life. And infinitely more terrifying.

He released her hand to position himself behind her, his hand now on her back to propel her forward. "Move!"

She felt the spray of sand against her legs as the bullets hit the beach.

Their pursuers were too close.

There was no way she and Michael could continue to out-run them.

Finally they pushed into the cover of the trees.

He didn't let her stop to catch her breath but led her deeper.

"Stop." He breathed the word softly, almost soundlessly.

Shannon halted beside him and saw that they were now fac-ing the beach less than fifty yards down from where they'd disappeared into the trees.

The beach onto which the Zodiac was now being dragged ashore.

Jazz was in front, pulling the bow of the craft with one hand, holding some kind of gun in the other.

"They can't have gone far." He dropped the boat, striding to-ward the opening between the trees where Shannon and Michael had disappeared. His hand gripped the weapon with easy famil-iarity, and she knew he was eager to start shooting again.

Rico stayed beside the boat, shaking his head. "We don't have time to go after them now."

"We can't leave them here." Jazz's voice was filled with anger, frustration.

In contrast, Rico's was controlled, almost unconcerned. "Where are they going to go?"

"That's not the point."

"That's exactly the point. We have other things to take care of first—we'll deal with the woman and Courtland when we get back."

"But—"

"We can't kill her yet, anyway, and if we don't make that shipment, A.J. will kill *us*."

Jazz hesitated a moment, then nodded.

Shannon felt some of the tension slowly seep from her body as she watched Jazz move back toward the Zodiac. But she didn't breathe until she heard the motor start up again, and she didn't speak until she saw the small boat heading back to the yacht.

"What are we going to do now?"

Mike had been prepared for the question. Unfortunately, he couldn't give her a more definitive answer than to say, "Hope the Sarsat beacon on the boat was working."

"What's a Sarsat beacon?"

"It's a distress signal sent via satellite to a search-and-rescue center. The coast guard might already be on its way." *If it was working.*

"Might?"

He should have known she'd pounce on that word. "Since the radio was destroyed, we have to consider the possibility that the emergency signal may have been, as well."

"Destroyed?" She frowned.

Damn.

"It had been tampered with," he admitted.

"Oh."

But it was obvious she didn't fully understand the implications of his explanation, and he didn't want to expand on the details right now.

"Let's take a walk around," he said. "Get our bearings."

He bent to retrieve the backpack, wincing when his arm flexed with the movement.

Frowning, he glanced at the bicep, at the sticky crimson fluid trickling down his arm. He'd felt the bite of the bullet, the searing heat as the metal projectile cut through the flesh, but he'd put it out of his mind. Now that more immediate dangers had passed, he knew he should take care of the wound.

It really wasn't deep, but in this environment, infection was a definite possibility.

"Which way—" Shannon gasped when she turned and saw the blood. "What happened?"

"Those weapons you were telling me about," he said. "Definitely AK-47s."

"You were *shot?*"

"Flesh wound," he said dismissively.

"There's an awful lot of blood...."

Her face seemed to drain of color right before his eyes, and he was afraid, for a moment, that she might pass out. "Are you okay?"

She drew in a breath, steadied herself. "I'm not the one who was shot."

He glanced at the wound, the blood still seeping down his arm. It really was minor—the bullet just having grazed the skin. "It's fine."

She shook her head and muttered something that sounded like "macho idiot" under her breath.

This time he did smile.

"Is there a first-aid kit in the backpack?" she asked.

"Yeah." He reached inside for the metal box with the familiar red cross on the top, scowling when he realized the box was wet, that everything inside the waterproof pack was wet. His scowl deepened when he realized there was a bullet hole in the fabric, and the canteen he'd packed was both broken and empty. He was almost more annoyed at the loss of the water than his injury. He bit back a curse and handed Shannon the first-aid kit.

She rummaged inside until she found an antibiotic wipe, gauze pads and tape. Her fingers were cool and gentle as she dabbed at the blood around the torn flesh.

The light touch reminded him of the way those same hands had skimmed over the bare skin of his chest, gripped his shoulders. The memory made him tense, tightening the muscles in his arm.

He swore.

She pulled her hand away. "Did I hurt you?"

Yeah, but the pain he was feeling had nothing to do with her nursing skills.

"No," he responded to her question, his voice sounding hoarse, aroused, even to his own ears.

She glanced at him warily, then away quickly, returning her attention to his arm.

He tried to focus on the scarlet blossom of a hibiscus flower visible in the distance, but his gaze kept being drawn back to Shannon. Her head was bent down as she applied herself to her task. Her long hair hung in a tangled, dripping mass down her back, but even the saltwater residue failed to dim its fiery color. Her neck was long and slender, the skin pale and smooth.

He wondered how she would respond if he dipped his head to nibble the soft lobe of her ear, press his lips to the graceful curve of her neck, touch his tongue to the racing pulse point at the base of her throat.

His eyes riveted on that pulse point.

It *was* racing.

She might project cool competence and a hands-off attitude, but Shannon Vaughn wasn't as unaffected as she wanted him to believe. Or maybe it was adrenaline that was causing her heart to pump so furiously.

He let his gaze drop further, to the wet T-shirt that clung provocatively to her generous curves. Her nipples pebbled beneath his stare, confirming that there was more than just adrenaline at work here.

She lifted his arm gently, to clean away some already dried blood, and his elbow brushed against her breast.

"Sorry."

"It's okay."

Her response was automatic, but he noticed that her cheeks had turned pink and her hands weren't quite as steady when she unrolled and tore off a piece of tape to fasten the gauze to his arm.

She definitely wasn't unaffected, and he suddenly wanted nothing more than to bridge the distance between them and cover her mouth with his own.

It was a natural desire under the circumstances—the result of adrenaline pumping through his own system. Because he understood the reaction, he was able to resist the impulse.

Besides, he knew one kiss wouldn't be enough. He wanted not just to taste her lips but to touch her all over. He wanted to hear her soft sighs and throaty whimpers as his hands moved over her naked flesh, to feel the yield of her soft curves to the press of his body as they merged together and finished what they'd started in her room.

He exhaled a ragged breath.

One kiss definitely would not be enough.

She finished applying the second piece of tape. Then she glanced up, her eyes locking with his, and he saw the desire that raged through him reflected in the dark-green depths of her gaze.

He heard her sharp intake of breath, noted the slight parting of her lips.

If he leaned toward her now, would she pull away?

Or would she meet him halfway?

He stepped back, away from Shannon, out of reach of temptation.

She closed the first-aid kit, put it away, then slung the bag over her shoulder.

"Let's go."

She sighed. "I'm guessing since Rico and Jazz left us here, there isn't anyone else on this island."

"That's right," he admitted. "We've landed on our very own

Gilligan's Island, and the first order of business is to find water and make shelter."

"*Make* shelter?"

He nodded.

"What do you plan to do, Gilligan? Build a little hut out of palm fronds?"

His eyes narrowed. As if her sarcasm wasn't enough, now she was insulting him. "Gilligan?"

She shrugged. "You were the one who brought up the show."

"But—Gilligan?"

"Believe me, I'd be much happier if you were a professor who could miraculously fabricate some kind of communication device out of coconut shells and vines."

Right now that would make him happy, too, but it wasn't going to happen. And although he had certain survival skills that no doubt would be useful in this situation, that wasn't one of them.

"You're the scientist," he reminded her. "I'll leave that up to you."

She looked around. "Well, I'm a little out of my element here."

"Then we'll have to give you another role." He decided turnabout was fair play. "Ginger or Mary-Ann?"

"Neither," she snapped.

But the idea was too intriguing to let go.

He let his gaze skim over her long, shapely legs, the softly curved hips, trim waist. He lingered for a moment on her full breasts, remembering the weight of them in his palms, the taste of her rosy nipples. His body responded predictably to the mental image as he continued his survey.

He took in the graceful line of her neck, the stubborn tilt of her chin, the tempting lushness of her lips. And the dark-green eyes that were currently spitting fire. Then there was the hair. He grinned. "Definitely Ginger."

She glared at him.

"She was so hot."

Shannon didn't say anything.

"Of course, there's something to be said for Mary-Ann's sweet innocence. And the way her curves filled out those little shirts and short shorts."

"You're a pervert."

"Just a healthy red-blooded man."

"Same thing," she muttered, pushing past him to lead the way.

Mike fell into step behind her, grinning as he watched her slim hips sway with every step.

Definitely Ginger.

Definitely hot.

Ginger.

Shannon huffed out an exasperated breath and pushed ahead through the trees. The man infuriated her. He was bold and arrogant and—dammit all—charming. He'd labeled her a sitcom-movie-star bimbo, but he'd done so with a slow, sexy smile, and she'd been ready to tumble into his arms.

Instead she'd done the smart thing: walked away.

Shannon had no idea where she was or where she was going, and she didn't care. She just needed to get away from Michael—to keep a safe, respectable distance and pretend her body wasn't still yearning to finish what they'd started in her hotel room last night.

Huffing out another breath she recognized that she wasn't mad at Michael; she was mad at herself.

She was a practical, rational woman with plans for her life that didn't include being kidnapped in Miami, shot at by killers or stranded on a deserted island.

Of course, nowhere in her carefully laid plans had she anticipated meeting Michael Courtland, either. And it was that first meeting—a seemingly chance encounter—which had fundamentally altered the path of her life. A path mapped out through careful consideration and meticulous planning—a path leading to career success and financial independence with no side trips for personal pleasures and no detours for emotional entanglements.

She pushed her way through the knee-high grasses, swatted at the bugs buzzing around.

Now she was in the midst of one hell of a detour, and all because she'd allowed herself to be seduced by a few kisses on a moonlit beach.

She was the only one to blame for what had happened between them. She could have—and should have—turned away from the attraction blazing between them. But he'd made her skin burn and her mind spin and her heart yearn, and she'd never felt any of those things before.

Her ex-husband had said she was a control freak. From her work in the lab to her responses in the bedroom, he'd accused her of rigid management of every aspect of her life.

Why can't you ever be spontaneous? Why can't you just let go and enjoy it? he'd said.

"It" being sex, of course.

Not that she didn't enjoy sex—she did. She just didn't understand why men were obsessed with it and women were supposed to get swept away by it. It was pleasant and pleasurable, but it had never been all-encompassing for her.

She'd never wanted it to be all-encompassing. She didn't want to chase after the elusive passion-of-a-lifetime as her mother had been doing for so many years.

Then she'd met Michael.

In six minutes he'd shown her more about passion than she'd experienced during the entire six months of her marriage to Doug. He'd made her feel both desire and desirable. He'd made her want things she'd never wanted: personal complications and emotional entanglements and uninhibited sex.

But she couldn't trust any of those feelings now. Their meeting hadn't been spontaneous or coincidental—it had been planned, a staged attempt to get close to her. And it was a blow to her pride to think his seduction routine had all been part of a design to keep her under his surveillance.

She thought of the heat in his eyes when he'd touched her, the passion in his lips when he'd kissed her. Had it all been fake?

She remembered the press of his body against her, the unmistakable evidence of his arousal, and managed a smile. Okay, at least she could be certain that something had been real.

She pushed the memories, the questions, aside.

What had happened with Michael in her hotel room last night was in the past; whatever his reasons for being with her then had absolutely no bearing on the predicament they were in now. And they were definitely in a predicament.

Stranded.

On a deserted island.

Together.

Her primary concern should have been the "stranded" part. Instead, all she could think about was that they were "together."

She needed to concentrate on Peart's threat and figure out some way to get off the island before he returned. That was certainly enough cause for concern without letting herself be distracted by this intense attraction that refused to go away.

She sent up a quick and silent prayer that the coast guard would show up to rescue them—soon.

Mike followed behind Shannon, preoccupied with his own thoughts. He didn't worry about where she was leading—the island wasn't big enough that he needed to be concerned they might get lost. He was more concerned with the possibility they might not find a source of fresh water.

In this heat, dehydration was a very real concern. Shannon was already showing the effects of fatigue. Her steps were lagging, but she continued along without protest. She couldn't have slept at all during the night, and he knew she had to be exhausted.

But she didn't complain, even though he knew her muscles had to be burning, the agony from the physical marathon she'd endured enough to make anyone scream.

And then she did scream.

Chapter 5

The reason for Shannon's cry was immediately apparent to Mike.

It was a brown-and-yellow boa, about six feet in length, and it was hanging from a branch immediately in front of her face. An unwelcome surprise, but also a harmless one.

Unfortunately, this snake didn't seem to know it should be harmless. As Mike watched, it somehow dropped from the low-hanging limb and managed to drape itself across the back of her neck.

Shannon stood perfectly still, her face white, her eyes wide, pleading.

"It's not poisonous," he reassured her, reaching for the snake.

As he did so, the reptile curled its body around her throat.

He cursed under his breath as he realized the stupid creature didn't seem to know it wasn't big enough to consume human prey. And while it didn't have any venom to worry about, there was a real possibility it could cut off Shannon's supply of oxygen.

He wrapped his fingers around the body, behind its head. The boa immediately flexed its muscles, tightening its coils in protest.

Shannon gasped and instinctively began clawing at it.

"Relax," Mike told her, forcing himself to do the same as he worked at untangling the boa. But the snake was determined to hold on, and he was having trouble getting a solid grip.

At last he managed to wrap his fingers around the body and unravel it from Shannon's neck. The creature responded to the indignant handling by twisting around his arm. If Mike hadn't been so concerned about Shannon, he might have been impressed by its tenacity. Instead, he was just pissed off.

Still holding the back of its head in one hand, he grabbed for the tail end with the other and stretched his arms apart so the snake couldn't maneuver into an offensive position again. He held the stance until it stopped struggling, then finally tossed it back into the bushes.

When he heard the rustle of it retreating through the long grass, he turned back to Shannon.

Her face was still white, her eyes still wide and filled with terror. And while she hadn't moved a single step since she'd first set eyes on the snake, her entire body was now trembling.

Mike gathered her close in an instinctive gesture of comfort.

A mistake, he realized immediately, because although she clung to him like a frightened child, she wasn't a child. The soft curves that pressed against him were definitely those of a woman—a woman he had no business putting his hands on. Not when her life was in danger because he'd left her alone when she was vulnerable.

But when he might have drawn away, she burrowed deeper against him.

"It's gone." He rubbed his hands gently down her arms.

She continued to hold on to him, continued to tremble.

"Snakes are pretty common here," he told her, "but they don't get much bigger than that one."

Despite his casual tone, he had to admit that he'd experienced a few moments of unease when the constrictor wrapped itself around her throat.

"It seemed big enough to me." She shuddered. "I'm terrified of snakes."

He could tell it was a difficult admission for her to make. A woman as fiercely independent as Shannon wouldn't easily admit to any kind of weakness, and he imagined that she'd only done so now because events of the past twelve hours had chipped away at her usually impenetrable facade.

"They're not among my favorite creatures in the world, either," he admitted.

"Really?" She asked the question with her face still buried in his shirt.

"Really." He brushed a hand over her hair, worked his fingers through the wet ends that were tangled together.

"Sharks scare me to death, too," she confessed softly.

"Sharks?"

She nodded. "While I was swimming, all I could think was that I'd rather die from a gunshot than be eaten by a shark."

"I don't think you need to worry that we'll find any hammerheads in the trees around here," he assured her.

She eased out of his arms, looked up at him with narrowed eyes. "Are you making fun of me?"

"No," he said honestly. "I'm just surprised that a woman who is worried about sharks would choose to jump off a boat in the middle of the ocean where the nearest landmass was miles away."

"Death at the hands of my abductors seemed imminent, while being eaten by a shark was only a possibility."

"Sharks or no sharks, you could have died in the water. From hypothermia or dehydration or any number of things."

She straightened her shoulders, lifted her chin just a fraction. "I know, but at least it was my decision."

He shook his head. There was no denying that the woman had guts. "Dylan warned me about your independent streak."

"Independence isn't a character flaw."

"It could be when it compels you to take a midnight swim in the middle of the ocean."

"What was I supposed to do?" she challenged. "Sit around and wait for you to rescue me?"

"Yes."

His response startled her into silence for a moment.

"I was finalizing my plans to get onto the yacht when you jumped off," he told her.

Her brows drew together. "How were you going to do that?"

"Trust me—I would have managed it."

"You keep insisting that I should trust you, but you haven't given me any reason to do so."

"I saved your life," he said. "Twice."

She nodded. "But I might never have ended up on Drew's yacht if you'd been honest with me."

"What do you mean?"

"If you'd told me that you were a private investigator when we first met, if you'd told me the truth about why you were in Florida, I would have been more wary when Drew showed up at my door with the same story."

He hated to admit it, but she had a valid point. "I didn't tell you at first because Dylan asked me to keep the surveillance low-key. He wasn't sure if there was any real danger, and he didn't want to worry you unnecessarily. And when Conroy was killed, he believed the threat had passed."

She considered his explanation for a moment. "Okay, that

was at first," she allowed. "What about later, when you introduced yourself to me on the beach?"

Mike hesitated, knowing this was where things got a little sticky. "I didn't tell you then because my reasons for being with you had nothing to do with my assignment."

She was obviously skeptical.

"I was attracted to you. It was as simple—" and as complicated "—as that."

Shannon pondered his words as she followed in his footsteps. After the snake incident, she was more than happy to let Michael lead the way through the trees, to struggle along behind him through the hanging vines and palmetto fronds.

It was as simple as that.

Except nothing was ever as simple as it seemed, least of all the attraction that still simmered between them. She could deny it all she wanted, but it was there—hanging in the air as thick and heavy and all-encompassing as the humidity.

And how completely inappropriate was that?

They were stranded on a deserted island, at the mercy of the elements and the bugs—she paused on that thought to slap at another mosquito on her arm—and deadly predators with no way to escape, and she was thinking about her nonexistent sex life.

A sex life that had almost been brought back into existence by Michael last night. Except that she'd kicked him out of her room because she'd been too stubborn and proud to admit that she was afraid. She couldn't help but think how different her situation might be right now if only she'd let him stay with her.

She wondered if they should discuss what had happened between them, then discarded the idea as quickly as it had come.

She didn't want to discuss it, she didn't even want to *think* about it. It was probably the last thing on his mind right now, anyway, after the events of the past few hours.

"Are we going to talk about it or continue to tiptoe around it?"

His question proved her wrong, unnerving her with the realization that his thought process had so closely paralleled her own.

"I'm perfectly happy to keep tiptoeing," she said.

"Figures," he grumbled. "Most women want to talk a relationship to death, but *you* don't want to talk at all."

"We don't have a relationship. And I'm willing to talk about anything but last night."

"Why?"

"Because it was a mistake—a glaring error in judgment." She flushed, realizing how incredibly insulting that sounded. "Not because of you personally, but because I don't do things like that."

He glanced over his shoulder. "Things like what? Taking strange men back to your hotel room?"

"Exactly like that," she agreed.

"Why not?"

"Because it's irrational and irresponsible."

"And you're always rational and responsible," he guessed. Except for last night... "Always."

"That doesn't sound like very much fun."

She shrugged. "Fun isn't high on my list of priorities."

"Maybe it should be. Maybe, if you let yourself have some fun every once in a while, you wouldn't have made such a—what did you call it?—glaring error in judgment."

"I thought we weren't going to talk about it."

"That wasn't a mutual decision. And I'm curious as to what may have inspired your out-of-character behavior."

She remained silent. A conversation, by definition, required more than one person, and she could end this one by simply refusing to be a part of it.

"If you don't know," he continued. "How can you be sure it won't happen again?"

He was deliberately baiting her, but she still couldn't prevent her instinctive and emphatic response. "It won't."

He turned to face her, forcing her to stop abruptly. He was close. So close she could feel the heat emanating from his body—heat that frazzled her nerve endings and scrambled her thought processes.

"How can you be sure?" he asked again.

She swallowed. "Because anything personal between us would be a mistake."

"The timing and the circumstances might not be ideal," he admitted. "But it's already personal between us."

She moistened her chapped lips with the tip of her tongue, realizing her mistake when his gaze zeroed in on her mouth.

"Isn't there some kind of rule against involvement with a client?"

His smile was slow, sensual. "I figured you for the kind of woman who would play by the rules, but I didn't expect you to hide behind them."

"I'm not hiding."

"And you're not my client," he pointed out.

"A mere technicality."

"An important distinction."

The insects continued to buzz around them, but she was oblivious to them now. She was oblivious to everything except Michael. She could see only him, the dark sheen of his hair, the undisguised hunger in his eyes, the sensual curve of his lips. She could hear only him, the steady rhythm of breath moving in and out of his lungs. She could smell only him, the elemental scent of male heat and earthy sweat. She'd worked in fragrance development early in her career at Divine Cosmetics. She understood the role of scent in triggering certain responses, but she'd never met a man whose natural essence triggered her own pheromones.

He leaned close, closer.

Was he going to kiss her?

Her breath caught in her throat.

Would she kiss him back?

No, definitely not.

She'd already told him, clearly and unequivocally, that what happened between them last night would not happen again. Yet less than three minutes later, she was fighting against the same desire that had compelled her earlier out-of-character behavior.

She took a careful step back.

His gaze followed her movement, then moved past her to something in the distance. "Look at that."

She exhaled an unsteady breath. "What?"

"Coconut trees."

She picked up her pace, perking up immediately at the thought of filling the empty hole in her stomach. Other than the bottle of water he'd given to her on the boat, she hadn't had anything since dinner last night.

Dinner with Michael.

She pushed the memory aside.

He was already crouching at the base of the tree, shaking his head as he examined and discarded samples of fruit on the ground.

"What's wrong?"

"These are too old."

"We can't eat them?"

He shook his head again. "The flesh will be hard and the water dried up."

"Oh." Her excitement fizzled like air escaping from a balloon, but he didn't seem discouraged. In fact, he was removing his shoes and socks.

She tilted her head back to look up at the top of the tree. "You're not really going to climb up there?"

"Do you have a better plan?"

"No, but—" She clamped her jaw shut as he looped his arms around the tree, gripping the back of it with his hands. She watched in amazement as he braced the soles of his feet against the trunk and seemed to walk up the tree, alternately moving his hands and feet as he ascended. Amazement turned to apprehension as she realized how far off the ground he was.

"Look out below," he said.

She stepped back as the first coconut thunked onto the ground near her feet. Another quickly followed. Then two more.

After a few more seconds passed, she looked up to see Michael working his way back down the tree. She tried not to stare, but she was mesmerized by the flex of muscles in his arms and legs. Muscles she'd explored with her own hands. She felt a quiver in her belly and tore her attention away to begin gathering up the coconuts.

He dropped to the soft ground and smiled. "Hungry?"

Her stomach growled, her mouth watered. She nodded.

He selected one misshapen sphere from the pile she'd made. The waxy, green covering split when he smashed it against a rock, then he dug his fingers into the fissure to peel back the husk and reveal the hairy brown inner shell.

Then he pulled a knife out of the pocket of his shorts, flipped it open. The lethal-looking blade glinted in the sun as he poked the point of it into one of the eyes, pushed it deeper, then twisted it back and forth, boring out the hole. When he was finished, he held the shell toward her.

She gratefully accepted the fruit, tipping her head back to taste the milk. It was watery and sweet, a glorious treat for her parched throat. After a few sips, she handed the coconut back to Michael.

He wrapped his fingers around hers, around the shell, and lifted his other hand to brush his thumb over her bottom lip. When his hand withdrew, there was a drop of milk on the pad. He lifted it to his mouth, licked it.

Something inside her quivered, and she felt her nipples pebble beneath the wet T-shirt.

His gaze dropped to the front of her shirt. There was no way he could miss her obvious reaction, not with the way the wet cotton clung to her like a second skin.

Then he raised the coconut to his mouth, putting his lips where hers had been. There was something strangely intimate about sharing the milk of this fruit with him, despite—or maybe enhanced by—the knowledge that only last night he'd had his tongue in her mouth…and other even more personal places.

"More?" he asked.

Her body ached, yearned.

Yes. More.

She finished off the juice and returned the shell to Michael.

He picked up the knife again and sliced through the shell, neatly splitting it in two. The flesh inside was milky white, glistening with moisture. He broke a piece off, held it to her lips.

She parted her lips to bite into the firm, crunchy meat.

He took a bite of the same piece, his eyes on hers, his gaze reflecting the heat she felt building inside herself.

She felt her breath coming faster, her heart pounding, and knew if she wasn't careful, she would end up jumping the man over a coconut. She didn't know what had gotten into her— she wasn't an impulsive person and she definitely wasn't the type of person to succumb to hormonal impulses. But there was something about Michael that tempted her to throw caution to the wind, even in these bizarre circumstances.

Or maybe it was the circumstances themselves that were causing her to act so irrationally. Yes, that made sense. It was adrenaline coursing through her blood, not desire. A natural and completely understandable response to the life-threatening situation she found herself in.

Satisfied that there was a reasonable explanation for her unreasonable behavior—even if it didn't justify her actions last night—Shannon picked up another chunk of fruit.

"How did you learn to climb a tree like that?" she asked.

"Practice."

It was an answer, but one that didn't give her any information. A deliberate evasion? she wondered. She didn't know. She also didn't intend to give up. If they had to be stuck on this island together, they might as well get to know each other.

"Did you climb trees in your backyard as a kid? Or work picking fruit when you were a teenager?"

"Neither."

"Or maybe you were separated from your parents as an infant, raised by apes like Tarzan, and therefore simply unable to carry on a human conversation."

His smile was wry. "That doesn't sound like such a horrible fate."

Before she could decipher his cryptic comment, he stood up.

"We need to keep moving," he said, already gathering up the rest of the coconuts. "To find water and shelter—hopefully before the storm hits."

She tipped her head back, noted the sunlight still streaming through the canopy of trees. There were some clouds that she could see, but nothing that suggested a storm. She rose to her feet, anyway, ignoring the protests of her aching muscles as she did so, because she knew that, regardless of the weather, water and shelter were essential to their survival on this island.

As she fell into step behind him, the sun beating down on them, she couldn't help asking, "Storm, huh?"

He chuckled. "Trust me."

Trust wasn't easy for her to give under the best of circumstances, but considering that he'd already taken a bullet for her, wrestled a snake from around her throat and scaled a tree for coconuts, she was willing to give him the benefit of the doubt. At least for now.

She followed him through the thick growth, ducking through palmetto fronds and battling with hanging vines. Although the lush, tropical vegetation sheltered them from the worst of the sun's rays, there was no escaping the oppressive humidity. Or the bugs.

Michael paused for a second.

"What's the matter?"

"Shh."

She fell silent, listening as he was apparently doing. She could hear the steady rustle of leaves and grasses, the incessant buzzing of insects and the occasional melody of birdsong—the same sounds she'd been hearing since they landed on this island.

But her guide obviously picked up on something else, because he pivoted about sixty degrees and started forward again. "This way," he said. "I can hear it."

"Hear what?"

"Water," he answered over his shoulder.

She nearly whimpered with relief. Although the coconut milk had taken the sharpest edge off her thirst, she desperately needed to rinse the dried salt from her skin and hair.

When they reached the source, she recognized the need to modify her plans. The stream wasn't even four feet across at its widest point and probably no more than a couple of feet deep. Still, it was clear and—when she stepped into it—blessedly cool.

When Michael had taken her onboard his boat, she'd felt as though she wouldn't ever get warm. The cold had seemed to penetrate her bones and chill her to the core. But after trekking through the tropical heat, her skin was now slick with perspiration, and the chilly water was undeniably refreshing.

She knelt down to dip her cupped hands into the stream, then sighed as she let the liquid trickle through her fingers. It was clear, probably spring fed, but she couldn't take the chance. As thirsty as she still was, she knew it needed to be purified before they could drink it. Even a sip of contaminated water could create bigger problems than dehydration.

"Do you happen to have a pot in that backpack of yours so we can boil some water?" she asked hopefully.

"No," he admitted. "But I have purification tablets. We just need a container."

She'd seen him remove the pieces of the shattered canteen from the backpack and knew it wasn't his fault they were unprepared. Still, she couldn't resist saying, "At least Gilligan had access to the cooking equipment from the *Minnow*."

"That's because the *Minnow* wasn't blown to bits," he said dryly.

She nodded, acknowledging the validity of his point.

"Of course, you're welcome to swim to the bottom of the bay to see if there's anything left to salvage."

"I doubt it would be worth the effort," she said. "And I've done enough swimming for a while, thanks."

"Then we'll have to get creative."

And saying those words, he pulled out a condom.

Chapter 6

Shannon stared at the square packet in his hand.

Obviously Michael believed in being prepared, but did he really expect—

She wouldn't let herself complete the thought. She refused to acknowledge the hot thrill of anticipation that coursed through her veins.

No, it wasn't excitement; it was anger. She was furious that he would make such an assumption. Regardless of what had happened between them last night, she had no intention of sharing any further intimacies with this man. And how could he even *think* about getting naked when their lives were in danger?

She forced a note of aloof disdain into her voice when she said, "You've got to be kidding."

He followed her pointed gaze and chuckled. "You think I want to have sex with you?"

Some of her indignant anger faded to confusion. Confusion gave way to embarrassment. "You...don't?"

His eyes raked over her boldly, then he smiled, a quick grin filled with blatantly masculine approval. "Oh, yeah." He waited a beat before adding, "But that's not what this is for."

The confusion returned. "I'd hardly profess to be an expert," she said. "But even in my limited experience, I'd venture to say that's *exactly* what a condom is for."

He quirked an eyebrow. "How limited?"

She felt her cheeks burn. "That's none of your business."

"It is if we're going to be lovers."

"We're not."

His grin widened. "Again, I beg to differ."

"You can beg all you want—it's not going to happen."

"By the time I'm finished, Ginger, *you'll* be the one begging."

It was a hotly spoken promise that caused her heart to skip a beat, but she was determined not to let him know it. "That's quite an ego you have, Gilligan."

She'd used the insult deliberately, hoping to annoy him, to reassert distance between them. A distance she needed him to acknowledge and accept, because when she was with this man, her hormones had a tendency to overrule her common sense.

Unfortunately, he didn't remind her of Gilligan at all. He was too tall, too strong, too elementally masculine. And the combination of his narrowed gaze and the dark stubble on his jaw made him look just a little bit dangerous. Temptingly dangerous.

"It's a water receptacle," he told her, choosing to let her comment pass without argument.

She frowned, not entirely sure she should believe him. "Do you really expect me to drink out of that?"

"Only if you're thirsty."

She glared at him.

"It's not my first choice, either. But it's the only thing we have that will hold enough water to let us safely use the purification tablets."

"How do you know it will work?"

"Basic training," he told her. "Nonlubricated condoms have several uses and are standard issue in most survival kits."

His reassurance made her feel only marginally better.

"We'll move back to the beach to make camp," he said. "But we'll need to take water with us."

"Why can't we make camp right here?"

"Because the sound of the stream might cover up other sounds we need to be listening for."

"Like rescuers?"

"Yeah," he agreed. "Or predators."

She knew he wasn't just referring to animals, but Rico and Jazz. Their promise to return was something that would weigh on her mind until she and Michael somehow managed to get off this island—*if* they managed to do so before Peart's men returned.

She sent up another silent prayer that the emergency beacon was working and the coast guard would find them first.

"Near the beach, we'll be able to hear any approaching vessels sooner and signal for help," he explained.

Again she read between the lines to hear what he wasn't saying: *or run for the hills.* Not that there were any hills on this island, nothing substantial, anyway. And if Rico and Jazz returned before they were rescued, they were going to be in trouble.

She shivered as a breeze rustled through the trees and clouds blocked out the sun.

Maybe he was right—maybe there was a storm coming.

Michael had found a bottle of purification tablets in the backpack and tucked them into his pocket. The condom was still in his hand.

"Are you really going to put water in that?" she asked, still thinking there had to be a better way.

He grinned. "Don't worry. There are several more in the pack if we need them for…anything else."

Shannon decided the best response to his suggestion was silence. She was feeling decidedly heated as a result of their sexual banter—damn, the man didn't even have to touch her to make her hot—and didn't want to encourage him to continue the conversation. So she was relieved when he rose to his feet, condom in hand and headed toward the stream.

He'd taken only a few steps, however, when he turned to glance back at her over his shoulder. "That ego you referred to earlier?"

"Yeah," she said hesitantly.

"I earned it."

She held her breath as she watched him walk away.

Saunter was more like it. His steps as arrogant as his words, his smile just confident enough to make her heart sigh.

Despite their almost constant verbal sparring, however, she was grateful Michael was stranded with her. He seemed to know so much about survival, while she was comparatively inept and generally helpless.

After snakes and sharks, there was nothing Shannon hated more than being helpless.

It was a feeling that stemmed back to her childhood. She'd grown up poor, not knowing from day to day whether there would be dinner on the table when she got home from school. Her father had been a laborer and he'd worked hard when there was work to be had. But he'd frequently been laid off or between jobs, and then the grocery money had gone to the landlord instead. Although her mother had worked prior to meeting and marrying Robert Vaughn, he'd been insistent that his wife did not need a job outside of the home.

Deborah had accepted her husband's decision, as she'd accepted that his authority was absolute in their home. She'd been completely in love, completely devoted.

Shannon had resented her mother's willing subservience almost as much as she'd resented living in poverty. She'd started waiting tables when she was fifteen, determined that she would go to college, that she would never subordinate her own ambitions or desires to those of a man.

Not that she'd wanted to live her life alone. No, she'd been young and naive enough to believe that she would someday meet a man who would be willing to accept her as an equal partner. And she'd foolishly believed Doug was that man.

When she'd finally accepted her mistake and walked away from her marriage, she'd made a new vow: to depend on no one but herself.

For the past nine years, she'd done exactly that.

But there was no denying that she needed Michael now. Although it grated to be dependent on someone else at this stage in her life, she was thankful for his presence. Not just his knowledge and competence in dealing with the necessities of survival, but his company.

Pride was a strange thing, she realized now. Pride was the reason her father had forbidden her mother to work outside the home. He'd needed to feel he was capable of providing for his family, even when he wasn't.

Shannon now realized she was guilty of the same stubborn pride.

It was pride that insisted she could go it alone when her heart longed for a partner with whom to share the burden. And it was pride that had made her send Michael out of her room last night when what she'd really wanted was to feel the support of his strong arms around her.

She'd blamed Michael for his deception—suggesting that his lack of disclosure was responsible for their current predicament. The truth was, they were both at fault.

And what did it matter who was at fault? The end result was the same. Regardless of who had done what, they were both stuck on this island, they were both probably going to die there.

She sighed wearily.

Michael had promised to do whatever was necessary to protect her—but he was only one man. If what she'd heard about Conroy's organization was true, there were legions of hired guns ready to do his bidding—ready to kill her. And Michael, too, for no reason other than that he'd already demonstrated a willingness to put himself in the line of fire for her.

She let her gaze drift over to where he was crouched by the stream—just in time to see him tug his T-shirt over his head. She stared, mesmerized, as he stripped away the garment.

The action couldn't have taken more than a few seconds, but it held her enraptured as the hem moved upward, inch by inch, exposing hard muscles, bronzed skin and a sprinkling of dark hair that arrowed into the waistband of his shorts.

Shannon felt her mouth go dry. Her palms tingled with the memory of sliding over that firm body. She continued to watch him, acknowledging that she was just shallow enough to be turned on by the sight of his gloriously muscled physique. The broad shoulders, mouthwatering pectorals and sleek, rippling abs. He was so primal, so perfect.

And while she wasn't afraid to admit she was attracted to him, she was cautious about pursuing that attraction. Because what had started as something purely physical was threatening to turn into a lot more.

She tore her gaze away, nibbled on her bottom lip.

The problem was that she was starting to *like* him.

He'd promised Dylan he would keep her safe, and he'd put his own life on the line to do so, proving that he was trustworthy and fearless. But she knew he would have done the same to protect anyone in danger, because he was innately honorable. And after rescuing her from the snake—she shuddered at the memory—he'd taken the time to comfort her and calm her fears, showing that he was also thoughtful and caring.

Yeah, she was definitely starting to like him, and the liking scared her far more than the chemistry between them.

Michael set the water-filled receptacle inside his T-shirt to support the fragile weight, then dropped one of the purification tablets into the condom before picking up the bundle and carrying it back to Shannon. He set it down carefully beside her.

"I thought I'd take a look around," he said, "if you'll be okay by yourself for a few minutes."

She glanced around uneasily, looking for snakes and other unknown dangers that might be lurking in the trees, just waiting for him to leave her alone. She was afraid, not just of what might happen in his absence, but of what might happen to him. "Maybe I should go with you."

He shook his head. "You should rest—try to rebuild your strength."

She couldn't deny that she was tired, but she wasn't ready to be left alone.

"Unless you're afraid to stay here by yourself," he said.

There was no censure in his voice, and yet she couldn't bring herself to admit it was true. To admit that sometime during the past hour they'd been traversing the island together, she'd come to rely on his knowledge and his guidance in an environment so far beyond her realm of experience she might as well be on another planet. Instead, she said, "Of course not. I wanted to wash some of this dried salt off my body and rinse out my clothes, anyway."

He nodded. "I won't be long."

Left to her own devices, Shannon decided that she would take advantage of Michael's absence to rinse off in the stream. She tugged the shirt over her head and unfastened the button on her skirt, reminding herself that her bra and panties were no more revealing than most two-piece bathing suits.

She moved into the water and dipped her hands to pick up

a handful of sand. She rubbed it over her body, removing any last traces of dried salt on her skin. Then she rinsed out her clothing, scrubbing the fabric against the rocks as women had done through the ages before washing machines. It was a bizarre thought, a surreal example of how far removed she was from the conveniences of her usual life.

She climbed out of the stream with her dripping clothes in hand and twisted the fabric to wring out the excess water, silently vowing she would never again complain about the two-dollars-per-load machines at the Laundromat. *If* she ever got back to civilization and had the opportunity to do laundry again.

She tried to banish the doubts and fears, but she couldn't see a way out of this predicament. The coast guard *might* be looking for them, but Rico and Jazz *knew* exactly where they were. And although she wasn't ready to give up, she knew that hopes and prayers weren't any match for the weapons those bad guys carried.

The sky overhead had grown increasingly dark as Mike trekked around, and the clouds were now low and heavy. When he got back to the stream, Shannon had finished bathing and was lying in the sun—no doubt trying to dry the wet T-shirt and skirt that were plastered to her body.

And what a body it was—long and lean with curves in all the right places. Except that this was the *wrong* place for him to be thinking such thoughts.

He stepped through the trees, striving for a brisk and impersonal tone when he spoke. "We're going to have to move fast if we want to beat the rain."

She immediately rose to her feet. An indication of surprise rather than compliance, he was sure. "Where are we going?"

"I found a cave not too far from here," he told her. "It will do until the storm passes. Can you grab the backpack?"

She did as instructed while he scooped up the water supply. He was grateful for her ready-and-unquestioning assistance, not wanting to admit how much the bullet wound in his arm was starting to ache. He made a mental note to ensure that Jazz was held responsible for that when he returned.

Peart's goons would return—of that Mike had no doubt. And although he almost relished the thought of facing off against the two men and making them regret what they'd put Shannon through, he knew his priority was to keep her safe. If he could get her off the island first, that would be best, but eventually Rico and Jazz would pay.

"Come on," he said, leading her into the brush just as the first drops of rain fell.

"How far is it?"

"Not far," he said. "But we'll have to move fast."

She picked up her pace.

Not fast enough.

The sky simply opened up, dumping torrential amounts of rain upon them. In less than half a minute they were soaked. Again.

"Here." He indicated the mouth of the cave he'd scouted out earlier.

Shannon was shivering already, her clothes sopping wet, but still she hesitated, eyeing the dark entrance warily.

"It's uninhabited." He stepped inside, leading the way.

She followed with obvious reluctance.

"Watch your head—the ceiling's low."

"I can't see anything."

The slight tremor in her voice prompted him to ask, "Are you afraid of the dark?"

"No—just of the creatures that might be lurking in it."

"I already told you it's uninhabited."

"Maybe no animals live here," she acknowledged. "But what if they use it to take shelter from the rain?"

"Then there would be evidence of occasional visits," he told her.

She fell silent.

"This should be far enough," he said, carefully setting down his bundle.

She dropped down beside him, brushing his injured arm in the process. He sucked in a breath, bit back the oath that sprang to his lips.

"S-sorry."

"It's okay." He willed the wave of pain to subside so his words would be true.

Shannon shifted away from him, just a little, and bumped into the pile of sticks and tinder he'd collected while she was bathing. She froze.

"There's something in here." Her whisper was strained. "A nest."

"It's only some wood and stuff I gathered to make a fire."

He heard her soft exhale. "S-something else you learned in basic training?"

"Yeah."

She fell silent again, but he could tell she had her arms wrapped around her knees, trying to preserve her body heat, trying not to shiver.

He reached for the backpack, his fingers brushing the bare skin of her thigh where her skirt had fallen open. The skin was soft, silky and covered with goose bumps. "I, uh, there's a blanket in here."

"O-okay."

Mike pulled the thermal covering out of the waterproof plastic case, then unfolded it and wrapped it around her shoulders.

"Th-thanks."

He knew sharing body heat would help warm her up a lot more quickly than a blanket, but under the circumstances, he didn't think that was a particularly good idea.

Instead he turned his attention to the contents of the backpack, retrieving the tin of emergency candles and waterproof
matches. He set one of the candles in place on the lid and lit
the wick. Immediately a soft glow illuminated their space.
It wasn't the same as a real fire, but it would provide a little
bit of heat in addition to light, without smoking them out of
the cave.

"Afraid of the dark?" she teased.

He smiled. No—afraid of the things he wanted to do with
her in the dark, although it wasn't an admission he was going
to make. "Maybe I am," he said instead.

"Then it's a good thing you brought candles."

Except that the flickering light somehow cast a romantic
glow in the darkness of the cave.

He shook his head. They were stranded inside a dark, damp
cave waiting for the imminent return of killers. There was absolutely nothing romantic about the situation—except for the
close proximity of a woman who made his hormones run
rampant and obliterated common sense.

He needed to ignore the hormones and retain that common
sense if he was going to get them safely off this island. But
still he wondered what would be the harm in passing a few
hours in the warm softness of her body.

Of course he knew that the harm would be in getting caught
by Rico and Jazz with his shorts down around his ankles. And
it was that threat he needed to remember—not the way her
lips had tasted or the way her body had arched against his, and
certainly not the soft murmurs of pleasure she'd made when
his hands had moved over her.

"What branch of the military were you in?"

Shannon's question proved that she wasn't preoccupied
with similar thoughts; the direction of the question effectively
cooled his own ardor.

"I was an army ranger," he said.

"I've heard about the rangers," she told him. "The most elite combat soldiers."

He tried not to remember how much pride he'd felt to have graduated from the grueling nine-week course beside his ranger buddy, how much it had meant to him to wear the coveted black-and-gold tab on the left shoulder of his uniform, how it had nearly destroyed him when Brent had been killed and he'd lost everything that mattered.

"How long were you in the army?"

"Six years."

"Why did you leave?"

He'd braced himself for the question. Since he'd left the service, it had been asked more times than he wanted to count. And it was the question he still couldn't bring himself to answer, falling back, instead, on his usual response. "I can't talk about my career—it's classified."

She narrowed her eyes. "If you don't want to talk about it, just say you don't want to talk about it."

"Fine. I don't want to talk about it."

He winced at the harshness of his words even before he saw the flicker of hurt in her eyes. He didn't mean to sound so abrupt, but his reasons for leaving the military weren't something he talked about. Even if he sometimes wished he could.

Because after seven years, his memories of that fateful day were still too fresh, his regrets too sharp. In the space of a few hours, he'd lost everything—the man who'd been his best friend in the world; a woman he'd cared for more than he'd expected; and the career that had given him a sense of direction and purpose.

"Fine," she responded, her tone matching his.

For several long minutes, the only audible sound was the pounding of the rain outside. A flash of lightning flickered, briefly brightening the interior of the cave. A few seconds later there was the low rumble of thunder.

"Sounds like it might be quite a storm," she finally said.

He recognized her statement as an offering of peace and, as it was more than he deserved, accepted it. "Afternoon storms are common in the tropics."

"Having never been to the tropics before, I wouldn't know," she said. "How bad is it?"

"Nothing unusual."

"Oh."

He managed a chuckle. "You sound disappointed."

"I was hoping the wind and waves might capsize the *Femme Fatale* and drown Rico and Jazz."

"Not likely."

Her sigh was heartfelt.

"I won't let anything happen to you, Shannon."

She didn't say anything.

"You don't believe me."

Still she hesitated. "I believe you'll do everything you can to protect me."

"But you don't think it'll be enough." He didn't know why her lack of confidence, her complete absence of faith, bothered him so much. It shouldn't matter what she thought or believed, except that her lack of faith was threatening to undermine his own confidence.

"I don't know if you can keep me safe," she admitted. "And I don't know that I'm comfortable with the thought of you—of anyone—putting their life on the line for me because it's their job."

It was his job—and it was personal. But at least both motives had the same objective: to keep her alive. And he would do it. He would concentrate on what needed to be done, focus on the essentials and forget that his errant hormones were preoccupied with getting her naked.

"You've never been to the Caribbean?" he asked, redirecting the conversation in response to her earlier comment.

"I've never been outside of the continental United States," she admitted ruefully. "Until now."

"Too bad your first experience had to be under these circumstances."

"Yeah."

"The Bahamian Islands really are beautiful," he told her. "But especially Exuma."

"What's different about that one?"

"It's still relatively unspoiled, not overrun with vacation resorts and tourists. The beaches are clean, the water crystal clear, and the weather absolutely fabulous."

"It sounds like you've traveled a lot."

He nodded.

"For business or pleasure?"

"Both. When I was a kid, I did a lot of globe-trotting with my parents."

In retrospect, he could appreciate the incredible experience he'd been given. At the time, however, he'd chafed against the strings that were attached to each opportunity. His father was fond of reminding him that with privilege came responsibility. Mike hadn't wanted either. It had been the main source of conflict between his father and him—until Mike had proven his determination to walk away from everything by joining the army.

"Later I moved around frequently with the rangers," he said. "I do a lot less traveling now, but I still enjoy getting away and seeing new places."

"Have you been to France?" she asked.

He remembered that he'd seen her reading a Paris guidebook on the beach. "A few times."

"I've always wanted to see Paris—the Louvre and Musée D'Orsay, the Eiffel Tower and L'Arc de Triomphe."

"It's an incredible experience—the art, the architecture, the ambience."

She sighed, a little wistfully. "I've been offered a job at Lilli Girard—an international cosmetics conglomerate based in France."

"Are you going to take it?"

"I've already said that I would."

"Then why do you sound hesitant?"

She shrugged. "Right now I have no idea when or if I'll get off this island."

"I'll do everything I can to make sure you get to Paris," he promised. "If that's where you want to go."

"It is. I've worked hard for this opportunity. I'm ready for a change."

Despite the assertion, he sensed she was still waging an internal battle about the decision to move across the ocean. "Won't you miss your friends and family?"

"Probably. Although to tell you the truth, sometimes my family drives me crazy."

"Isn't that what makes them family?"

She smiled. "Maybe."

"Who, in particular, drives you crazy?"

"How much time do you have?"

He shrugged. "It doesn't sound as if this rain is going to let up for a while."

"The most obvious insanity starts with my mother," she told him. "Deborah Vaughn-Clayton-Morningstar-Turner-Sutherland, and her never-ending search for the illusion of a happily ever after. Her fifth wedding is one of the reasons I came to Florida."

"And yet you don't seem happy about it," he noted.

"I didn't come to share in the celebration. I came to avert, or at least delay, the exchange of vows."

"Why?"

"Because she barely knows the man. I booked a flight into Fort Lauderdale—because that's where she was living—only to find she'd moved to Miami with him. She met him five weeks ago. And now she's gone off to some tacky chapel in Vegas to marry him."

"Which part is it that you don't approve of?"

Shannon sighed. "All of it—although I know it has nothing to do with me and I shouldn't care that she's setting herself up for yet another heartbreak."

"Is that why you didn't go to the wedding?"

"That—and the fact I wasn't invited."

Despite the casual tone, he sensed that she was hurt by the slight. "Even after you came all the way to Florida to see her?"

She shrugged. "They claimed to want a private ceremony. I think my mother was afraid I'd voice my objections to Elvis."

"Would you?"

"Probably not," Shannon admitted. "I might have little faith in their future together, but I can't deny that she seems happy with Ray. At least for now."

He ignored the last part of her comment and asked, "What do you know about husband number five?"

"Not a lot, except that he's a successful—and apparently very wealthy—businessman. She met him while she was waiting tables at some country club."

Outside, the pounding of the rain slowed.

"Do you think she's marrying him for his money?" he asked.

"No. My mother is a lot of things, but she's not a gold digger. Her commitment to my father was proof of that fact." She shook her head. "Undoubtedly she's marrying Ray because she believes she loves him."

"Maybe she does. And maybe he loves her."

She shook her head again, obviously unconvinced. "Now you sound like my sister."

"You said it's an illusion. Happily ever after," he prompted. "Is it personal experience that has made you so cynical, or your mother's previous four marriages?"

"I'm not cynical," she denied. "I'm realistic. Not many marriages succeed in this day and age."

"My parents have been married for thirty-seven years."

Shannon pulled the blanket tighter. "Is that single example supposed to make me believe in fairy tales?"

He smiled wryly. "Hell, no. My parents are miserable together—they're just too stubborn to admit it."

"Why would anyone want to live like that?"

It was the same question he'd wondered about for years. The question he'd learned the answer to only when he'd almost fallen into the same trap himself. "Because there's comfort in the routine, in being with someone rather than being alone."

"Only until you realize that you can be lonely even when you're not alone," Shannon said.

He nodded, surprised that her statement so closely mirrored his own thoughts.

"I like being alone sometimes," she admitted. "But I'm glad I'm not now. I don't know what I would do if I was here on my own."

"You don't have to worry about that," he promised her.

He didn't need to remind her that their greatest worry wasn't being alone or stranded—it was the imminent return of Peart's men.

Chapter 7

The funeral of Zane Conroy was well attended. The private chapel overflowed with associates who had come to pay their respects, and curiosity seekers who came to gawk at the dead man they hadn't dared glance toward when he was alive. Only one came to mourn.

There were several cops discreetly sprinkled among the guests, to take careful note of who was there and hopefully pick up on snippets of conversation.

As if it wasn't obvious to everyone in Conroy's organization who they were and the reason for their presence.

Except that it wasn't Conroy's organization anymore.

Her brother was dead.

Alysia blinked back the tears that burned, and dabbed the corner of her eye with a lace hanky.

There had been a meeting last night, hosted by her husband, Andrew, with the expectation of being handed the reins of power. She knew he was disappointed it hadn't turned out that way.

She knew he'd married her because she was a direct link to Zane. Now that Zane was gone, he'd expected that connection to be recognized and his years of service rewarded.

He'd certainly been with the organization longer than A.J.

But A.J. had known, better than anyone else, how to manipulate Zane. In recent years, A.J. had been an invaluable part of the organization, coming through for Zane in critical situations where others had already failed. And Zane had made sure everyone knew the role A.J. had played in things.

Alysia was surprised by the ease with which A.J. had taken control, but not displeased. As much as she loved her husband, she didn't want him taking over where her brother had left off.

It was a dangerous job. Zane had always tried to shield her from the darker aspects of his business, but she knew only too well exactly what it entailed. And she'd worried about him. He'd disregarded her concerns, insisting that without risk there was no reward.

Well, he'd taken one too many risks—and now he was dead.

She didn't want to see the same thing happen to Andrew.

She knew he was disappointed and resentful that he wasn't sitting in the top spot, but he'd managed to get past his personal feelings to be here for her. He slipped an arm across her shoulders now, and she let her head fall back against his shoulder.

She heard the almost imperceptible click of a shutter, knew the picture would show up in tomorrow's paper. Just as she knew there would be other photos taken, other names noted by both the cops and the reporters. But the buzz was all about A.J. She could feel the anticipation, hear the murmurs in the crowd.

"Is he here?"

"How long has he worked with Conroy?"

"What does this mean for the structure of the organization?"

She hated it. All of it. Her brother wasn't even in the ground and he was forgotten. She wanted to scream, to force their attention back to the man being buried, to demand justice for the way his life was taken away.

But she wasn't the type of woman to act on impulse or indulge in emotional displays. Her brother had raised her to be steady and strong, and he needed her to be that now.

She bit her lip. Hard.

They were all opportunists and gossipmongers, hypocrites and small-town cops. She refused to let any of them see her cry.

Shannon had been joking—

She tried to think back to their conversation. Was it only earlier that day? So much had happened in the space of the past twenty-four hours she wasn't even sure what day it was anymore.

But when Michael had suggested building shelter, she'd been joking when she'd challenged him to build a hut out of palm fronds. It turned out that was exactly what he had in mind.

She stared at the pile of leaves and branches she'd helped him gather and hoped he knew what he was doing. She stifled her doubts and questions—of course he knew what he was doing, he had ranger training and condoms in his survival kit—and watched as he demonstrated the proper technique for weaving the leaves together. When she'd shown she was capable of continuing with the assigned task, he moved on to making the framework for the roof and walls, using vines to tie branches together. He seemed to know exactly what he was doing and how to do it, while her efforts seemed clumsy and protracted.

"If we were trapped in a research facility, I wouldn't need your step-by-step instructions to complete the most basic tasks," she noted.

"If we were trapped in a research facility, we wouldn't be worried about crawling insects and rain."

"I just want you to know that I'm not a complete idiot," she continued. "I just don't have experience with this sort of thing."

"Not many people do." He'd already completed one section of frame and was starting another, but he paused to glance up at her. "Not many people have honors degrees in chemistry, either."

His comment made her feel marginally better—until she remembered that she hadn't told him about her education.

"How did you know about my degree?" She shook her head, already guessing the answer to her question. "You did a background check on me."

"It's standard procedure," he said unapologetically.

She fell silent.

"Why did you choose to study science?" he asked.

"Because it's fascinating and because elements and formulas are consistent and dependable."

He knotted the vine around the corner, then made a loop at the other end. "Has everything else in your life been so undependable?"

"Of course not," she denied, refocusing her attention on her own work.

"Then why do you feel the constant need to assert your independence?"

"Maybe I don't like to depend on other people, but that doesn't mean I can't." She flexed her fingers as she reached for another branch. "Like now, for example."

Obviously finished with his own task, he started to help her with the weaving.

She decided she was grateful for, rather than resentful of, his obvious expertise. "I was wondering about something."

He lifted a brow. "What's that?"

"You said the communications system on your boat had been tampered with."

"Yeah."

"Why would they disable the radio and not the engines? Why would Peart let you follow him?"

"That's a question only Peart can answer for certain," he said.

"But you have a theory."

He shrugged. "I don't know where exactly Peart fits into Conroy's organization. But I know—knew—Conroy. He was more than the leader of a crime syndicate—he was a gambler and a hunter. There was nothing he enjoyed more than pitting himself against others—to test their fortitude and worthiness.

"My guess would be that Peart planned this as a last tribute to his former boss. He wanted me to come after you so that he could play his own game of cat and mouse. Maybe even to prove his worth as a leader in the organization."

He'd suspected he was being set up, and he'd come after her, anyway. The realization staggered her. What kind of man risked his life for a stranger? Because, despite what had happened between them last night, they were strangers. Even though he'd been hired to watch out for her, he couldn't be expected to sacrifice his own life to save hers. Especially considering that she'd fought his efforts at almost every turn.

"Thank you." She said it softly, finally saying the words she should have spoken hours before. Many times before. When he'd found her exhausted and shivering in the water, when he'd forced her to jump off the boat, when he'd put himself between her and Jazz's gun. The realization of everything he'd done—everything he was still doing—was overwhelming.

He shook his head. "I don't want your gratitude, only your cooperation. When I tell you to do something, I need to know you'll do it—no questions asked."

It wasn't an unreasonable request, but she couldn't promise him anything except to say, "I'll try."

"I need you to do more than try."

"I know I owe you a lot. I owe you *everything*," she amended. "But unconditional trust isn't something that comes easily to me."

"Why?"

"Does it matter?"

"Under the circumstances, yeah, it does. If we're going to get off this island alive, I need your trust and you need to get over whatever is preventing you from giving it to me."

"Okay. I'll get over it."

"Tell me about it," he said gently.

"Why?"

"Because talking can be therapeutic."

She laughed. "Yeah. I can picture you stretched out on a psychiatrist's sofa, spilling the intimate details of *your* life."

He winced at the unlikely scenario. "I just meant that it might help to share your feelings with a friend."

"And that 'friend' would be you?"

"Why not?"

A valid question considering there was no one else around to talk to. But that fact didn't make her any more eager to spill the messy details of her life. "Let's just say someone I trusted implicitly used that trust to take advantage of me."

"Your ex-husband," he guessed.

Obviously her short-term marriage nine years earlier was something else that had come up in her background check.

Shannon nodded, confirming his suspicion. "We worked at the same cosmetics company. I was in product development, Doug was in marketing."

She paused, still reluctant to admit the extent of her husband's betrayal—and the depth of her own naiveté.

Michael remained silent, threading the woven panels through the crosspieces of the frame, waiting for her to continue but not pressuring her to do so.

She was grateful for his restraint. After all these years, the lies and deceptions still hurt. But maybe he was right. Maybe she needed to talk about what had happened in order to let go of it.

So she took a deep breath and continued. "He had some innovative marketing ideas, including marketing inside information about the products I was developing to other companies."

"Ouch."

She didn't know if it was the distance of nine years that finally allowed her to view the painful interlude with more objectivity or his unquestioning sympathy, but she somehow managed to smile. "Yeah, it hurt. I nearly lost my job because of Doug. I *definitely* lost my naiveté."

"I can see why you have trust issues."

"Among other issues, apparently."

He glanced up, lifted a brow in silent question.

She shook her head, stifling a yawn. "I think that's enough baring of my soul for now."

"I'm here," he said, "if you want to bare anything else."

This time she laughed. "I'll keep that in mind."

Mike secured the shelter to the ground with pegs he'd carved out of wood and stood back to survey the finished product, pleased to note that it blended almost invisibly into its surroundings.

Satisfied with the completion of one important task, he sat down with his knife and another stick to begin another.

Beside him Shannon yawned again.

He wasn't surprised that she was obviously exhausted. His energy was flagging, too, but his body was trained to go for days with nothing more than brief snatches of sleep. Hers wasn't.

"What else should I be doing?" she asked.

"There's nothing else to do."

"Then why are you sharpening that stick?"

Her body might be fatigued, but her mind was still sharp. "Would you believe that whittling is a hobby of mine?"

"No," she responded immediately.

He chuckled. "I'm making a spear to catch a fish for dinner."

"I could help," she said.

"It's not a two-person task."

She looked as if she might protest further, but whatever she intended to say was stifled by another yawn.

"Why don't you take a nap?" he suggested. "Someone needs to test out our shelter."

She managed a smile. "Is that supposed to make me feel useful?"

"You'll be more useful if you're rested."

"All right," she relented, obviously too tired to do anything else.

Mike waited until she'd crawled into the shelter, then made his escape quickly, before he did something incredibly stupid like succumb to the urge to lie down beside her and cradle her in his arms. She needed to sleep, and he needed to concentrate on getting them dinner.

As far as priorities went, seducing Shannon Vaughn wasn't even in the top ten—at least not until they made it back to Florida.

It took Mike longer than he'd expected to catch a decent-size fish for their dinner. Working with only the stick he'd fashioned into a spear and trying to evade the sharp teeth of the many barracuda while he aimed for one was an onerous task. But at last he nabbed one that would be big enough for their dinner. After it was caught, he cleaned and skewered it, ready to cook it in the pit he'd set up on the beach.

He peeked into their new shelter and confirmed that Shannon was still sleeping. He was tempted to leave her until morning. It would certainly be easier for him if he could avoid more personal interaction with her.

The attraction between them was too powerful to be denied, and he knew it was inevitable that they would become lovers. It wasn't a matter of if, only when. He also knew that the when couldn't be now—not when he needed to keep his wits about him to ensure they both made it off this island alive.

When Dylan had first approached him about this assignment, Mike had been reluctant, assuming it would turn out to be nothing more than glorified babysitting detail. But it wasn't the most mundane task he'd ever been asked to perform, and as he'd had nothing else going on at the time, he'd accepted.

Then he'd seen Shannon's picture, and he'd been hooked. Not just because she was beautiful, but because he was intrigued by the contrast of strength and vulnerability in the depths of her stunning green eyes. Still, the tug he'd felt in looking at her picture hadn't begun to compare to the full-blown assault on his senses the first time he'd seen her in living color. It was a purely physical attraction, no doubt about it.

But as he'd continued to watch her from a distance, something had changed. During the days, she played with her nephew, splashing in the water, building sand castles on the beach, eating ice cream under the shade of a striped umbrella. Her nights, after Jack had gone to bed, were spent sitting alone on the balcony of her hotel room with the inexplicable glint of tears in her eyes. And the primal lust in his blood shifted to something else, something softer and stronger but equally compelling.

Then all hell had broken loose in Fairweather. In the altercation that had killed Zane Conroy, Shannon's sister had been wounded. Dylan had come to Florida to take Jack back to his mother, and Shannon had been alone.

The next day she'd taken a stroll on the beach. There had

been no way Mike could follow her without being seen, so he'd approached her—one vacationer striking up a conversation with another. He hadn't anticipated that the sparks would be flying from both directions. He'd certainly never intended to kiss her.

Now there was no going back. No way to turn off the feelings she stirred inside him. But he could—and would—set them aside to do what needed to be done.

It was his job to take care of Shannon. And as much as she needed to rest, she also needed to eat.

He ducked into the shelter. She was sleeping with the blanket tucked around her, the ends clutched tightly in her fists. Her hair was a spill of auburn silk against the lush green of the palm fronds that covered the ground. The soft cotton of her sleeveless top clung enticingly to her breasts, and the side of her skirt had fallen open again, exposing a tantalizing glimpse of creamy thigh.

He felt a stirring in his blood, heat in his belly.

He stayed back, as far away from her as possible inside the confined space.

"Wake up, Ginger."

She didn't respond to his summons.

Resigned, he moved closer, touched his hand to her shoulder. "Come on, sleepyhead."

She snuggled deeper into the thin blanket, mumbled, "Tired."

"I know," he said, and then, as if of its own volition, his other hand reached out, brushed a stray lock of hair off her cheek. "But you need to eat something."

"Not hungry."

He smiled at her stubborn denial.

She was probably starving, which she would realize as soon as she woke up.

He nudged her again; she didn't move.

Okay, he could think of one thing that would surely penetrate her subconscious. But as certain as he was that the tactic would rouse her from slumber, he was even more certain she wouldn't appreciate it.

Now that the thought had crossed his mind, however, he couldn't shake it.

"Last chance, Ginger. Either you wake up right now, or I'll be forced to take drastic action."

He could have raised his voice, or shaken her again. He did neither of those things, because he'd decided he wasn't in such a hurry anymore. He didn't want her to wake up just yet. Not until he'd had a chance to taste her again.

She sighed in her sleep, turned her head slightly.

Her face was tilted upward now, her lips mere inches from his own.

He was insane to even be considering this. She'd made it more than clear she thought it was a mistake to pursue the attraction between them, and yet he couldn't stay away. Her life was literally in his hands, and all he could think about was getting his hands *on* her.

He stroked a finger down her cheek, along her jaw.

Her lips curved slightly, temptingly, and she murmured, a soft sound of acquiescence that went straight to his gut.

It was obvious she was dreaming about something—someone. He pulled his hand away. He couldn't do this—he couldn't take advantage of her vulnerability.

"Michael."

Oh, hell.

She was dreaming about him—and he wasn't strong enough to resist the whispered plea.

He slid his mouth over hers.

She responded immediately to the gentle pressure of his kiss, her lips parting, welcoming. And his whole world tilted on its axis.

His intention had been to wake her. Instead he found himself being drawn into her dream—reality fading into something softer, sweeter. Something he wished would never end.

The blanket slipped from her fingers as she lifted her arms to wind them around his neck, pulling him closer. He needed no more urging.

His hand moved from her waist, over her rib cage, brushing the side of her breast.

She moaned softly.

He cupped the gentle swell, stroked his thumb over the already beaded nipple, felt the shudder run through her.

She moaned again, arching toward him.

His body reacted instinctively, immediately.

Suddenly she froze.

Her eyes flew open. "Wh—what are you doing?"

His fantasies came crashing down around him, but somehow he managed to smile. "I was trying to wake you up."

She unwound her arms from around his neck, placed her palms on his chest and pushed him away. "I'm awake," she said coolly.

"So I see." He moved away reluctantly.

She pushed herself into a sitting position, brushed her hair away from her face. "You might have considered saying, 'Wake up.'"

"I tried that."

She looked skeptical.

"And I tried shaking you. You sleep like the dead," he told her.

"An appropriate analogy," she said dryly. "Considering that someone wants me dead."

He wanted to assure her that nothing would happen to her on his watch, but they'd already had this conversation. She wasn't ready to accept the lengths to which he would go to protect her, and her skepticism was threatening to erode his own confidence. So he only said, "It's time for dinner. You need to keep up your strength for when Rico and Jazz come back."

Chapter 8

Shannon blinked in the brilliance of the sunlit afternoon. She felt as though she'd been sleeping a long time and had been certain it must be night. The unexpected brightness left her feeling confused and strangely disoriented.

Or maybe that was the aftereffects of Michael's kiss.

"What time is it?" she asked.

He glanced at the watch on his wrist. "Almost five."

As if on cue, her stomach growled.

She scented the fire even before she noticed the telltale curl of smoke rising into the air. He'd set a couple of Y-shaped sticks into the ground on opposite sides of the circular stone pit he'd built and placed the skewered fish between them, high enough it was out of reach of the flames.

"Are you sure it's safe to build a fire here?" she asked.

"There's hardly any breeze now, and it's well out of reach of the trees." He turned the end of the stick, rotating the fish.

She shook her head. "No, I mean, won't it give away our location?"

"Peart's men already know we're here," he reminded her.

She sat down beside the fire, her ravenous appetite suddenly gone. "We're going to die here, aren't we?"

"No, we're not."

He made the statement simply, with an absolute confidence that somehow managed to reassure Shannon even as she wondered at it. "But what can you do? How can we possibly hope to evade them indefinitely?"

"We don't have to evade them indefinitely," he said. "Only long enough to circle back and trap them."

"You're kidding."

He shook his head. "This is what I'm trained to do."

"I wouldn't know," she said. "Apparently it's classified."

He remained silent, but she had too many unanswered questions to let the subject drop.

"Let's suppose you do manage to trap Rico and Jazz," she allowed. "How is that going to get us off this island?"

"We'll take Peart's yacht."

"What if Peart comes back with them?"

"I can handle Peart."

Now that she knew he'd been an army ranger, she figured he'd earned the right to sound so sure. He'd obviously survived dangerous situations before, and she had to believe that this one would be no different.

"I guess if I had to be stranded here, I'm glad it's with someone who has some survival training."

"Except that you wouldn't be here if I'd been honest with you in the first place," he said, reminding her of the accusation she'd thrown at him earlier.

"I don't really blame you," she said.

"You should."

His response startled her.

He was angry with himself, she realized. Because he felt responsible for their current predicament. Because she'd made him feel responsible, blaming him when there should never have been any blame assigned.

But Michael took his responsibilities seriously and held himself to high standards. She knew he would do whatever was necessary to ensure he didn't fail her.

The knowledge didn't make her feel any better. She derived no comfort from knowing he would put his life on the line to save hers—as he'd already done when he'd put himself between her and the bullets Jazz shot at them.

He'd been dismissive of his wound, and it obviously wasn't a life-threatening injury. But it could have been, and that realization shook her to the core.

"It wasn't your fault any more than mine," she said. "And you did save my life. Twice."

He didn't respond to her comment as he removed the fish from the fire, carefully cutting it away from the stick and dividing it into two empty coconut shells. He passed one of the makeshift bowls to her. "Watch for bones."

She was hungry and she accepted the offering with a heartfelt, "Thanks."

She picked up a chunk of the flesh and popped it into her mouth. It was hot but tender, with a mild and inoffensive flavor. "This is good."

He smiled at the obvious surprise in her voice. "It's not French champagne and Russian caviar, but it's edible."

"I think I'd rather have this."

"You're not a woman of expensive tastes?"

"I'd choose a peanut butter and jelly sandwich over fish eggs any day."

He made a face.

"You don't like PB and J?"

"I don't think I've ever had it."

She was shocked by this disclosure. "Not even when you were a kid?"

He shook his head.

"What kind of deprived childhood did you have?"

He laughed again, but there was a hint of strain in it this time. "You can't imagine."

"What about mac and cheese?"

He shook his head again.

"Hot dogs?"

"A ballpark staple," he said. "But only with mustard."

She smiled. "Maybe your taste is salvageable, after all."

They ate in silence for several minutes. Shannon noticed that the sun was starting to dip toward the horizon, but she knew they still had several more hours of daylight. To do what? Watch the water and hope for a rescue? Hope it wasn't Peart's yacht that appeared in the distance?

Not wanting to think about what could or might happen, she focused on her food. "Thanks," she said again. "For catching and cooking dinner."

"You're welcome."

"I wish I could make more of a contribution. So far I haven't managed to do much more than get your boat blown up."

He dumped the fish bones into the fire. "Actually, it was my sister's boat."

"Uh-oh."

"Yeah. She's not going to be too happy about that."

Shannon could imagine. She remembered how annoyed she'd been when Natalie borrowed a skirt from her closet once and spilled grape juice on it. Of course, they'd both been in high school at the time and although she'd planned to wear the skirt to a job interview the next day—it was only a skirt. On second thought she couldn't imagine how Michael's sister would react to the destruction of a boat that probably cost more money than Shannon earned in a year.

"Are you close to your sister?" she asked.

"Close enough that she trusted me with the keys."

She smiled at the warm affection in his voice that belied the casual statement. "Do you have any other siblings?"

He shook his head. "Only Rachel."

"Does she live in Florida?"

"For the past couple of years. She travels around a fair bit in her business."

"What does she do?"

He leaned forward, poking a stick into the glowing embers. "She's, uh, in the hospitality industry."

"What does she think of your job?"

"She likes the P.I. gig better than when I was in the army. At least I'm usually within cell phone range so she can call me daily and nag at me about something."

"And you love her for it," she guessed.

"Despite the nagging, I do."

"Why did you become a private investigator?"

"Why do you suddenly have so many questions?" he countered. "You didn't seem half as interested in making conversation last night."

"Neither did you," she pointed out. "Although I realize now that may have been because you already knew a lot more about me than I could have guessed."

She winced at the trace of bitterness evident in her tone, and hoped he wouldn't comment on it.

His next words obliterated that hope. "That bothers you?"

She shrugged, pretending it didn't. "I thought we were on equal footing."

"You thought we could have a night of wild sex and then go our separate ways without ever seeing each other again."

"Isn't that what you thought?" She stared into the flames as she asked the question, hoping it would be a little easier to have this suddenly awkward and intensely personal conversation without looking at him. Still, she heard the smile in his response.

"Actually I was hoping for two or three nights."

She managed to smile at his teasing but shook her head. "I'm not good with relationships—casual or otherwise. And last night was completely out-of-character behavior for me that would not have been repeated."

"It was out-of-character for me, too," he said. "I've never gotten involved, or even been tempted to get involved, with the subject of an assignment before."

She remained silent.

"Aren't you going to ask why I did this time?"

"I figured it was a convenient way for you to keep an eye on me."

He pinned her with a steely gaze. "That's insulting to both of us."

"What was I supposed to think?"

"That I was attracted to you."

"That is what I thought—until I found out Dylan hired you to watch out for me."

"Do you really believe that I would have slept with you just to keep tabs on you?"

"I don't know. I don't know anything about you," she reminded him.

"Well, let's get one thing perfectly clear," he said, suddenly angry. "What happened between us last night had absolutely nothing to do with my assignment. In fact, had I been thinking about the job—as I should have been doing—it never would have happened.

"I made a mistake. I let my personal feelings interfere with my duty to protect you. As a result—this is where we are. Believe me," he said fervently, "it's not something I planned as a surveillance tactic."

Despite the harshness of his tone, his words caused a strange warmth to seep through her veins.

He *was* attracted to her.

This strong, sexy man was attracted to *her.*

But maybe that was only because they hadn't actually completed the act.

Her heady sense of power fizzled away.

"Speaking of surveillance," she said, in a determined attempt to redirect the conversation, "what made you decide to join the army?"

"I thought we agreed we weren't going to talk about my military career."

"That wasn't a mutual decision," she said, turning the words he'd spoken earlier back on him. "Besides, I didn't ask about your career *in* the army, only why you signed up."

"I enlisted because of my father."

"Was he in the military?"

Michael smiled. "No. I was trying to get away from him. It's not that he was a horrible father or a bad person," he explained. "It's just that we couldn't agree on what career path I was supposed to follow."

It was the first insight he'd given into his personal life, and she was surprised by how eager she was to hear more. "What did he want you to do?"

"Get a business degree and work for him."

His words and his tone left her in no doubt how he felt about that idea.

"My father has his own business," he continued. "Actually, it's a business my great-grandfather started. Then he passed it down to my grandfather, and my grandfather passed it to my father."

"You didn't want to carry on the family tradition?"

"I know I should have been grateful for the opportunity he offered me, but I always felt trapped by his expectations. I needed to make my own way, to prove to him—and maybe to myself—that I could.

"He wanted me to go to college, so I did. I stayed in school long enough to get my MBA. Then, the day after graduation, I joined the army."

"What happened to make you leave?" She knew this question pushed at the No Trespassing signs he'd already established, and she was fully prepared for another refusal to talk about his military career.

He shook his head. "You don't let up, do you?"

"You were the one who said that talking could help."

"I meant help *you*."

"Why can't it work both ways?"

He didn't respond for so long she thought he wasn't going to answer. Then he finally said, "A friend of mine was killed in Righaria."

"Where's that? I've never heard of it."

"It's a small African country just west of Somalia. We were there at the request of the UN," he explained. "To help restore control to the proper authorities. Because although Righaria has a democratic government, at least on paper, in reality it's controlled by drug lords. Unfortunately, no one outside of the rightful government wanted us there.

"It was a bad situation from the beginning. We couldn't walk down the main street without risking our lives. But we knew the risks—we were prepared for them. We were brothers more than soldiers, and we looked out for one another.

"Brent and I were even closer than most. We'd been buddies in ranger training and became best friends. Neither of us was thrilled about going to Righaria, but at least we were going together.

"I was supposed to be watching his back…" His voice trailed off as he shook his head. "I'd met a woman at a little café in the center of town a few weeks earlier. We were two

Americans drawn together by the commonality of being foreigners in a hostile country."

"You fell in love with her," she guessed.

He laughed shortly. "I was young. Lisa was even younger. I thought I loved her, but maybe I just loved the distraction she provided.

"I never intended to get involved with her," he continued. "But somehow it happened, anyway. And when I found out about the raid we'd planned, on the building next door to where Lisa was staying, I went to warn her. I wanted her to leave the city, go somewhere safe.

"While I was gone, there was an attack on our camp. Brent was killed."

She laid her hand on his arm, wishing now that she'd never asked about the circumstances that precipitated his leaving the army. She'd been curious about this man who'd already risked his own life to protect hers. Now she was starting to get a clearer picture, starting to understand his determination to protect her—as if keeping her safe might somehow compensate for the fact that his friend had died. But she'd never intended to hurt him by bringing up such an obviously painful subject.

"It wasn't your fault," she said gently.

"I should have been there." His voice was thick with grief and guilt.

"If you'd been there, you might have been killed, too."

"I should have been there," he said again. "It was my responsibility to watch his back—as he always watched mine. Instead I was with Lisa. And then Lisa was gone, too."

"Gone?" she asked cautiously, silently praying that the woman he loved hadn't been killed, too.

"She heard about Brent's death and came to see me at the base. But I didn't want to see her, not then. She left Righaria with her brother the next day."

"Tell me about Brent," she said, hoping the suggestion would help him focus on his friend's life rather than his death and forget about the woman who'd hurt him so deeply when she walked out on him.

"He was twenty-six years old, the youngest of three brothers, and engaged to be married when he was killed. Tara, his fiancée, was four months pregnant."

She heard the anguish in his tone, felt her own throat tighten as she thought of the young woman, widowed before she was even married, carrying the child of the man she'd loved. She could guess how Michael had responded to that situation. "What did Tara say when you asked her to marry you?"

He turned his head, surprise momentarily replacing the grim despair she'd glimpsed in his eyes. "How'd you know I proposed?"

She smiled. Yeah, she was starting to get a very clear picture. "It's the kind of thing I suspect you'd do—try to right a wrong, accept responsibility for something that couldn't possibly have been your fault."

"That's what Tara said when she refused my offer."

"Do you still keep in touch with her?"

He nodded. "She finally got married two years ago."

"And the baby?" she asked gently.

"Brent, Jr. He's five now."

She smiled again. "You're a good man, Michael."

He shook his head, almost vehemently. "A good man would have made sure Brent made it home to become a husband and a father."

"Are you going to punish yourself for the rest of your life because you couldn't? Is that why you put yourself between me and Jazz—do you think you have to sacrifice yourself to be forgiven for what happened to Brent?"

"They gave me a citation for bravery," he admitted, his voice choking on the words. "Because I walked through gunfire to bring him out. And I accepted it, because I didn't—couldn't—admit to anyone that it was my fault he was dead."

Her heart ached for him, for the way he'd suffered, the pain he still endured.

"Tara forgave you," she said gently. "The only thing left is for you to forgive yourself."

"I thought you were a chemist—not a psychologist."

"As it happens, I have a minor in psychology," she said. "And what *you* have is textbook survivor's guilt."

"Thanks for the diagnosis, Ginger."

"Now you're lashing out at me because you want to keep me at a distance."

His smile was slow, seductive. "I'd prefer to keep you close—real close."

"Another textbook trait—using physical intimacy as a substitute for emotional closeness."

"I don't need a textbook to know that I want you naked and under me."

"Do you think a few crude words and heated looks are going to scare me?"

His eyes glittered in the firelight. "You should be scared. I'm not the nice guy you want me to be."

It was a warning, and a not-so-subtle one at that. But Shannon was tired of running, tired of being afraid. "Maybe I don't want you to be nice."

He moved closer, his knee brushing against hers as he deliberately invaded her space. "What do you want?"

Sparks zinged through her, incinerating her bravado.

What was she thinking, engaging in this kind of suggestive banter? Not only was it inappropriate under the circumstances, but Michael was clearly out of her league. He was a man with a world of experience she couldn't begin to comprehend, whose simplest touch tempted her with the promise of something more. And she was a woman who'd spent so much time convincing herself she was content, she was scared to reach for something more.

"I just want us to get along."

He trailed a finger down her arm, barely skimming her flesh and yet somehow branding her with his touch. "I want us to get along, too."

Her skin burned from the brief contact—and got hotter with wanting more. "You're deliberately misunderstanding me."

"I don't think I'm misunderstanding anything." His finger skimmed upward this time. "I think you're afraid to admit what you want."

She batted his hand away. "That is such a typical male response. Everything's about sex, and if a woman doesn't want to have sex with you, she has some kind of problem."

"Except that you *do* want to have sex with me."

She opened her mouth to deny it.

"You do," he insisted. "I see it in your eyes, in the way you respond to my touch, the way your pulse races and your breath quickens."

"I will admit to a certain physiological response," she said, unable to refute his observations.

"You want me."

She hated the smugness of his tone. Hated even more that it was true. "Maybe I just want a distraction from the situation."

He shrugged. "And since we've already established that I want you, why are we talking about sex instead of having it?"

"Does that sort of blunt approach usually result in women tumbling into your bed?"

His gaze dipped to her mouth. "Is that a hypothetical question or are you asking for permission to tumble?"

"Purely hypothetical." Still torn between the conflicting urges of advance and retreat that were warring inside her, she nevertheless felt guilty for misleading him. "Despite the impression I may have given you, I'm not really into sex."

His eyes lifted to meet hers, narrowing speculatively. "What do you mean, you're not into it?"

She shrugged and looked away, struggling to find the right words to ensure she wasn't sending the wrong kind of signals. Because despite what had almost happened in her hotel room the night before, she wasn't a promiscuous woman. In fact, in all of her thirty-three years, she'd been intimate with only two men.

The first was Doug, and after she'd left him, she'd been full of recriminations and self-doubts. Following the divorce, she'd focused her attention exclusively on her career and repairing the damage her ex-husband had done to it.

Three years ago she'd met Ron. He wasn't the first man she'd dated since her divorce, but he was the first one she'd slept with. The first one she'd felt a strong enough attraction to that she'd wanted to prove to herself she wasn't the inept, inexperienced lover Doug had accused her of being. Except that a few nights with Ron had only confirmed her ex-husband's opinion.

Shannon had resigned herself to the knowledge that she just wasn't a passionate woman. Until she'd met Michael and he'd made her feel passion she'd never even imagined.

"When you invited me back to your hotel room last night, it wasn't for coffee," he said.

As if she needed to be reminded. "Last night was an aberration."

He shook his head, as if he couldn't believe what she was telling him. "Do you even *remember* last night?"

She looked away, her cheeks infusing with heat. Of course she remembered it. Every second of it. Every kiss, every caress. In torturously vivid detail. The problem wasn't remembering, it was trying to forget—trying to focus on their circumstances here and now, on the inherent dangers of being trapped on this island, on battling the elements and trying to prepare for Rico and Jazz to return.

Dangerous Passions

"That wasn't me," she finally responded.

His smile was slow, seductive. "Oh, baby, that was *so* you. It was you and me and the chemistry between us without any hang-ups to get in the way."

Her face burned hotter. "I obviously wasn't thinking very clearly. I had a lot on my mind."

"Such as?"

"Such as the fact that my mother was getting married for the fifth time and my sister had almost been killed and I'm supposed to be moving to another continent in a few weeks."

He considered her explanation for a moment, then shook his head. "You weren't thinking of any of those things. You weren't thinking about anything but mindless, sweaty sex."

"You're confusing your fantasies with reality," she said.

He smiled again. "My fantasy was about to become reality," he told her. "You were half-naked and writhing beneath me, practically screaming my name."

"I don't writhe," she said coolly. "And I definitely don't scream."

He quirked a brow. "Never?"

"I'm a Type-A personality," she said. "I don't like to relinquish control."

"Maybe you just haven't been with anyone who made you want to give up control." He leaned forward so that his mouth hovered mere inches above hers. "Or maybe you need to be with someone who's willing to take it."

Chapter 9

A few inches.

Mike was tempted to breach the distance, lower his head and cover her lips in a long, slow kiss that would obliterate all of her misconceptions.

She wouldn't resist.

Despite her verbal protests, her body language was telling a whole different story.

Her eyes were wide and dark—not wary but curious. Her lips were softly parted and angled slightly toward him. Her breathing was shallow and just a little bit fast. Oh, yeah, she was interested.

"You're thinking about it," he said. "Wondering."

She swallowed, but didn't deny his assessment.

He brushed his thumb over the curve of her bottom lip, felt the tremble in response to his touch.

Her tongue swept over her bottom lip, tracing the path of his finger in an erotically enticing motion.

If he kissed her, here and now, he had no doubt they'd finish what they'd started last night. But while there was a part of him that desperately wanted to move them in that direction, he couldn't do it. Not now.

Even if he could forget about Peart and Rico and Jazz for a while—and he had no doubt that he could if he was naked with Shannon—there were other considerations.

Most notably the fact that she wasn't ready. Her body might quiver from his touch, but her heart and mind were still holding back, and he didn't want to push her into anything.

Or maybe it was guilt that held him back.

Because while he was trying to break through her barriers, he was carefully maintaining his own. He'd told Shannon more about his past than he'd ever shared with another woman, but there were still certain facts she didn't know—revelations about his life that he wasn't ready to make.

He didn't enjoy the deception, but he enjoyed having the opportunity to explore the attraction between them and know it was real. He'd dated too many women over the years who had been interested in him solely because of his family's connections and wealth. Shannon didn't know he was anyone other than Michael Courtland, Private Investigator. She wasn't using him to get ahead or advance any kind of personal agenda. In fact, she didn't seem to have any expectations at all.

The realization intrigued him as much as it mystified him, and he took a mental step back, needing some time and space to think about it.

"It's starting to get dark," he said.

She exhaled slowly.

He saw the swirl of emotion in her eyes—the mixture of relief and regret.

"I guess the coast guard isn't coming today."

"Doesn't seem likely," he agreed.

"Which means the beacon probably wasn't working," she said, speaking the words he hadn't wanted to say aloud.

"Even if it wasn't, Detective Garcia will be expecting to hear from me soon. When he doesn't, I'm sure he'll investigate."

She frowned. "Who's Detective Garcia?"

"A friend of Dylan's with the Miami P.D."

"Oh." She fell silent again, no doubt contemplating the same questions that occupied his mind.

How long would Garcia wait to hear from him before suspecting that something had gone wrong? How long would it take to establish a search party? Where would they begin? And how could they possibly track down Mike and Shannon before Peart's men returned?

They were questions she didn't want to ponder, reminders of a situation that was out of her control.

"What are we supposed to do in the meantime?" she asked.

"All we can do is wait."

It wasn't the answer she wanted, but she knew it was an honest one.

"In that case," she said. "I'm going to turn in."

"Good idea."

"What about you?" she asked, then cringed at the question that sounded too much like an invitation.

To her relief Michael shook his head. "I'll stay here until the fire dies down."

She crawled into the enclosure, relieved that she didn't yet have to face being in this narrow space with him. She stretched out on top of the palm fronds that covered the ground, careful to stay on her side, then pulled the thermal blanket over her.

She shivered. It was likely eighty-five degrees outside, and she was shivering. It was possible her body hadn't completely recovered from her swim, or she might have caught a chill when she got soaked by the rain, or maybe it was fear that was responsible for the bone-deep chill. Fear that Peart would come back before the coast guard. Fear that despite all of her best efforts—and Michael's, too—she would be captured again. Fear that A.J. would kill her.

She shivered again and stared through the opening of the shelter at the dwindling fire, tried to envision a roaring blaze. But the visual exercise did nothing to ward off the chill that ran straight through to her bones.

She wished Michael was beside her. Maybe then she'd be shivering with something other than cold or fear. She pushed away the thought and tugged the blanket tighter. The last thing she needed was any more complications in her life.

Yet she couldn't stop thinking about the way he'd kissed her, couldn't help remembering how it felt to be touched by him. The memories caused a warm heat to suffuse her body. Okay, so maybe she needed to think about Michael instead of the fire, so long as she remembered her resolution not to turn any of her sexual fantasies into reality.

It was a long time later before he finally crawled into the shelter. When he did so, Shannon kept her eyes tightly closed, tried to suppress her shivers and ignore his presence.

But he seemed to anticipate her needs, sliding closer to wrap his arms around her. "Just relax." He murmured the words gently. "Sleep."

How could she when the warmth of his body was already seeping into her chilled skin, infusing it with heat, awareness, desire? How could she possibly sleep when his proximity was inducing all kinds of erotic fantasies in her mind?

She wondered what would happen if she turned so that she was facing him. Would he anticipate her wishes? Would he kiss her the way only he'd ever kissed her—until everything inside her was soft and warm?

Just thinking of those kisses made her sigh.

She yawned and snuggled closer against him.

And finally she slept.

It was a new experience for Mike—waking up with a woman he hadn't had sex with.

Come to think of it, it was a rare occasion to wake up with a woman he *had* had sex with. Because while he enjoyed the physical act, sleeping together suggested a level of intimacy he wasn't entirely comfortable with.

Using physical intimacy as a substitute for emotional closeness.

Shannon's words echoed in his mind.

It irritated him that she was right.

And yet, somehow, here he was—with this stubborn, opinionated and incredibly sexy woman asleep in his arms. Her head was nestled on his shoulder, her back flush with his chest, the curve of her derriere against his groin. And instead of making him want to bolt, it somehow felt natural.

Or as natural as anything could feel under these unusual and extraordinary circumstances.

She murmured in her sleep, then turned over so that she was facing him. Her breasts, soft and full, were pressed against his chest.

She shifted again, sliding one knee between his legs and pressing her body closer to his. Mike felt all the blood drain out of his head and migrate much further south.

She was killing him here.

The worst of it was, she seemed to have no clue about the effect she had on him, no understanding of her innate sensuality.

She laid her hand on his chest, and he wondered if she could feel the way his heart was pounding beneath her palm. The way she made his heart pound.

He tried to focus his thoughts, to remember all the reasons

he'd taken that step back. But all he could remember was the taste of her.

Her eyelids fluttered, then opened. The cloudy confusion of slumber slowly cleared away to reveal an awareness and desire that rivaled his own.

He should draw back.

She should push him away.

Neither of them moved.

For several long moments their gazes stayed locked together in wordless communication.

He wanted her. There was no denying that. But wanting her was a distraction he couldn't afford right now. Rico and Jazz could return at any time and he had to be ready.

"It's, uh, time to get up," he said.

Her eyes flickered with a disappointment quickly masked. Now she did draw away, forced a smile. "What's for breakfast? Fish or coconuts?"

Shannon knew she should be grateful for his restraint. So long as they were stuck on this island, danger continued to hover over them. It was hardly an appropriate time to let herself be carried away by passion.

Except that, for the first time in her life, she wasn't *letting* anything happen. Her desire for Michael was unprecedented, the yearning simply beyond her control.

Yes, she should be grateful for his restraint. Especially since she apparently had none where he was concerned.

By the time Michael came back, with another coconut and a few small, overripe bananas for their breakfast, she'd accepted that he'd done the right thing in walking away. The smart, sensible thing.

She'd also decided that she was tired of being smart and sensible. Smart and Sensible had been her motto—and yet she'd somehow ended up stranded on a tropical island hiding from killers. Obviously Smart and Sensible wasn't working for her.

And if she was going to die on this island, which she knew was a definite possibility, she was going to make sure she lived every minute she had left to the fullest.

"I took the binoculars up to the top of the hill," he said, peeling back the skin on one of the bananas. "There's a lot of traffic on the water, but nothing close enough to signal to. No sign of the coast guard and, so far at least, no sign of Peart's yacht, either."

"I hate the waiting," she said. "Knowing they're coming back, but not knowing when."

He nodded and bit into the fruit.

When she'd jumped off the *Femme Fatale,* she'd thought she was making an escape. Now it appeared she'd only delayed the inevitable. Rico and Jazz would come back for her, and she would have to face whatever fate A.J. had in store.

She should have just stayed on the boat, because now Michael was in just as much danger as she was.

"Isn't there anything else we could be doing—instead of just sitting here and waiting?"

"We could build a raft."

The casual tone with which he made the suggestion convinced her he could do so without any great difficulty.

"But on the water we'd be exposed and essentially defenseless," he explained. "I know it's frustrating to sit and wait, but I really believe we're safer here."

She couldn't argue. Michael had proven time and again that he had more experience and expertise in this kind of situation.

Instead, she peeled her own banana, forced herself to eat despite her sudden lack of appetite.

She didn't want to think about Rico and Jazz anymore, to speculate about what would happen when they returned. She especially didn't want to consider that this day could be her last. But it was a possibility she had to acknowledge and she decided that she was going to live this day rather than regret it. She was going to go after what she wanted—open herself up to passion and possibilities.

"If all we have to do is sit and wait, why can't we have sex?"

He nearly choked on the banana he'd been munching. After he'd finished coughing and swallowing he asked, "Did you just say what I think I heard?"

She hadn't expected to have to say it again. But she'd made up her mind and she wasn't going to back down. "I want to have sex with you, Michael."

He shifted away from her—clearly establishing both a physical distance and an emotional withdrawal.

Yesterday such a response would have obliterated her resolve. But today she was a stronger—or maybe just more desperate—woman.

"I'm not asking for a relationship or a commitment," she told him. "I just want to forget, for a while, that every minute on this island could be my last. I want to forget that when Jazz and Rico return, we could both end up dead.

"And the only thing I can think of to possibly drive those thoughts from my mind is sex. No strings attached."

It was every man's fantasy.

A beautiful woman offering the joys of passion without the constraints of a relationship.

But Shannon was offering it under false pretenses—because she believed she was going to die.

"I'm not going to let anything happen to you," Mike said, somehow managing to find his voice.

"As much as I know you want to, you can't make that kind of guarantee." The words were spoken with gentle conviction as she moved toward him.

Two steps, and she'd breached the distance that separated them. She pressed her lips to the side of his jaw.

He grabbed her arms, intending to push her away before he completely forgot the assignment to protect her, his own convictions and everything else but his desire for her.

"I'm not asking for any guarantees." She flicked her tongue against his earlobe, then nipped it gently. "I'm asking you to help me forget—just for a little while."

Maybe a stronger man could have refused, but he couldn't. Especially not when she pulled his head down to kiss him.

The touch of her lips was tentative at first, an innocent passion, softly questioning. Her eyes remained open, searching his. It took every ounce of willpower he possessed to control his response, to let her set the pace.

He felt the tension ease from her body as her eyelids drifted downward and her lips parted.

He'd always thought of kissing as a kind of foreplay, a necessary precursor to the more physical aspects of sex. Not that he didn't enjoy kissing, but it had always been a means to an end.

He realized now, kissing Shannon, that he had underestimated both the power and the satisfaction of this simple act. Her lips yielded, parting willingly to the pressure of his. But it was a sharing rather than surrender—a mutual exploration and reciprocal pleasure.

There wasn't just heat, there was warmth—a sweet and gentle warmth that stirred something deep inside him. Was this what she'd been referring to? Was this the emotional intimacy he'd avoided for so long? The possibility was unsettling. No matter how sweet it was, he wasn't ready to succumb to it. Not yet.

But he was more than ready to give himself over to the physical intimacy they both craved.

He fisted his hand in her hair and tilted her head back to deepen the kiss.

There was no hesitation in her response, no resistance.

Her mouth was hot and hungry now. Her hands eager and adept. Her curves, pressed against him, perfect. The complete package was pure seduction.

He slid his hands beneath the hem of her T-shirt, his fingers skimming over the satiny softness of her skin, searching—and finding—the front closure of her bra.

He released the simple clasp, filled his hands with the luscious weight of her breasts.

She gasped as his thumbs stroked the already-rigid peaks.

He trailed kisses across her jaw, down her throat, teasing her with his teeth and his tongue. His three-day growth of beard rasped against her tender skin, but she didn't seem to mind.

He tugged the T-shirt over her head and tossed it aside. Then pushed the straps of her bra down her arms and discarded the scrap of peach lace as well. Her skirt followed, and a pair of wispy peach bikini underwear after that.

He tumbled with her to the ground.

Desire was like a trapped animal set free. It attacked him with sharp claws, sank into him with jagged teeth, overpowered him with ravenous hunger.

When he'd thought about making love with Shannon—and there was no denying that he'd thought about it—he'd planned to take things slow.

There was no going slow for either of them now.

He might have worried except that her response was as primitive and unrestrained as his own.

He slid his hands up the back of her thighs, over the curve of her bottom. Her skin was soft, smooth and supple.

She was like a marble goddess in the dappled sunlight. Her long, fiery hair flowed over her creamy shoulders to the round fullness of her breasts. Her waist was slender, her stomach flat, her legs long and lean. She was almost too perfect to be real—definitely too soft and warm to be taken on the hard barren ground.

"Wait a sec." He kissed the furrow in her brow. "I'll be right back."

Shannon watched as he disappeared into the shelter, returning a moment later with the blanket and a condom.

"It's not a feather mattress," he said. "But it should be an improvement."

It was a sweet and thoughtful gesture. She knelt on the center of the blanket and smiled at him. "It's perfect."

He knelt beside her. "I know I'm crazy for even asking this, but are you sure this is what you want?"

If she'd had any lingering doubts at all, his question—the very fact that he'd paused long enough to ask it—alleviated the last of them.

She met his gaze evenly. "I'm sure."

Then, in case he needed more convincing, she reached down between them to slide her fingers inside his briefs and wrap around the hard length of him.

"Shannon."

She didn't know if it was a plea or a warning. She didn't care. She slid her fingers upward, then slowly downward again.

His breath hissed through clenched teeth.

She pushed him back onto the blanket and tugged his briefs down over his hips. Then she knelt over him, leaning down to press a hot, wet kiss to his mouth as her hand resumed its stroking motion.

She felt needy; she also felt empowered. Because as much as she wanted him, she knew he wanted her, too. She'd never realized how good it could feel to have a man want her. The naked desire in his eyes left her in no doubt that he did.

The thrill of satisfaction, the sense of power, went to her head, made her giddy—and maybe just a little bit reckless.

"Shannon."

It was a growl this time, definitely a warning.

And the only one she got before he'd reversed their positions, effortlessly flipping her onto her back and bracing himself over her.

He laved her breasts with his tongue—stroking, sucking. Sensations bombarded her, overwhelmed her.

She wasn't innocent, but she felt as though she'd never been touched before. She'd certainly never been touched the way Michael was touching her. She'd never felt the way he made her feel.

She arched against him, instinctively thrusting her hips against his.

She heard his groan and repeated the action.

He swore this time, then grasped her hips in his hands.

"I think you need to work on relinquishing some of that control," he told her.

The words, equal parts threat and promise, sent a surge of anticipation through her veins.

He quickly sheathed himself with the condom then shifted toward her, so the weight of his arousal was positioned at the juncture of her thighs, against the softness of her femininity. The pressure was subtle, yet undeniably arousing. Even more so when he began to rock gently, teasing the aching nub with slow strokes while his hands continued to roam over her body, and his lips continued to torment her breasts.

She felt the pressure building inside her.

Slowly. Relentlessly. Inexorably.

Until finally, the world exploded into a spinning kaleidoscope of blinding light and color.

Michael couldn't think of anything more satisfying than watching Shannon—the self-proclaimed master of planning and control—lost in the throes of passion.

He watched her eyes glaze, felt the shudders rack her body.

Her hips arched, positioning the tip of his erection at the center of her slick heat.

"Now, Michael."

It wasn't a plea, but a demand.

Only yesterday they'd argued about whether or not they'd become lovers. She'd denied the possibility; he'd said she'd beg for him.

They were both wrong.

He didn't want her to beg.

He wanted her exactly the way she was now, gloriously sensual and uninhibited.

He thrust forward and into her in one smooth motion.

She gasped at the invasion, but any concerns he had about hurting her were obliterated by her throaty murmurs of approval. She ran her hands over his chest to his shoulders, linked them behind his head to tug his mouth down to hers. Then she slid her tongue in and out of his mouth, mimicking the rhythm of mating, telling him in no uncertain terms what she wanted.

It was what he wanted, too. But there was so much more he wanted to share with her, so much he wanted to show her. At the very least, he wanted to take his time, prove he was capable of a certain amount of finesse. Her provocative kisses and searching hands made that next to impossible.

Type-A personality or not, she was writhing beneath him— just as he'd imagined. But the soft, sexy sounds she was making went beyond anything he'd imagined, the throaty sighs and moans nearly driving him wild.

His hands fisted into the blanket as he fought for control that was rapidly slipping out of his grasp. Control that was wrenched completely away from him when she wrapped her endlessly long legs around his waist and pulled him even deeper into her.

He stopped fighting and gave in to the overwhelming need.

They moved together—racing higher, harder, faster—until space and time were nothing but a blur and the world outside of this moment nonexistent.

He was vaguely aware of her nails biting into his shoulders, of her body arching. She shuddered as the climax ripped through her. His own immediately followed, leaving him spent, stunned, shattered.

Chapter 10

"Get dressed."

Michael pulled away from her abruptly, scooped up her clothes and practically threw them at her.

Shannon clutched the garments to her chest, stunned.

After the most incredible sexual experience of her life, she was completely unprepared for such an immediate and abrupt withdrawal. Her body was still quivering and he was already tugging on his shorts.

"I didn't expect promises or flowers," she said coolly, slipping her arms through the straps of her bra. "But I didn't think a little postcoital civility would be too much to ask."

"What?" Fully clothed now, he stared down at her, uncomprehending.

She tugged her T-shirt over her head.

Then she heard it, the low drone in the distance. Her heart, still pulsing erratically from the passion they'd just shared, skipped a beat. "Is that a boat?"

"Yeah. What did you—oh." He crouched down beside her, cupped her cheek in his hand. "Did you think I was in that much of a hurry to be finished with you?"

She shrugged, unwilling to admit that was exactly what she'd thought.

He kissed her gently, soothing the unintentional hurt he'd caused. "I have to go check this out."

"Of course," she agreed immediately.

"But I'll make this up to you later." He brushed his lips over hers again. "I promise."

She shook her head. "No, it's okay. I overreacted."

His gaze was steady. "It's not okay. And I'm not finished with you or this conversation, but we'll have to postpone both until later." Then he jogged away with the binoculars in hand.

Nerves skittered like Ping-Pong balls inside her belly as she waited for him to return.

This was it—the moment she'd been alternately anticipating and dreading—the moment when they found out if it was Peart's men or the coast guard who would come for them first.

Shannon figured it made sense to be ready to leave regardless. She folded up the blanket and shoved it into the backpack.

When Michael returned, the grim expression on his face confirmed her fears before he spoke.

"It's the *Femme Fatale*."

She swallowed the panic that threatened to choke her, forced her voice to remain steady when she asked, "What are we going to do now?"

"You're going back to the cave."

"But you said it was too obvious."

He nodded. "If they were to arrive unexpectedly. But we know they're coming, and I'll make sure they don't make it that far."

"What are you going to do?"

"Please, Shannon. Just go to the cave. It's the safest place for you."

"Dammit, Michael, do you really think I only care about myself?"

"No." He took her hand, linking their fingers together and leading her away. "But your safety is my priority right now."

"What if something happens to you?"

"Nothing's going to happen. Shannon, you have to trust me."

"It's not a matter of trust," she insisted. "It's a matter of probabilities. There are two of them, and they have very big guns."

Despite the tension of the moment, he turned to grin at her. "Don't you know it's not the size of the weapon but how you use it that counts?"

Maybe he could joke about this, but she couldn't. "Well, the last time they used it, you got hurt."

He glanced at the white gauze pad on his arm, as if he'd forgotten it was there. "Lucky shot," he said dismissively.

"Not lucky for you."

He ignored her comment, not speaking again until they'd reached the cave.

"I'm going to leave this with you." He held out his gun.

She swallowed, eyeing the weapon uneasily. "Why?"

"Because if anyone else shows up here, I want you to shoot them."

"I don't—I've never—"

He put the gun in her hand, wrapped her fingers around it. "Just aim and pull the trigger."

"But if I have this, you'll be unarmed."

"I have the knife."

But how effective would a knife be against the automatic weapons Rico and Jazz carried?

"I don't need the gun," he said patiently. "I'm trained to handle this kind of situation."

"But there must be something I can do to help. I could create a diversion or—"

"Shannon, I need you to stay here. I'll be able to focus better if I'm not worried about you."

She hated being tucked away in a safe little corner while he risked his life, but she would do it because he'd asked.

"Okay?" he asked gently.

No, dammit, it wasn't okay. She wasn't okay. She was terrified.

But she swallowed her fear, accepting that their best hope of survival was to trust that Michael knew what he was doing. She bit back any further protest. "Okay."

He nodded brusquely and took a step toward the entrance of the cave before turning back to her again. "One more thing."

"What's that?"

"Don't shoot me." Then he kissed her, a brief but firm press of his lips against hers. "Because I will be the one who comes back. I promise you that."

Shannon bit down hard on her lip as she watched him go.

He strode confidently out of the mouth of the cave and disappeared into the trees, never once looking back. She wondered if she'd ever see him again, then banished the thought from her mind.

He'd promised to come back. She had to believe in him, she had to trust that he would do as he said. Any other scenario simply wasn't acceptable.

She sat down on the stone floor of the cave, her back to the wall, and trained her weapon on the narrow opening. The gun felt awkward and heavy in her hand. She'd never wanted to own a gun. She'd never even handled one before, and she had serious doubts about whether she'd actually be able to use it.

Her stomach churned at the thought of pulling the trigger, but Michael had told her to shoot. And because she trusted him, she would do what needed to be done.

The gun trembled slightly in her grasp; a trickle of perspiration slipped down her spine.

She almost couldn't believe it was happening—the final showdown. She couldn't quite grasp that this ordeal would soon be over and she and Michael would be on their way back home.

She swallowed and tightened her grip on the gun.

Or they would both be dead.

Mike had taken some time while Shannon was sleeping the previous afternoon to familiarize himself with the topography of the small island, noting natural barriers and hazards in preparation for this situation. While he'd hoped a quick rescue by the coast guard would eliminate the need for a confrontation with Peart's men, he was prepared for any contingency.

Having left his Glock with Shannon, he knew his best hope against two heavily armed men was to divide and conquer. Fortunately for him, Rico and Jazz had decided the most expedient way to track down their missing prisoner and her bodyguard was to split up, each covering one half of the island perimeter before moving inward.

While Peart's men had demonstrated some competence with weaponry—as evidenced by the destruction of Rachel's boat and the wound on his arm—he could only guess what other training or skills they might possess. It was possible they were nothing more than hired thugs, but he was going to assume they'd been professionally trained and make his own plans accordingly.

As Rico and Jazz went their separate ways, Mike opted to target Jazz first. The location of the cave on the west side of the island would put him in closer proximity to Shannon, and Mike wasn't taking any chances with her safety. Although he had faith that she would pull the trigger if confronted by either of their pursuers, it was a confrontation he wanted to avoid. He'd lived with the responsibility of taking another person's life, and even when the circumstances were justified, it was an onerous burden—a burden he didn't want her to have to bear.

Anticipating Jazz's course, Mike made his way down to the beach, leaving a deliberate but not obvious trail for him to follow. It was almost too easy to then circle back around and attack from behind—a quick blow to the back of his neck as he simultaneously wrenched the weapon from his grasp, then an upward swing with the butt of the gun to the side of his head. It was over in seconds without any blood being shed.

Unfortunately, he didn't have any handcuffs, but he managed to restrain Jazz's hands and feet with zip ties from the backpack, then fashioned a quick rope out of the malleable vine that was abundant on the island to secure him to a leaning but sturdy palm.

One down, he said to himself, as he set off in search of Rico.

Jazz's cohort proved to be a more worthy adversary.

It took Mike almost twenty minutes to locate him. Close to twenty minutes of careful silent tracking, and with every minute that passed his concern for Shannon grew. He knew he should be focusing on Rico, but he couldn't stop worrying about Shannon.

Until the snap of a twig immediately refocused his attention. Then every muscle in his body tensed in preparation for the final assault.

Shannon had no way of marking time while she waited for Michael to return. No way of knowing how long he'd been gone.

The cave was dark, and even if she'd had the emergency candles, she wouldn't have dared to light one. Michael was the only one who knew where she was, and she wanted to keep it that way.

But the darkness and emptiness and silence grated on her nerves. She could hear nothing but the beating of her heart, a sound that seemed to echo so loudly in the empty space she was certain it would give away her position to anyone in the vicinity.

After what seemed like hours, she heard something else.

She held her breath, listening.

There it was again.

Footsteps?

Yes, she was almost certain of it. There was someone outside, moving toward the cave.

Her breath caught in her throat.

Michael?

The initial glimmer of hope faded. If it was Michael, he would have called out to her. He wouldn't make her sit here and worry—he would let her know he was safe.

She tightened her grip on the weapon. Her stomach no longer rebelled at the thought of having to shoot. If Rico or Jazz had hurt Michael, she would gladly pull the trigger.

"Shannon?"

Michael.

She tucked the gun into the waistband of her skirt before racing toward the mouth of the cave. She stepped on something, felt a brief, stabbing pain in her foot, but didn't stop.

He dropped the backpack when he saw her, and she launched herself into his arms, mindless of the newly acquired weapons slung over his shoulder.

He hugged her tight. "I told you I'd come back."

She stepped out of his embrace, her throat inexplicably tight. "I knew you would."

He smiled at this manifestation of faith as Shannon finally acknowledged the weapons slung over his shoulders.

"Did you get those from Rico and Jazz?" she asked.

"Yeah."

"But how—" She stopped herself. She didn't care what he'd had to do to get them. The only thing that mattered was that he'd come back, as he'd promised he would do.

But he anticipated her unspoken question, reached out a hand to gently stroke a finger down her cheek. "I didn't kill them. I could have," he admitted, dropping his hand away. "I wanted to, to make them pay for what they put you through. But I didn't. I only disarmed them and tied them up. It's up to the authorities to decide their fate now."

She couldn't deny she was relieved. If it had been a choice between Michael and Rico and Jazz, she would gladly have traded the lives of Peart's two goons for this man. But while she wouldn't have blinked if Michael told her he'd killed them in self-defense, she didn't want any blood shed for vengeance. His restraint proved to her, once again, that he was an honorable man. A man worthy of the trust she'd finally allowed herself to give him.

"Are you ready to get off this island?" he asked.

She nodded. "More than ready."

He reached for the backpack again, paused. "Christ, Shannon. What happened?"

"What?" She glanced down, surprised by the crimson stain in the sand. "Oh. I must have cut myself on something."

He dropped to the ground beside her, gently lifting her foot to examine the injury.

"There'll be a lot more of her blood on the ground if you don't put your hands in the air right now, Courtland."

Everything inside Mike froze.

Later he would wonder how he could have been so preoccupied as to let Peart get the jump on them. Later there would be plenty of time for self-recriminations. For now, Mike needed to figure out how the hell he was going to extricate himself and Shannon from the mess he'd just dumped them into.

He'd been a fool to accept Rico's assertion that Peart was still in Pennsylvania, to believe he wouldn't have time to get there and back despite the private planes and helicopters that were at his disposal. It was a stupid mistake that could end up costing Shannon her life.

No, he wouldn't let it. He would find a way out of this.

The AK-47s he'd liberated from Rico and Jazz were still slung over his shoulder. But Peart was also armed, his finger at the ready on the trigger of his weapon. Mike was certain he could take Peart out in less than a second, but he couldn't risk the possibility that Shannon might get caught in the crossfire. Which meant that for now he'd have to stall while he considered other options.

"Get up, Courtland," Peart said. "Slowly."

He rose to his feet, stepping in front of Shannon to shield her with his body as he did so.

"Miss Vaughn will relieve you of your weapons. One at a time," he said to Shannon, "touching only the barrel."

Mike remained motionless while Shannon moved to his side. Her gaze was steady on his, silently communicating her faith and belief in him. He hoped like hell that trusting him wouldn't be her last mistake.

The first gun removed, Peart instructed her to take three steps forward and place it on the ground. The same routine was followed for the second gun, while he just stood there, helpless to do anything else.

"If you're going to kill us," Shannon said, "why don't you just do it?"

"Are you in that much of a hurry to die?"

"I just don't like being a pawn in someone else's game."

"It won't be for too much longer," Peart told her.

"Maybe not for me," she agreed. "But how much longer are you going to jump through hoops for A.J.?"

Peart made no verbal response to her taunt, although Mike saw the way his jaw clenched and his eyes narrowed.

"Ginger," he warned softly. "It's not smart to piss off the guy holding all of the weapons."

"Good advice." Peart turned his gaze back on Shannon. "Because if my finger so much as twitches on this trigger, you'll be dead before your body hits the ground."

"How would you explain that to A.J.?" Shannon asked, apparently undaunted.

If Mike didn't believe Peart was looking for an excuse to pull the trigger, he would have reached forward to clamp his hand over her mouth.

"Accidents happen." He gestured with the weapon. "Now step back beside Courtland."

She stepped back, seemed to lose her balance as she favored her injured foot.

Mike automatically reached out, his hand going to her waist to steady her. His heart nearly stopped when Peart sighted the weapon on her.

"Do you really want to test me?" he snarled.

"Sorry," she mumbled.

But Mike knew that she wasn't, that her stumble had been deliberate. And with the familiar weight of his Glock now nestled in his palm, he sent up a silent prayer of thanks for her bold action and quick thinking.

But he still didn't know if he could risk drawing the weapon on Peart with Shannon so near.

"Do you hear that?" she asked.

Mike strained his ears but couldn't hear anything.

"It sounds like a helicopter. Maybe it's the coast guard."

Peart, obviously uneasy about the possibility of anyone being witness to this abduction at gunpoint, glanced up.

It was the moment Mike had been waiting for.

He shoved Shannon out of the way, swung his weapon toward Peart and fired.

Shannon drew in deep gulps of the salty air as the boat skimmed across the water. The wind was cool on her face, the light spray of water welcome evidence that they were finally on the move.

She didn't turn around to watch the island fade into the distance, hoping her memories of the past two days would disappear as easily.

She could still hear the echo of those gunshots ringing in her ears.

It had happened so fast. A split second that stretched into an eternity.

And then the rescue boat had finally arrived and the authorities had been contacted. Peart was airlifted to the nearest hospital, Rico and Jazz taken into police custody, and she and Michael were on their way back to Miami.

He was on the bridge now, talking to Garcia. Then he looked up, an easy smile creasing his face as his gaze locked with hers.

He made his way across the deck toward her, carrying a first-aid box in his hand.

"Are you okay?" he asked.

Somehow she managed a weak smile. "I'm feeling a little shaky," she admitted.

"Adrenaline crash," he told her. "You've had a hell of a day."

"How about you? Or was it all in a day's work?"

"Hardly. I had some very bad moments when Peart was pointing that weapon at you. Although I was almost ready to kill you myself for baiting him."

"I wanted his attention on me so you could make your move," she explained.

"Well, you succeeded." He slid his arm around her shoulders, hugged her tight. "And although I still wish you'd played a more passive role, you did good."

She wasn't usually an emotional person. She certainly wasn't the type to indulge in overt displays and had never been particularly susceptible to tears. But when he took her in his arms, when she felt the warm strength of his embrace, she couldn't hold back the sob that tore at her throat as she finally accepted that everything could have ended differently.

Michael brushed a hand over her hair, stroked it down her back. She buried her face against his chest, trembling with the onslaught of emotions, too overwhelmed to be embarrassed by her tears.

"It's okay," he said softly.

She could only nod, clinging tighter to him.

He didn't say anything else, he only held her until her tears were finally spent and her trembling had subsided.

"I'm sorry. I don't usually have meltdowns like that."

"I'd say you're entitled." He kissed her lips gently. "Now are you going to let me take a look at the gash on your foot?"

With everything that had happened, she couldn't believe he was concerned about such a minor injury. "It's fine."

"If you don't let me take care of it, I'll get the medic."

She sighed and lifted her foot for a quick visual inspection.

Shaking his head, Michael knelt beside her. "I'm going to have to clean this," he said, already uncapping the bottle of antiseptic.

She nodded, then sucked in a breath as he poured the liquid over the cut.

"Sorry." He winced in sympathy with her pain.

When he'd finished flushing the cut, he covered it with a sterile gauze pad. She watched in fascination the careful attention he gave to the task. His touch was firm yet gentle, as careful as though he was Prince Charming about to fit her with Cinderella's glass slipper.

Prince Charming? Cinderella?

It was then she knew she was in trouble.

Big trouble.

And this time it had absolutely nothing to do with Andrew Peart or Rico or Jazz or the mysterious A.J.

It was because she'd fallen in love with Michael.

Chapter 11

Panic expanded inside Shannon's chest. It wasn't the life-or-death kind of panic she'd experienced facing Peart's gun, but it was panic nonetheless.

Love?

No way.

She didn't do love under the best of circumstances, and the past few days had been anything but.

No, it wasn't love.

It was relief, adrenaline, excitement, gratitude.

Anything but love.

"Better?" Michael asked.

She stared at him blankly, her mind still reeling.

"Your foot," he clarified.

"Oh. Yeah. Thanks."

"You'll still need to have it looked at when we get back to Miami. It probably needs a few stitches."

She nodded. "Any idea when we'll get back?"

"About another hour or so."

She nodded.

It seemed unreal that a mere three hours could bridge the distance that only this morning had seemed an insurmountable obstacle.

"Thank you," she said.

"For?"

She smiled. "Keeping me alive."

He tucked a blowing strand of hair behind her ear and smiled. "It was my pleasure."

She knew he wasn't talking about his safeguarding her but about the intimacy they'd shared. She felt the responding heat building inside her and reminded herself that what had happened between them on the island was over. It had been a moment of insanity, nothing more. Definitely *not* love. And the sooner they got back to the mainland and she went home, the sooner she could forget the ridiculous notion.

"I hope it won't be difficult to get a flight back to Chicago."

Michael's smile faded. "Are you in that much of a hurry to leave?"

She looked away. "There's no reason for me to stay in Florida any longer."

"Until the police have identified and apprehended A.J., you're not safe going anywhere."

"What if they never find this A.J.? You can't keep tabs on me forever."

"It won't be forever," he promised. "Probably just a few more days."

A few more days with Michael.

It was tempting, and it was because she was tempted that Shannon knew it was a bad idea.

"I want to go home."

"I can understand that you want to get your life back to normal, but you're still in danger."

"Maybe Peart only came after me because I was here—a convenient target."

"That's a possibility," he agreed. "But now you *are* the target. You've managed to escape from him and evade him, and though he won't be coming after you anytime soon, it's likely that A.J. will send someone else."

"I can't understand why someone would go to this much trouble to retaliate for the fact that my sister was there when Zane Conroy was killed. It wasn't even Natalie who killed him—she was just unfortunate enough to get caught in the middle."

"You don't have to understand it, you only have to believe it. These people follow their own rules, not anyone else's."

"Are you trying to scare me into staying?"

"I want you to be aware of the facts. And the fact is, I'm not letting you go back to Chicago."

Mike regretted the choice of words as soon as he'd spoken.

Sure enough, after a brief moment of stunned silence, Shannon's eyes flashed—sparks of molten fury in the emerald depths.

"You're not *letting* me?" she enunciated carefully, her tone deliberately controlled.

He almost smiled. But that, he knew, would be an even bigger mistake.

"You have no identification and no credit card to buy a plane ticket," he reminded her. "How do you expect to go anywhere?"

"I'll call my sister. She can wire me money for a bus ticket."

He should have expected she'd have a ready answer. And maybe it wasn't such an unreasonable one, but he wasn't willing to back down on this. "Or you could just stay in Miami a few more days."

"Do you really think I should just continue my vacation as if the past three days never happened?"

"I'm not suggesting you go sightseeing," he said patiently. "I'm just asking you to stay so that I don't have to follow you halfway across the country on a bus."

"You don't have to follow me anywhere."

"Until A.J. is locked up, I'm sticking to you like glue. It's your choice whether that's in Florida or somewhere else."

"Even if I wanted to stay," she said, "as you've pointed out, I have no cash or ID for a hotel room."

"Don't worry about that."

"I *hate* when you do that."

Her vehemence surprised him. "Do what?"

"Tell me not to worry. Or tell me to trust you. Three days ago I didn't even know you. Then you waltzed into my life and took right over."

He was silent for a long minute, considering her position. "I apologize if it seems that I've taken over your life," he said. "But I'm not going to apologize for looking out for you. I'm trying to keep you safe, and it isn't always convenient to answer a dozen questions in the process."

"Fine. I could see that, when we were on the island, trying to stay two steps ahead of Rico and Jazz and Peart. But right now, when the most immediate concern is sunburn, you'd think you could give me the courtesy of some answers."

She was right, of course. He was just accustomed to giving instructions and having them followed. And while Shannon may have let him call the shots while they were on the island, she had no intention of letting him continue to do so.

"You're right," he agreed.

Some of her anger faded, but she remained wary.

"I should have discussed the plans with you."

"The plans being?" she prompted, when he failed to divulge any more information.

"I told you my sister works at a hotel in Miami," he reminded her.

She nodded.

"I contacted her to make her arrangements for us to stay there."

"Why couldn't you just tell me that? Why is everything such a big secret with you?"

"Maybe it's a throwback from my military career—sharing information on a need-to-know basis."

"Well, I don't appreciate you pulling rank on me."

He reached for her hand and was relieved that she didn't tug it away. "Will you stay in Miami, anyway?"

She smiled. "Only because I want to see your sister's reaction when she finds out about her boat."

He was grateful for the smile, suspecting it might be the last one of hers he saw for a while. Because when they got back to Miami, his biggest secret would be blown out of the water. And he had no idea how she would react to it.

Shannon sat in the back of Garcia's car and watched the familiar sights of the city speed past her window. It had been hours since they'd arrived back in Miami—hours that had been spent first in the police station and then at the hospital. Nine stitches and a tetanus shot later, she wasn't sure which she resented more—Michael's insistence on remaining at her side throughout the ordeal in the E.R. or the burning pain of the injection that lingered in her arm.

The injury to her foot would heal, but Michael's vigilance wasn't likely to change anytime in the near future.

She sighed, accepting that she wasn't annoyed with him so much as she was disappointed in herself. She'd actually enjoyed having him hover over her, appreciated his solicitous attention. For a woman who had been independent for so long, his concern and consideration were irresistible.

In fact, there were too many things about him that were irresistible. The warmth of his eyes, the strength of his arms, the slow, sexy smile. The way he looked at her, touched her, kissed her.

She gave herself a mental shake to banish these traitorous thoughts. Now that they were off the island, she needed to reassert her independence, to stand on her own two feet. Except that right now she didn't even have shoes for those feet, no money to buy shoes, and the thought of lying down on an honest-to-goodness mattress with real sheets was too tempting to resist.

"Here you are," Detective Garcia said, interrupting her thoughts.

Shannon frowned as he pulled up at the back entrance of an obviously exclusive hotel.

She looked down at her bare feet, torn skirt, dirty T-shirt, then at Michael. "You've got to be joking."

"I wish I was," he said grimly, sliding toward the door.

She didn't move. "I can't go in there looking like this."

He reached for her hand, tugging when she resisted his attempt to help her out of the vehicle. "As you're aware," he said, "our options are severely limited."

"And *limited*—at least in my mind—means we find a budget hotel on a dead-end street—not a five-star luxury resort."

There was no doubt in her mind that the pink stone building with its elaborate cornices and gleaming windows was a five-star resort. The ornately scrolled *C* etched in the brass plate beside the service door further confirmed this belief.

In fact, that symbol was vaguely familiar to her, but before she had time to wonder where she might have seen it, Michael was ushering her toward the entrance.

"My sister will be so glad you approve," he said, leading her into the chaos of the hotel kitchen at the height of dinner hour.

The scents registered first: grilled meats, spicy sauces, sweet cakes. Then the sounds: dishes clattering, pots clanging, voices murmuring. And the vision: at least a half-dozen chefs in white aprons bustling about from chopping blocks to stovetops in a meticulously choreographed production.

The swinging door pushed open to admit a busboy with a heavy tray and, on his heels, an immaculately dressed woman.

The manager, Shannon guessed. Her black skirt and tailored jacket were designer, her dark-blond hair secured in a neat French twist, her gray eyes sharp and assessing. But more than anything else, it was the air of authority she carried with her that told Shannon this was the woman in charge.

She prepared herself to be turned back out onto the street and was stunned when the woman's lips curved, only seconds before she threw her arms around Michael.

"I've been so worried about you."

"Hey, Rach."

His sister, Shannon realized.

She could see it now—the family resemblance. Despite Michael's disheveled appearance and decidedly masculine features, there were definite similarities in the shape of the face, the color of the eyes, the curve of the lips.

"Sorry to intrude at mealtime," he said to his sister.

"You know I'm always happy to see you. Not so happy to hear about my boat," she continued. "But relieved to know that you didn't blow up with it."

"You're all heart," he said dryly.

Rachel grinned and turned to her. "You must be Shannon."

She could only nod, feeling filthy and self-conscious in the presence of this together, professional woman. She usually was such a woman, but now—covered in dirt and sweat and bug bites—she felt completely out of her element.

"I'm guessing you probably want a bath and a bed—not necessarily in that order."

"Definitely in that order," Shannon said. As exhausted as she was, no way was she climbing between the sheets until she'd scrubbed the two days' worth of dirt and grime from her skin.

"And food," Michael added.

"Dominic is grilling red snapper with plantains and sweet potatoes tonight."

"We'll keep that in mind," he said.

"Just call down to the kitchen when you decide," she said, pressing two keycards into his hand.

"Did you remember what I told you about the registration?"

She nodded. "Harold Jessop is in Room 1027, Lillian Baines in 1029. And if anyone comes looking for you, I'm sorry, but I haven't seen my brother in several days."

He grinned. "Thanks, Rach. I owe you."

"Big-time," she agreed cheerfully. "But we'll talk about that after you've had a chance to rest."

Then suddenly her eyes filled with tears, and she wrapped her arms around him and hugged him close.

"You're going to get your pretty clothes all dirty."

"I don't care." She held on a moment longer to prove it. "You really scared me this time, Michael."

"I'm sorry."

"Yeah, well—" she pulled back, sniffled "—don't ever do that again."

Then she turned to Shannon, the professional smile back in place. "I hope you enjoy your stay at the Courtland Resort Miami."

A.J. was furious.

Not only had Peart failed to apprehend the woman and the P.I., he'd gone and gotten himself shot in the process. He was one of the organization's top men and he'd embarked on the pursuit armed with plenty of firepower and two assistants. Yet somehow Courtland had bested all of them.

A.J. didn't tolerate second place.

Ever.

The crystal tumbler of whiskey smashed against the door frame, raining shards of glass and drops of Chivas.

Obviously it had been a mistake to entrust such a crucial task to anyone else—a mistake that would soon be rectified.

A.J. knew which hotel they were at and what rooms they were checked into. The information had been relayed by a well-paid informant on the Courtland staff almost as soon as the phony registrations were logged into the computer at the front desk.

Courtland obviously thought he could keep the woman safe there, and with good reason. Security at the hotel was top-notch, with video cameras in the lobby, the halls and each of the stairwells and elevators.

But A.J. knew that nothing was impenetrable, no one was ever truly safe. And though it was tempting to launch the next attack in that direction to make the point, it was what Courtland would expect.

No, it was time for a subtle change of tactics. Shift the target, change the rules. Make Courtland play the game.

But there was one other loose end to take care of first.

Shannon knew now why that scrolled *C* had seemed familiar—it was the logo on more than a thousand Courtland resorts and hotels around the world. In fact, she'd stayed at a Courtland resort in San Francisco once—on her honeymoon with Doug.

Michael slipped the keycard into the slot, pushed the door open when the signal blinked green and stepped back so Shannon could precede him into the room.

She moved past him, her feet sinking into the soft rose-colored carpet. The floor-to-ceiling windows were draped with velvet curtains and the walls were papered in silk. And then there was the bed—wider than she was tall, covered in a silk brocade spread and piled high with fluffy pillows.

Every detail was perfect. Of course, nothing less than perfection was tolerated at a Courtland resort.

She wondered if it was that kind of pressure that had driven Michael away from the family business and into the army. She shook off the instinctive sympathy that stirred inside her.

"You haven't said two words to me since Garcia dropped us off," he noted.

She had plenty she wanted to say but no idea where to begin. She crossed over to the window, pulled back the heavy drapes. "I'm surprised you couldn't swing us a couple of rooms overlooking the beach," she said.

"I figured you'd seen enough water for a while."

She turned away from the window to face him. She couldn't believe that, even now, after everything they'd been through, he was continuing to be evasive.

"Have you ever heard of Howard Vaughn?" she asked him.

His brow furrowed. "The *New York Times* bestselling novelist?" he asked cautiously.

She nodded.

"Of course," he said.

"Well, here's a newsflash," she said. "We share the same last name, but we're not related in any way. In fact, we've never even met."

He sighed. "You're ticked about the Courtland thing, huh?"

"The Courtland thing"—as if it was merely an insignificant detail and not an integral part of who he was.

"When I asked you about the accommodations you'd arranged, you told me your sister worked at a hotel in Miami."

"She does."

"Wouldn't it have been more accurate to say she *owns* the hotel?"

He selected a bottle of water from the top of the bar, twisted the cap. "Actually she only owns twenty-four and a half percent of it."

"How much do you own?"

He took a long swallow before admitting, "The same. My dad holds the remaining fifty-one percent."

"Why didn't you tell me?"

"Because it wasn't relevant," he said simply.

She stared at him. "Your family owns one of the largest hotel chains in the world—how is that *ever* not relevant?"

"Because it's theirs, not mine."

"You just admitted that you own almost a quarter of the company."

"Only on paper. I have less than zero involvement in the day-to-day operations of the business."

They'd had this conversation already, but when he'd first told her about his decision not to work for his father's business, she hadn't realized what that business was. "How does your family feel about that?"

His smile was strained. "They're still convinced I'm going through a rebellious phase—that I'll come to my senses one day."

"Your parents must be pleased that your sister's involved in the business, at least."

"You'd think so," he agreed. "But that's a whole other story."

She realized he wasn't being deliberately evasive, he was just explaining the situation as he saw it. She also realized that if they'd had other options, he wouldn't have chosen to come to this hotel, either. "So why are we here, Michael?"

He recapped the empty water bottle and tossed it into the garbage. "Because we need to keep a low profile and I couldn't think of another hotel that would accept our phony registrations without question. Because I know the security of the hotel and believe I can keep you safe here. But mostly because the next time I make love with you, I want it to be in a real bed."

Chapter 12

Shannon snapped her jaw shut.

Whatever other questions she'd intended fled at the naked desire in his eyes, the answering heat that pulsed through her own veins.

"Oh."

He smiled wryly. "I don't think I've ever seen you at such a complete loss for words."

"I'm surprised," she admitted. "I figured that what happened between us on the island happened because we were on the island, and the way it ended…" She trailed off, aware that she was rambling incoherently.

"I promised to make it up to you," he reminded her.

She remained silent.

"You didn't think I actually meant it, did you?"

"You don't owe me anything, Michael."

He took a step closer, brushed a strand of hair off her

cheek. "I want to be with you, Shannon. The question is, what do you want?"

She swallowed, not willing to admit how much she wanted to be with him. Because wanting equaled vulnerability, and this time she was determined to protect her heart.

"I don't know," she lied.

He studied her for a long moment, his expression unreadable.

The close scrutiny reminded her of her disheveled appearance—the dirty clothing, unwashed hair. On the island there had been no point in worrying about something she couldn't fix. But since she'd stepped off the boat in Miami, she'd been increasingly aware of how ghastly she looked.

"I want a bath," she decided. "A long, hot bath."

He nodded. "There are bubbles, creams, lotions—everything you'll need—in the bathroom. I'll go next door to my room and give you some privacy."

"Your room?"

"I know what *I* want," he told her pointedly. "The rest is up to you."

Shannon watched Michael disappear through the connecting door, feeling oddly bereft by his easy retreat. And yet she knew it was for the best. There was no point in sustaining a relationship that had no future.

She passed a mirror on the way to the bathroom and grimaced. She could see why he'd retreated. Obviously Michael thought she needed a bath as much as she did.

She peeled her T-shirt over her head and unfastened her skirt, tempted to toss both items in the garbage except that she didn't even have a change of clothes. At least there was a complimentary robe on the back of the bathroom door—that would suffice until she had a chance to send her clothes down to the laundry.

That decision resolved one of her immediate problems, but what was she going to do about Michael?

He'd asked what she wanted. The answer was simple: she wanted to spend the next week locked in this room with him, just the two of them—together because they wanted to be and not because circumstances had forced them into proximity.

But it was crazy to even dream of something like that. Even on the island she'd accepted that their time together was limited—and that was before she'd known he was a Courtland.

She shook her head, still reeling from that little bit of information. She felt like such an idiot for not making the connection, for not even suspecting.

Now she'd somehow found herself involved, irrationally and impulsively, and with a man who lived in the same world as her ex-husband. A world she'd never managed to fit into.

Even if she wasn't already in love with Michael—and she was sure she wasn't—she knew it would be easy to fall. And if she fell in love with him, she'd be opening herself up to the same heartbreak all over again.

She wished Natalie was here. Not that she necessarily wanted to talk to her sister about these chaotic emotions, but she did want to talk to her. To know that she and Jack were safe, that any problems she'd encountered in her dealings with Zane Conroy had died along with Conroy.

The need to hear her sister's voice was suddenly more pressing than anything else. She forgot about the bath for a few more minutes and dialed.

"Shannon—I've been going out of my mind with worry. Where are you? Are you all right?"

The welcome sound of Natalie's voice brought tears to her eyes. The obvious concern in her tone helped Shannon hold them in check. "I told you I'd call when I got a chance."

"I know. But Dylan expected to hear from Mike yesterday and when he didn't, we started to worry that something might have happened. Dylan was even thinking about flying down to Florida to track you down."

"That's not necessary," Shannon assured her. "Everything's fine here."

"Are you still with Michael?"

"Yes," she admitted, then quickly changed the subject before her sister could pursue that avenue of inquiry. "Have you heard from Mom?"

"The new Mrs. Sutherland called me from Vegas last night," Natalie said. "And she sounded very happy."

Shannon couldn't hold back the sigh. "Doesn't she always?"

"I really think it's different this time."

"That's because you're an eternal optimist."

"Maybe I do want it to be different," Natalie admitted. "I want her to be happy. I want *you* to be happy."

"Marriage isn't the answer for everyone." But she realized that she sounded more wistful than disdainful and only hoped her sister wouldn't pick up on it.

She should have known it was a futile hope.

"Just because Doug didn't love you doesn't mean the right man won't," Natalie said gently.

"I'm not sure I believe there is a 'right man' for everyone," Shannon told her. "And I have too much going on in my life to even think about things like that right now."

This time it was Natalie who sighed. "Does that mean there weren't any sparks between you and Michael?"

There were so many sparks she sometimes felt as though she might spontaneously combust when she was with him. But she decided it was best to keep those details to herself rather than fuel her sister's overactive imagination.

"How's my nephew's baseball team doing?" she asked instead, hoping to make her sister forget about Michael.

"Terrific," Natalie said, launching into the subject with enthusiasm. "They're on a three-game winning streak, and Jack hit a home run last game."

"I can't wait to see him play."

"He'd love it if you came out to a game."

Shannon promised herself she'd make it to the ballpark before the end of the season—because next year she'd be on the other side of the Atlantic Ocean. "Be sure to give him a big hug and a kiss for me."

"I will," Natalie said.

Her doubts and confusion about moving to France aside, Shannon felt marginally better after talking to her sister. If nothing else, saying the words out loud to Natalie reinforced her belief that she had neither the time nor the inclination for romantic entanglements.

A mutually satisfying physical relationship was one thing—falling in love was something else entirely. Something she wasn't prepared to do—not after only a few days, and definitely not with someone like Michael. Not again.

Forcing those thoughts out of her mind, she finally headed into the bathroom.

Andrew Peart had survived surgery.

He'd suffered significant internal bleeding as a result of his wounds and what was likely permanent damage to his shoulder. Despite this, the doctors told his wife they were optimistic about his recovery. He was young and healthy and obviously had a strong will to live. For now, however, he remained in intensive care and under police guard in the hospital.

Alysia was allowed to visit her husband, but she wasn't permitted to be alone with him. The cop who was posted outside the room followed her inside, and she had to endure his silent but undisguised scrutiny while she held Andrew's motionless hand between her own.

She was concerned about the fact that he hadn't yet regained consciousness, but the doctors assured her that was normal. His body had suffered significant trauma and undergone major surgery, but there was no reason to think he wouldn't come around in a day or two.

She brushed a lock of hair away from his forehead.

Truth was, she was glad he wasn't awake. Because she knew that, as soon as his eyes opened, the room would be filled with cops interrogating and harassing him. He didn't need to deal with that right now, not after everything he'd already been through.

She squeezed his hand as a lone tear trickled down her cheek. She couldn't believe how close she'd come to losing him. And so soon after her brother's tragic death.

It was so unfair. How much was one woman supposed to endure? How many losses could she bear?

She brushed these questions away along with her tear. She wasn't going to lose Andrew. He was her husband, her partner.

Till death do us part.

Shannon decided to take a shower before her bath. When she realized how much dirt and grime was stuck to her body, she decided the last thing she wanted to do was soak in it. After wrapping her foot in a laundry bag to keep the stitches dry, she turned on the spray. She scrubbed her body thoroughly with a puff and scented shower gel. And she washed her hair—three times. Then, when she was sure that she was clean, she filled the tub with hot water, added a generous amount of foaming bubbles and finally relaxed.

She felt as though she'd been on the island for weeks instead of only days. Her body ached with fatigue and tension, but both slowly drained away into the soothing warmth of the water, the fragrant froth of the bubbles.

She only wished she could empty her mind so easily. But no matter how hard she tried, she couldn't stop thinking about Michael.

Dammit—she didn't need the complication of these unexpected feelings. And she couldn't afford the heartbreak that would inevitably follow if she succumbed to them.

Just because Doug didn't love you doesn't mean the right man won't. Her sister's words haunted her, tempted her.

Except that there was no way Michael could ever be the right man for her.

Men like him didn't fall in love with women like her. Men like him had sex with women like her, but they fell in love with and married women of their own social class and tax bracket. Doug, of course, had been an exception—but only because she had something he wanted.

She couldn't imagine there was anything she had that Michael would want for the long term. She wouldn't delude herself into thinking she was anything more to him than a temporary diversion. And that was a role she couldn't continue to play—not if she wanted to keep her heart intact.

She pulled the plug and stood up, grabbing a thick terry towel and vigorously scrubbing it over her body as she contemplated the night ahead of her.

Michael was in his room. Maybe he was even waiting for her to knock on the adjoining door. He'd made it clear that the next move was hers. But she wasn't strong enough to take that step. She wasn't brave enough to risk her heart again.

She shoved one arm into the oversize robe, then the other, then belted it securely around her waist. She was going to stay in her own room, order up a hot meal from room service, then climb between the fresh crisp sheets of a real bed and sleep for at least twelve hours without interruption—without dreaming about Michael.

Except that when she opened the bathroom door, he was there. Beside a small round table set for two with pressed linen, sparkling crystal and gleaming silver. There was music—soft and sultry jazz playing in the background. And flowers. A vase overflowing with creamy white roses, the scent of their fragrant blooms filling the air with a sweet, heady perfume.

But it was the man who caught and held her attention.

He was dressed in clean khakis and a yellow polo shirt that stretched across his broad shoulders, the color emphasizing the bronze tan of his skin.

Her mouth actually watered looking at him.

"Michael."

It was all she could manage, but it must have been enough because he smiled in response and stepped toward her. She felt herself tremble as he reached for her, taking each of her hands in one of his own.

"I know I said it was up to you," he said. "But I couldn't resist a little persuasion."

"It's…incredible."

"I wanted to take you out," he said. "Somewhere romantic for dinner and dancing. But under the circumstances—and considering the fact that you have nine stitches in your foot— I thought it best if we stayed in."

She smiled. "It was a nice thought."

"Are you hungry?"

"Starved," she admitted, remembering her decision to order up room service, her determination not to think about Michael. Both of those resolutions had been undermined by his actions, but she wasn't the least bit sorry.

"I took the liberty of ordering for both of us." He lifted the domed lids to reveal their dinner. "Peanut butter and jelly."

Then he pulled a bottle out of the wine bucket, popped the cork and poured into the two crystal flutes on the table.

She smiled. "Champagne?"

"You chose the meal, I chose the wine." He set the bottle back into the bucket, picked up the glasses, handed one to her.

She stared at the bubbles rising in her glass. Skippy and

Cristal—they were as different, and as incompatible, as she and Michael were.

"American peanut butter and French champagne don't go together," she said softly.

"Says who?"

Was he making a point—or was she reading too much into a simple gesture?

She took a sip of the wine and moved closer to the table, smiling at the neatly cut triangles of bread on the elegant china platter. "I can't imagine this is a staple of Courtland clientele."

"The Courtland organization prides itself on responding to the needs and desires of its guests. Although somebody needs to remind our current chef of that fact—apparently he threatened to quit over my request."

She smiled. "You're kidding?"

He shook his head. "There might have been a mutiny in the kitchen if Rachel hadn't managed to soothe his temper—or maybe it was his ego."

"I would have been more than happy with anything off of the regular menu," she told him.

"That's because you're starving," he reminded her, then pulled back a chair for her to be seated. "Let's eat."

She watched as he chewed a corner of his own sandwich, slowly, hesitantly. Finally he swallowed.

"Well?"

He took a long sip of champagne. "It's different."

"It's a classic," she corrected, popping another bite into her mouth. "And delicious."

They ate in silence until the platter of sandwiches was empty. Michael may not have been thrilled with the menu choice, but he'd obviously been as hungry as she was.

He topped up her glass with more champagne. "Feel better now that you've eaten?"

She nodded and reached for her wine. "I can't remember when I've enjoyed a meal more."

"I'm sure anything would have been an improvement over charred fish and overripe bananas."

"It was more than just the sandwiches," she said. "You didn't have to do any of this, Michael."

"I wanted to."

"Why?"

"Because I wanted to give you a memory that might help erase some of the horror of the past couple of days."

"It wasn't all bad," she said. "Aside from the bullets and the bad guys, the snakes and sleeping on the ground."

"You won't have to sleep on the ground tonight," he assured her.

She glanced over at the wide bed on the other side of the room and couldn't help but wonder if he would be sharing it with her. Michael followed the direction of her gaze, his own darkening with promise in response to her unspoken question.

Which was why Shannon was completely taken by surprise when he said, "There are some great movies on TV tonight."

She traced the base of her glass with the tip of a fingernail, puzzling over his statement. "You want to watch a movie?"

He reached across the table to take her hand. "What I want is to make love with you, Shannon. Slowly, thoroughly and endlessly."

His thumb stroked over her wrist, and she knew he was aware of how fast her pulse was racing.

"But I also want to spend time with you. Time just being with you, without worrying about any danger that lurks around the corner or any complications that tomorrow might bring."

Whatever plans she'd had to keep an emotional distance melted into a soggy puddle at his feet—along with her heart.

"Now I'll ask you again," he continued. "What do you want?"

"I think…I'd like to watch a movie with you." Then she smiled. "Later."

Chapter 13

Mike sat at the little table with a cup of coffee in front of him and wondered how it was possible that he could feel such a sense of peace and contentment.

It wasn't just sexual satisfaction—although there was certainly that—but a deeper intimacy and emotional connection he'd never experienced with any other woman. In fact, nothing had ever seemed as right as just being with Shannon.

Was this love?

The question would ordinarily have sent him into a tailspin. He wasn't looking for love. He wasn't looking for anything more complicated than what they'd already shared: mind-boggling, body-numbing sex. Mutually satisfying and definitely temporary.

Except that the thought of Shannon walking out of his life when this situation with A.J. was finally resolved made something inside him ache.

He wasn't ready to let her go.

Not yet.

Maybe not ever.

Okay—that thought gave him pause.

He'd known Shannon less than a week, it was ridiculous to think about spending the rest of his life with her.

The last thing he needed or wanted was to be tied to any one woman forever. He had no intention of signing himself up for the kind of misery that permeated both of his parents' lives. Not after the close call he'd had with Tiffany.

He'd started dating her about a year after he'd come back from Righaria. He'd been looking for something or someone to fill the gaping void of having lost Brent and Lisa and his career, and Tiffany had seemed…suitable.

He winced at the word but couldn't deny it was appropriate.

She'd been attractive, sophisticated and intelligent. And if there was no real passion between them, they'd at least been friends. Most important, being with Tiffany meant that he wasn't alone. Because when he was alone, he was haunted by the nightmares of Righaria and the uncertainty of what he was going to do with the rest of his life.

He'd known he wasn't in love with her, but he'd thought they could make their relationship work. She'd been supportive and sympathetic, encouraging him to take his time to figure out what he wanted to do with his life.

And then he'd overheard a conversation between Tiffany and his mother, in which Tiffany had promised she would convince Michael to take a position at Courtland Enterprises. He might not be thrilled with the idea at first, she'd admitted, but as soon as she got pregnant with their child, she'd make him see that it was the best way to provide for his family.

It was the wake-up call Mike had needed, and he'd walked away from Tiffany without a backward glance.

After that, he'd been determined to keep his relationships simple. No expectations, no promises, no disappointments.

And he'd done so—until Shannon. Until this morning, when he'd awoken with her in his arms, their naked bodies tangled together, and he'd realized he didn't want to let her go.

He looked up as she stepped into the room. She was just out of the shower again, wearing only a hotel robe, her hair still damp, her skin glowing.

He'd never seen Tiffany so completely without artifice. But even dressed to the nines in her designer clothes and flashy jewels, she'd never looked as perfect as Shannon did right now.

She inhaled deeply, smiled. "Please tell me that's coffee I smell."

"Genuine Columbian," he told her.

He poured another cup as she sat down across from him.

She didn't seem to notice that the lapels of her robe gaped open, exposing the creamy curve of one breast—but he certainly did.

She sipped, then sighed blissfully. "I can't believe it's been three days since I've had a cup of coffee," she admitted. "I really missed this."

It was the expression on her face—the pure and simple pleasure—that erased the last of his doubts.

This was the woman he wanted to be with forever.

Maybe it was fast, maybe it was crazy to make the decision over morning coffee, but there it was. He was in love with Shannon, and he wanted to spend the rest of his life with her.

Except that Shannon intended to take a job in France, which threatened to put a major kink in his plans.

"Are you still planning on going to Paris?"

She seemed as startled by the abrupt question as he was.

"I've already told them I would take the position."

"With your qualifications and experience, you could probably get a job anywhere."

She nodded. "But this is an incredible opportunity for me."

"It's also three thousand miles away from your family." Three thousand miles away from *him*. But, of course, he left that thought unspoken.

"Natalie and Jack are one of the reasons I made this decision in the first place," she reminded him. "Because I realized how empty my life was when they moved out of Chicago.

"Now Natalie and Dylan are going to be married, Jack's finally getting the father he deserves, and my mother and her new husband are on their honeymoon. It's a good time for me to make a fresh start, too."

"What about us?"

She didn't look at him as she refilled her cup. "This is just an interlude in both of our lives."

"It can be more."

She shook her head. "If this situation with Peart hadn't existed, we would never even have met. We certainly wouldn't be where we are right now.

"I'm not going to deny that I've enjoyed the time I've spent with you—at least the parts where we weren't running from bullets—but I don't make life-altering decisions in highly emotional circumstances."

"Like your mother," he guessed.

"Because it's not smart," she corrected. "I refuse to let a temporary affair influence this kind of decision, and our lives are too different for this to be ever anything else."

"Because I'm a Courtland?"

"That's part of it," she admitted.

He almost laughed at the irony. Most of the women he'd been involved with in the past viewed his name and birthright as assets. Because of her ex-husband, Shannon believed they were liabilities. Mike mentally cursed the man who'd been unable to appreciate this incredible woman and then compounded his mistake by making her feel unworthy just because she hadn't been born to the same social class.

"But it's only part," she told him.

"Okay—what are the other parts?"

She wrapped both hands around her cup so tightly her knuckles turned white. "Do you really want to make a list of all the reasons a relationship between us could never work?" she asked softly.

"No," he said evenly. "I want to make a list of the reasons you *think* it couldn't work so I can disprove them one by one."

"I'm just trying to look at this situation objectively."

"Well, before you arrive at any final conclusions, there's one more factor you need to put in your equation."

"What's that?" she asked warily.

"The fact that I love you."

Shannon's heart skipped a beat. Hope? Or fear?

She wasn't entirely sure which part of her instinctive reaction was stronger. She only knew that she couldn't allow herself to be swayed by his words or let her own emotions cloud the issue.

Right now she wanted nothing more than to stay with Michael. But those feelings were a product of these extraordinary circumstances. Since the moment she'd arrived in Florida, her life had erupted into chaos. She couldn't allow herself to be influenced by hormonal impulses that grew out of that turmoil.

"I love you, Shannon."

He said it again, so simply and easily she ached to believe him, and to share the feelings in her own heart.

"We've known each other a matter of days," she said, hoping to point out the absurdity of the situation to him as well as to herself.

"Maybe it doesn't make sense. Nothing about this situation has made sense," he admitted. "But when I woke up this morning, with you in my arms, I thought, This is how I want to wake up every morning for the rest of my life.

"Believe me, that isn't a thought that has *ever* crossed my mind before. And although I'll admit to an immediate and subsequent thought that I'd probably lost my mind, it's true."

She sighed. "Why are you bringing this up now?"

"Because I know that as soon as this situation with A.J. is cleared up, you'll be on your way back to Chicago trying to pretend none of this ever happened."

"I wouldn't ever wish away the time I've spent with you." She set down her empty cup and moved away from the table. "But I also won't make it into something it isn't."

"You're not giving us a chance to see what it could be."

"Maybe if we'd met in a different time and place, under different circumstances—normal circumstances. But how can any of this be real?"

"It doesn't get any more real than this," he told her.

Then he crushed his mouth down on hers.

Shannon responded to his kiss willingly, her arms wrapping around him, her body pressing against his. She could deny her emotions, but Mike knew she couldn't deny this.

The passion between them was incredible, and if it was all she could accept for now, it would be enough. He certainly wasn't going to complain about having a warm and willing woman in his bed. He also wasn't going to give up convincing her that what they had found together was so much more.

Starting now.

He'd just eased her back onto the mattress when a knock sounded at the door.

She pulled him down with her. "Did you order breakfast?"

"Not yet."

"Then let's just ignore it."

He wished he could. "There's a clearly displayed Do Not Disturb sign on the door," he told her. "Which makes me think I know who it is."

Shannon sighed as the knock sounded again.

He moved away from her reluctantly to peer through the security viewer, his scowl not easing as he turned the handle of the door. "Why did I ever think I could expect any privacy here?" he muttered.

"Why did you?" his sister asked, pushing past him without waiting for an invitation. She smiled at Shannon, evidently not surprised to find her in his room. "Good morning."

"Good morning," Shannon murmured in return.

"Sleep well?"

Shannon's cheeks flushed prettily. "Very well, thanks."

"What are you doing here?" Mike interrupted the social pleasantries to ask his sister.

"I wanted to let you know there's a delivery coming up." As if on cue, there was another brisk knock. "Right on time."

Mike let his sister respond to the summons. Then he could only stare as the bellhop pushed a luggage cart laden down with boxes and bags into the room.

Rachel helped the man unload the packages onto the bed. "Thanks, Carlos."

"You're welcome, Miss Courtland." He gave a slight bow and disappeared out of the room with the cart.

"What is all of that?" he demanded.

"'All of that,'" she said, "isn't for you."

She turned to Shannon. "I noticed you didn't have any luggage with you and thought maybe you could use a few things."

Mike shook his head. Only his sister would refer to a mountain of clothes and accessories as "a few things."

"I guessed at the sizes," Rachel continued, "but if there's anything you don't like or that doesn't fit, you can exchange it at one of the boutiques downstairs."

She smiled. "As comfortable as our complimentary robes are, I thought at some point you might want to get dressed."

"I do," Shannon finally responded. "But I can't possibly keep all of this. There's no way I could ever pay you back."

"Don't worry about that," Rachel said. "I charged everything to Michael's account."

"*My* account?"

His sister grinned. "I knew you wouldn't object," she said. "After all, you did blow up my boat."

"The boat was insured."

"That's hardly the point. Anyway," she continued, "I also came up to let you know that someone stopped by the front desk this morning looking for you."

He forgot about her shopping spree as every nerve-ending in his body went on full alert. "Who was it?"

"Someone named Garcia."

Some of his tension eased. "*Detective* Garcia?"

"Yeah, that would be the one."

"Did he say what he wanted?"

She shrugged. "Just that he was trying to get in touch with you."

"Why didn't you let him come up?"

She widened her eyes in feigned innocence. "I have no idea where my brother is, Detective. I haven't seen him in several days."

Mike groaned; Shannon smiled. "That is what you told her to say," she reminded him.

He turned back to his sister. "When I told you not to tell anyone where we were, Rach, I didn't intend for you to lie to the police."

Rachel only shrugged again. "He ticked me off—banging on my door at 7:00 a.m. as I was getting out of the shower. I did suggest, however, that if he wanted to come back at a more-civilized hour, I might be able to give him some more information."

"I'll bet he was thrilled by that."

"Give me some credit," she chastised him. "If he'd given

the impression it was anything urgent, I would have brought him to your door myself. He said he'd be back around nine."

"It's almost that now," Shannon said.

"I'll give him a call, anyway. Hopefully I'll be able to talk him out of pressing charges against my interfering sister for obstruction of justice."

She grinned unrepentantly. "Or not. He was kind of cute—and I've never been in handcuffs."

Mike shook his head. "Don't you have a hotel to run?"

"I'm going." But she kissed his cheek, then turned to Shannon. "You should try the Belgian waffles with fresh strawberries and whipped cream for breakfast. Giselle's pastries are to die for."

"Aren't you curious about what's in those bags?" Mike asked after Rachel had gone.

Shannon was just staring at the packages, looking a little overwhelmed. "I don't know where to begin."

He picked up a small pink bag. "This one looks interesting."

Inside was a tissue-wrapped package. Inside the tissue were a couple of scraps of butter-colored lace.

He slid a finger under the strap and whistled appreciatively, holding it up for Shannon to see. "My sister might be a little excessive at times, but I can't fault her taste."

She snatched the bra from his hand. "Unless you plan on wearing it—hands off."

He grinned. "I don't think I'll be putting it on, but you can bet I'll be taking it off."

"Weren't you going to call Detective Garcia?" She turned away from him and started rummaging through the bags Rachel had brought.

"I hate it when the real world intrudes on my fantasy."

"I don't want to know what you were fantasizing about."

"Silk 'n' Sensations."

She paused in the act of unfolding a pair of linen pants.

"When we first met, I wondered why you looked familiar," he continued. "But I only just realized it now. You were a lingerie model."

"A lifetime ago," she admitted, selecting a sleeveless peach-colored top to go with the pants.

"I thought you were a research scientist."

"I am. I modeled to pay my way through college."

"And I looked at those magazines to fuel my dreams through college."

"Pervert. And they're not magazines, they're catalogs."

"Whatever." He grinned.

She shook her head.

"It's not something you should be ashamed of."

"I'm not ashamed of it," she denied. "I just got tired of people making judgments about me because of it."

"Like carrying around the Courtland name."

"Maybe," she allowed.

"Is that why you gave it up?"

"It was more a matter of scheduling. It just got too hard to juggle both jobs. And then—" she shrugged "—when Doug and I got married, he didn't really approve."

"What's not to approve of?"

She found a pair of sandals, slipped them on her feet to try the size. "He said it was false advertising."

"Damn push-up bras," he said. He'd experienced the disappointment of unwrapping a tempting package—and finding there was nothing but packaging. Having already had the privilege of exploring every inch of Shannon's naked body, however, he knew that wasn't a concern.

She forced a smile. "Not the merchandise—me."

He sensed some pretty heavy undercurrents that she was trying to skim over. He forgot about the yellow lace and took her hands, turning her around to face him.

"Do you want to explain that to me?"

"I'd rather not."

But he wasn't prepared to let it go. Not this time. "Your ex-husband did a real number on your self-esteem, didn't he?"

"It was a long time ago."

He remembered their early conversation on the island, her claim that she wasn't into sex, didn't like giving up control. As if making love was some kind of battle to be won or lost rather than an experience to be shared and enjoyed. "Not long enough if you're still letting his opinions influence your actions."

"I'm not." She tilted her head back and brushed her mouth against his. "Not anymore."

He slid his arms around her waist, drew her closer. "Maybe you should prove it to me."

She laughed, as he'd hoped she would, some of the shadows lifting from her eyes.

"Let me put on some clothes first, then you can take them off me."

Shannon felt a hundred percent better after she was dressed. She had to agree with Michael—his sister had exquisite taste. She'd gone through the array of tops and bottoms carefully, selecting items that would mix and match and hopefully not make too huge a dent in her savings account. Because despite what Rachel had said about charging the items to her brother, Shannon was determined to pay him back for her clothes.

She was just running a brush through her hair when Detective Garcia arrived. Although she wanted to know how the investigation was coming along, his presence in the hotel room made her uneasy—the outside world intruding on the private paradise she'd shared with Michael.

"Peart came out of surgery with flying colors," the detective told them, gratefully accepting the cup of coffee she offered. "I'm not sure whether that's good news or bad, but that was the word from the hospital this morning."

"Have you talked to him yet?" Michael asked.

Garcia shook his head. "Hopefully tomorrow. I have, however, talked to both Enrico Ramirez and Jefferson Washington."

Rico and Jazz, she realized.

"Neither of them said a single word about A.J."

"I guess it was too much to hope otherwise," Michael said.

"I didn't expect much," Garcia agreed. "But I thought we'd at least get a hint of something. What we've got is nothing.

"That's one of the reasons I wanted to meet with Ms. Vaughn." He turned to her, opening a folder on the table. "I've got some surveillance photos I want you to take a look at. I know you didn't see anyone other than Rico, Jazz and Peart on the boat, but someone else might have been hanging around the hotel prior to your abduction."

Shannon nodded, willing to do anything to help finally end this nightmare. "I'll try."

Garcia spread a series of photos over the surface of the table. "Take your time and look at each person individually, see if you recognize any faces or even any features."

She went through the photos once, and then again. No one looked familiar to her.

"I know it's a long shot," Garcia said. "But I'll leave the photos with you while I check in at the station. Maybe something will click for you."

"I hope so."

But as she continued to stare at the faces after Garcia had gone, she couldn't help but feel disappointed at the lack of recognition.

Michael brought her a fresh cup of coffee. "While you're doing that, I'll order up some…" His words trailed off.

She glanced up to see him staring transfixed at the photos. "What?"

"Breakfast," he said. "I'm going to order breakfast. Did you want to try the Belgian waffles?"

"Sure." But her focus was still on the pictures and his reaction to them. "You recognized someone, didn't you?"

He hesitated before saying, "I don't know. Maybe."

"Who is it?"

He shook his head. "It's no one related to this investigation. It was just someone who looks like someone I knew a long time ago."

Although she was disappointed by his unwillingness to confide in her, Shannon didn't press him for more information. She knew that sharing his bed didn't give her the right to ask questions or make demands. Sex and intimacy were two entirely different things, as Michael's withholding of information proved.

Shannon continued to study the photos, anyway. And by the time Garcia returned she had, if no answers, at least a question.

"Who is she?" she asked, indicating the photo of a tall, blond woman, stunningly beautiful in a black sheath dress.

"Alysia Peart," Garcia told her.

"Andrew Peart's wife?"

The detective nodded. "Many expected that when Conroy was killed, Peart would take over. Not just as a reward for years of dedicated service, but because he was married to Conroy's sister."

"What's her middle name?" Shannon asked.

He frowned at the question but opened his notebook and thumbed through the pages. "Eleanor."

"Oh." So much for her brilliant theory. There was no way to get "A.J." from Alysia Eleanor Conroy Peart.

But then Garcia read aloud, "Alysia Eleanor Jacobs Peart."

Alysia Jacobs.

A.J.

"She's actually Conroy's half sister. Different fathers," he explained. "Conroy's father was involved in some smuggling operation overseas, left his wife alone for a couple of years. When he came back and found out that his wife had a child by another man—he was furious. Even more so when he realized she'd given the girl her real father's name. It was a blow to his pride, a smear on his reputation. In a fit of rage—he killed her. That's the story, anyway.

"The murder was real," he continued. "That was proven in court—Zane Conroy saw the whole thing, testified against his father at trial. But the motive is speculation."

Shannon wasn't concerned about an old killing but about the more recent attempts on her life.

"What do you know about A.J.?" she asked hesitantly.

"Too little," he admitted. "Our best information is that he joined the organization only three or four years ago, but rapidly proved himself indispensable to Conroy. He salvaged projects that others had jeopardized, allowing Conroy to save face and millions of dollars.

"In the process, he's proven himself to be ruthless and relentless. One night he took out four of our undercover operatives with a long-range rifle and without ever being seen."

She frowned. "Then how do you know it was A.J.?"

"Because after they'd been shot, he carved his initials into their skin—*A* on one cheek, *J* on the other."

Shannon shuddered at the mental image. At the same time, this gruesome revelation confirmed her suspicion. "You keep referring to A.J. as 'he,'" she said. "Have you ever considered the possibility that A.J. might be a 'she'?"

Garcia frowned. He opened his mouth to speak, no doubt to point out the ridiculousness of her suggestion. Then he looked at the scattering of pictures and closed his mouth, nodding slowly. "There are a lot of women who move in these circles, but they're wives or mistresses, not players."

"But Alysia appears in quite a few of your photos." She selected those images and set them aside. "And in each of these, she's with a different man."

"And most of them hold key positions in the organization," Garcia admitted. But then he shook his head. "There's still a major hole in your theory."

"What's that?" she asked.

"Zane Conroy did everything he could to shield his sister, to conceal the truth about his business from her. He would never have allowed her to get involved."

"Not knowingly."

Garcia was silent for a long moment, considering. "You think Conroy's sister could have assumed an alias and infiltrated his organization, to the point of becoming not only one of his most trusted employees but his successor to power, without Conroy ever knowing who she was?"

Maybe it wasn't the most obvious scenario, but Shannon couldn't shake the feeling it was the right one.

"What you described—the carving of the assassin's initials in the victims' flesh—was an act committed by someone who craved attention and recognition," she explained. "Someone who had something to prove to Conroy."

Garcia looked at Michael, as if to ask if he was buying in to this theory.

"She has a minor in psychology," Michael said.

The detective shook his head. "Damn, I hate to admit this, but in a twisted way, it almost makes sense. We've been running in circles for the past three years trying to get a handle on this guy—because we were looking for a guy."

Michael picked up one of the photos, stared at the woman for a long moment. "Do you really believe Alysia Peart could be A.J.?" he asked skeptically.

"I believe it's worth looking into," Garcia said.

"Then there's something else you should know."

Chapter 14

Garcia had ordered round-the-clock security on Andrew Peart. Not just to prevent a possible escape attempt, but to protect him. A trusted employee in A.J.'s organization, it was unlikely he would reveal any useful information to the police. But there was always a possibility, and others in the organization would want to eliminate that possibility.

The only visitor so far had been Peart's wife.

When Garcia arrived at the hospital to ask her a few questions, he was advised that she'd gone down to the chapel about half an hour earlier.

He headed down to the chapel.

A few minutes later a pretty, dark-haired, dark-eyed nurse showed up at Peart's room pushing the pole-mounted blood pressure monitor.

She smiled at the officer seated outside the door. "I'm on the last hour of a twelve-hour shift." She sounded grateful at the prospect of ending her long day. "How about you?"

"I'm here until six o'clock tonight," he told her.

"Not a very exciting job."

He shrugged. "Could be worse."

"I suppose." She smiled again. "Well, I've gotta check on the patient. Dr. Rawlings expects that he'll be coming around soon."

"My boss will be happy to hear that. He's been chomping at the bit to talk to this guy."

"I'll keep you posted," she said, moving past him and into the room.

The patient was, in fact, starting to come around.

His head moved restlessly on the pillow, his eyelids fluttered.

She attached the blood pressure cuff to his arm. "Just want to make sure everything's still in proper working order," she told him.

His eyes flickered open. He seemed confused, disoriented at first. She knew the wig and contact lenses contributed to his confusion, but she was confident he would recognize her voice.

"I'm here to take care of everything," she told him.

Some of his tension seemed to ease as he sank deeper into the pillows.

She removed the cuff, set the BP monitor aside and took the syringe from her pocket.

She didn't hesitate, refusing to let her personal feelings interfere with what needed to be done. He was the only one who could identify her, and right now that made him a liability.

Just a little injection into his intravenous tube, and it would all be over in minutes.

She bent to press her lips to his and whispered softly.

Till death do us part.

Mike was glad when Garcia finally left, although he knew the detective's departure wasn't likely to put an end to the inquisition. He was more surprised than relieved when Shannon didn't say anything at all.

"I can almost see the questions scrolling through your mind," he said.

She only shrugged. "I can't deny I'm curious about some things. But I figured if there was anything you wanted me to know, you'd tell me."

"Is that why you're upset—because I didn't tell you I thought Alysia was Lisa?"

"I'm not upset."

He didn't believe her denial for a moment. "I didn't tell you because I didn't believe it myself, not until Detective Garcia revealed her last name was Jacobs."

"You don't owe me any explanations," she said, in the same infuriatingly level tone.

"I wasn't deliberately hiding anything from you, Shannon."

"It doesn't matter."

"Yes, it does." He put his arms around her, kissed her gently. "Because you matter to me."

She didn't exactly melt, but she didn't push him away, either. He figured that meant he was on his way to being forgiven.

"Do you really think Alysia is Lisa?" she finally asked.

"I know it seems like an incredible coincidence, but the more photos I look at, the more I'm convinced," he said. "Then again, I haven't seen her in almost six years, so I could be wrong."

"You never saw her again after you left Righaria?"

He shook his head. "I made a half-hearted effort to find her once, but she seemed to have disappeared and I didn't really pursue it because I didn't want to be reminded of that time and place in my life."

"Now this is bringing it all back for you," she said softly.

"Not really," he denied. "A lot more time has passed since then, everything is different now."

"Why was Lisa in Righaria?" she asked.

He'd wondered the same thing—why a young American college student would be spending her summer vacation in a politically unstable country most people couldn't find on a map. When he'd asked Lisa the question, she'd told him that her brother was in town on business and she'd come with him so they could spend some time together.

At the time, Mike hadn't thought to ask any questions about the nature of that business. Of course, he hadn't known then that her brother was Zane Conroy.

But even if Conroy's reasons for being in Righaria were suspect—as they undoubtedly were—his sister could hardly be blamed for something she'd known nothing about.

Or had she?

That was a question he couldn't answer with any degree of certainty. Because as much as he wanted to believe Lisa was an innocent bystander, he just didn't know.

Still, it was too much of a leap from an awareness of her brother's illicit activities to becoming a hired assassin and infamous crime boss.

"You haven't answered my question," Shannon reminded him.

"I don't know why Lisa was in Righaria," he admitted.

"I'm not making accusations," she said. "I'm trying to find answers."

"So am I." And yet there was a part of him that dreaded what those answers might be.

"If Lisa is Alysia," Shannon said, "and Alysia is A.J.—"

"I don't believe Lisa is A.J.," he interrupted.

She frowned. "You were the one who made the connection."

"Lisa isn't A.J."

"I can understand why you don't want to believe—"

"Don't try to psychoanalyze me, Shannon."

He caught the flash of emotion in her eyes, but it was gone almost as quickly as it appeared. Now she did pull away from him.

He hated knowing that he'd hurt her. He hated even more

the way she continued to distance herself from him, to deny her own feelings.

"I was only trying to help," she said stiffly.

He sighed. "I know. I'm sorry."

She turned back to him. "I'm not sure this is a question I should ask, but I need to know—do you still have feelings for her?"

"No." His response was immediate and definite. "I might have doubts about her knowledge of Conroy's business, but there are no doubts about that. Whatever was once between us was over a long time ago."

"I wonder if she feels the same way," Shannon said.

He frowned. "What do you mean?"

She hesitated again. "I was thinking that there have been too many bizarre coincidences since we met on the beach that night. So many that maybe they aren't coincidences at all."

"Lisa isn't A.J.," he said again. "But even if she was, do you really think she had some master plan to bring us together before she killed us?"

She shook her head. "No. I think maybe she decided to kill us because we were together."

"Huh?"

"When I came down to Miami with Jack, it was because Conroy was making threats against my sister, and Natalie was concerned about her son. You admitted yourself that there was never any real belief that we would be in danger here. In fact, Conroy didn't even seem to know that I existed. He never so much as mentioned my name to Natalie.

"But if Conroy was keeping tabs on Jack and he sent someone—Peart or anyone else—down here, that someone might have realized we were being watched from both sides. Since you made no attempt to hide your identity, it's not such a stretch to think that Conroy knew you were here. And if Conroy knew, A.J. did, too.

"Then Dylan took Jack back to Fairweather, but I stayed, making a convenient target for A.J. with the added bonus of her former lover thrown into the mix."

He shook his head. "That is the most convoluted logic I've ever heard."

"It is convoluted," she agreed. "But it's also more logical than all of this just being some big coincidence."

He shook his head again. "It sounds like highly imaginative fiction."

"Maybe you're right to be skeptical," she said. "But if I'm right, you can bet that A.J. has one heck of a finale planned for all of us."

Shannon awoke the next morning to the welcome smell of fresh coffee and the not-so-welcome sound of banging.

She sat up in bed, pushed her hair away from her face. "This was not how I planned to start my day," she grumbled.

Michael pressed a cup of coffee into her hands. "It's not what I had planned, either," he said. "But it doesn't sound like something we can ignore."

She indulged in a long sip before setting her cup aside. "I guess I need to get dressed."

"You can go next door to do that while I see who's at the door." He kissed her softly, briefly. "If it's my sister, I'll kill her quick so we can get back to other things."

But when Shannon returned to his room a few minutes later, she found it wasn't Rachel who'd interrupted their morning but Detective Garcia.

"Andrew Peart is dead," he told them.

Shannon was stunned by his pronouncement. "Yesterday you said his prognosis was good."

"Yesterday his prognosis *was* good. Last night, he was murdered."

"How?"

"An injection of succinylcholine chloride into his bloodstream."

"What does that do?" Michael asked.

"It's a paralyzing agent," Shannon told him. "Commonly used to facilitate tracheal intubation in emergency rooms or provide skeletal muscle relaxation during surgery."

Garcia nodded. "That's exactly what they told me at the hospital. Except that the dose given to Peart could only have been intended to kill him."

"Do you have any suspects?"

"A.J.—Alysia—whoever the hell she is—tops my list," Garcia said. "There was a bag found beside the garbage bin in the ladies' bathroom. In it was a dark wig, colored contacts, hospital scrubs, running shoes and the empty syringe. It was as if whoever killed him wanted everything to be tied up in a neat little package for us. The only thing missing was a freaking bow.

"Alysia Peart hasn't been seen at the hospital since, and no one has been able to reach her to notify her of her husband's death."

Shannon shook her head. "It was somehow easier to accept that she'd done all those other things than to believe she would kill her own husband."

Garcia's mouth twisted in a wry smile. "It happens a lot more than you want to know."

"Do you have any evidence that ties this to A.J.?" Michael asked.

"CSI has the package. They're looking for something to link the items to our suspect. One of her own hairs left inside the wig, DNA off a contact lens, a fingerprint on anything. If there's something to be found, they'll find it," he said.

Shannon nodded, mentally crossing her fingers that this development would be the break the police needed, that A.J. would be found and this nightmare would end.

"We appreciate being kept up to date with the investigation," Michael said, "but I get the feeling there's another reason you're here."

"There is," Garcia agreed. "The killer's hospital identification read Lillian Baines."

Shannon's blood chilled as he recited the alias on her hotel registration.

Michael slid an arm around her and pulled her close to his side in an instinctive gesture of protection. "She knows we're here."

A.J. was a firm believer in the value of knowledge and the benefits of careful planning. It was why the file with Michael Courtland's name on it contained thorough and detailed information about every aspect of his life. From his exclusive prep school to Harvard, from his stint in the army to his partnership at Courtland & Logan Investigations. There were the names of friends and business acquaintances, the phone numbers and addresses of women he'd dated. A general outline of his daily routine, notes about his usual hangouts.

And there was information about his family—extensively and meticulously researched, if not very interesting.

He wasn't close to either of his parents. Martin Courtland was a third-generation hotelier and a single-minded workaholic who'd had little time for either of his children. Barbara Price Courtland was a typical socialite who liked Armani, diamonds, and gin martinis—all of them in quantity.

It was Michael's sister, A.J. had known early on, who would be the key. He would do anything for his sister.

Family loyalty was an admirable and respectable trait, and one that was easily exploited. For that reason, there was also a file on Rachel Courtland, her schedules and routines tracked and noted.

Michael's sister was a creature of habit. She worked out in

the hotel gym on Mondays, Wednesdays and Fridays—a strenuous weight-lifting and grueling cardio routine that kept her in top physical condition. But on Tuesdays and Thursdays, she left the sanctity and security of the resort to run along the beach. Early, before the sun was high in the sky, from Scenic Drive to Oceanview Park.

The only time the routine varied was if it rained.

A.J. pulled off to the side of the road, peered through the windshield into the cloudless sky and smiled.

Something was wrong.

Mike awoke suddenly with his heart pounding and knots in the pit of his stomach. He exhaled a slow, unsteady breath when he saw Shannon still sleeping beside him.

She was safe—and he was going to ensure that she stayed safe. But the uneasy feeling persisted, forcing him out of the warmth of the bed, away from her comforting presence.

He scrubbed his hands through his hair and fervently hoped he was mistaken. Crossing to the window, he peered between the curtains. It was early, but the sun was already bright in the sky.

"Michael?"

He pulled the curtains closed and turned back toward the bed. "I didn't mean to wake you."

Shannon slid out from beneath the covers, tucked her arms into a silky sage-colored robe—another one of Rachel's selections—and wrapped the tie around her waist. At any other time he would have protested the covering of her glorious naked body, but his mind couldn't embrace the welcome distraction this morning.

She moved closer. "What's wrong?"

After only a few days together, he hadn't expected she would be so attuned to his mood. And though he was touched

by her obvious concern, he was reluctant to admit his unease.
"I couldn't sleep."

"Tell me why," she said softly.

"You'll think I'm crazy," he said.

"Tell me anyway."

He managed a smile. "I just got a feeling, all of a sudden,
that something is wrong—or is going to be."

"Have you had this kind of feeling before?"

"A few times," he admitted. "The night Brent was killed.
The night I didn't want to leave you in your hotel room."

"The night I was kidnapped."

"Yeah."

She didn't say anything else, only wrapped her arms
around him and held on. It didn't change anything, but it did
give him a small measure of comfort.

He sat there with her for several minutes, alternately cursing the unwelcome premonition and trying to figure out what
it could mean.

They both jolted when the phone rang.

He stepped past her but hesitated before picking up the receiver, already knowing that this call was the reason he'd
woken and that his questions were about to be answered.
"Hello?"

"Hello, Michael."

Something about the voice nudged at a memory in his subconscious, momentarily overriding the realization that no one
should know he was here. "Who is this?"

There was a soft laugh. "I know it's been a long time, but
I didn't think you'd have forgotten."

No, he hadn't forgotten. He'd just hoped like hell he was
wrong. "Lisa."

He heard Shannon's soft gasp, saw her sink back down
onto the edge of the mattress.

"Then you do remember."

The satisfaction in the voice on the phone refocused his attention. Despite this confirmation, however, he was still having trouble getting his mind around the facts. Lisa was Alysia, and Alysia was A.J.

Except that the woman he'd known so many years ago had been young and carefree, full of joy and hope. How could she be responsible for the things A.J. had done? What could have happened to turn her into a killer?

"What do you want, Lisa?"

"I have a proposition for you," she said. "A once-in-a-lifetime opportunity, you might say—and you have the lucky task of choosing the life."

"What are you talking about?"

"Shannon Vaughn," she said. "I understand the two of you have become quite…close during the time you've spent together. I have to wonder how close, how much she means to you."

More than he'd ever wanted or expected. More than anything else in the world. But there was no way he would admit his feelings to the woman who'd threatened to kill them both.

"Get to the point."

"The point is that you have a decision to make—who means more to you—the woman currently sharing your bed…or your sister?"

He didn't—couldn't—speak.

"Think about it, Michael. Think about the choice you'll make this time. I'll call you back in half an hour."

"Wait—"

"Half an hour," she said again, then disconnected the call.

The next twenty minutes were a complete blur in Shannon's mind.

From the moment Michael hung up the phone, he'd been in constant motion. He'd made call after call. To the direct extension of his sister's office, which connected to her voice mail. To Rachel's cell phone, and her voice mail again. Then, finally, in despair and desperation, to Detective Garcia.

Now his hotel room was filled with people, planning and strategizing, trying to anticipate A.J.'s next move. Through it all, Michael remained calm, outwardly controlled.

But Shannon knew it was a facade. It couldn't be anything else. Inside, he had to be torn apart by the thought of Rachel in danger, and furious that there was absolutely nothing he could do about it.

She thought about how crazy she'd been when she'd heard—secondhand and after the fact—about Natalie being taken hostage by Zane Conroy. Even knowing her sister was safe hadn't alleviated the stark terror of imagining how she must have felt to be held at knifepoint.

She knew that what Michael was going through right now had to be a hundred times worse.

If A.J. had asked for any amount of money, she knew he would gladly have paid. But A.J. had asked for something he felt honor-bound to protect: Shannon's life.

It was Garcia's idea to bring in a female police officer— Laura Flaherty—who was of similar height and stature to Shannon. He believed that with a wig to approximate Shannon's hair length and color, Flaherty would resemble Shannon closely enough to fool A.J. at a distance. As soon as A.J. got close enough to recognize the mistake, Flaherty would take her into custody.

It sounded like a reasonable enough plan, except for one thing.

"She doesn't expect you to accept her offer." Shannon took Michael aside to warn him. "A.J. will never believe it if you agree to the trade. She'll know you're setting a trap for her."

"Then why would she have made the offer?" he asked.

As certain as she was that A.J. had no intention of dealing

one hostage for another, she hadn't been able to come up with a satisfactory answer to that question.

"I don't know," she admitted. "Maybe she did it just to torment you. To make you think you have to make a choice."

He scrubbed his hands over his face. "I don't think it's that complicated. Lisa wants revenge for her brother's death. She's not thinking about anything else."

"You're underestimating her. You still see her as the woman you knew in Righaria. A woman you were once intimately involved with. And because of that, you don't want to accept what she's capable of."

"She won't hurt Rachel," Michael said. "It won't gain her anything."

Shannon wished she had the same confidence, but she couldn't forget Detective Garcia telling them about the four undercover operatives A.J. had killed. Maybe it had been a desperate attempt to earn her brother's respect. Maybe it had been a way to establish a reputation for herself. Or maybe she'd killed simply because she could.

"You're not looking at this objectively," she warned.

"It's hard to be objective when my sister's life has been threatened."

She understood his frustration, and she hated that she was the cause of it. "That's not what I meant."

"What did you mean?"

"You're emotionally involved with Lisa, too. Your past with her is interfering with your ability to see the situation clearly."

"I can't believe she would harm Rachel," he said again. "It's not that I don't believe she's capable—I just can't let myself consider the possibility."

She knew what he was going through. It wasn't that long ago that her own sister's life had been in danger.

"I would do anything for Rachel," he continued. "Anything but make the trade Lisa asked for."

Shannon nodded. "Don't you think Lisa knows that?"

He met her gaze, finally allowing her a brief glimpse of the pain she knew was tearing him apart inside.

"I just need to concentrate on the plan to get her back," he said. "I can't let myself consider that this might end any other way."

"It won't." It wasn't an empty reassurance but a promise, and she would do anything to keep it. "While you're discussing strategy with the cops, I'm going into the other room to make a phone call."

He caught her hand as she turned to leave the room. "Who are you calling?"

She hated to lie to him but knew her deception was necessary. "My mother."

He frowned. "I thought she was on her honeymoon."

"They flew back last night," she told him. "And with everything going on...I just want to talk to her."

"Okay," he relented.

Shannon slipped into her room through the adjoining door, pulling it closed. Her heart was pounding fiercely, her palms were damp.

She glanced at the clock—7:54.

She rubbed her palms down the front of her new shorts.

It was possible that she was the one who'd misjudged A.J., that she was waiting for a call that wouldn't come. But she didn't think so.

Why had A.J. taken Rachel? Was she a decoy—to divert Michael's attention so she could get to Shannon? Or bait—to bring Shannon out of hiding?

It was 7:56.

She sat down behind the desk and tried to will the phone to ring. Except that she wasn't sure she wanted it to. Not really. What she really wanted was for Michael and Detective Garcia to come up with some foolproof plan that would bring Rachel back safely and put A.J. behind bars forever.

But it did ring, startling her from her introspection and confirming her fears. She grabbed the receiver, tried to ignore that her fingers were trembling as she brought it to her ear.

"H-hello?"

"I thought you might be expecting my call."

A.J. sounded pleased, and Shannon faltered at the obvious satisfaction in her voice. She'd warned Michael that the offer from A.J. was a game, and she was playing right into it. Though she was even more wary now, she was determined to see it through.

"I figured if you knew where to find Michael, you'd know where to find me," she said.

"Clever girl."

"Where's Rachel?"

"If I told you that, it would spoil all my fun."

"Is that what this is—fun?"

"It's certainly entertaining to see what's going on in that room. All those cops, plotting and planning."

Shannon twisted the phone cord between her fingers. Was A.J. only guessing that Michael would have called the police? Or did she somehow know exactly what was happening next door? Had she planted some kind of listening device in the room? Did she have the hotel under visual surveillance?

"It would be even more entertaining to send a little gift to the party," A.J. continued. "Maybe a bullet straight into the center of Michael's chest."

Shannon swallowed back nausea. She refused to believe that A.J. could see him, target him. She had to be bluffing. "If you're in a position to shoot him right now, you could just as easily shoot me. Why haven't you?"

"I've never been fond of execution from a distance," A.J. said. "It's so impersonal."

The smug tone was really starting to get on her nerves. "Then why don't you tell me what it is you want me to do?"

"I want you to make the trade we both know Michael won't." A.J. paused a moment, letting the words sink in.

"If I agree to this, you'll let Rachel go?"

"Of course," A.J. promised. "And, as an extra bonus, I'll let your lover live."

Shannon didn't hesitate. "Where should I meet you?"

"At the Clam Digger in half an hour."

"What is that? *Where* is it?"

"It's an abandoned warehouse south of the marina. Take a cab to the corner of Walkerton and Rexford Streets, then walk three blocks north."

She scribbled the name and directions onto the message pad and glanced at the clock again. Taking a deep breath to steady the quiver of nerves in her belly, she tore the page and tucked it into her pocket.

"One more thing," A.J. said. "If I see anyone else near that building—I don't care if it's a homeless beggar or a lost tourist—Rachel will die."

While Michael was strategizing with the police who had established a temporary command post in his hotel room, Shannon alternated between trying to figure out how to slip away and second-guessing her agreement to meet with A.J.

She wanted to tell Michael about A.J.'s call. She knew he would do anything to get Rachel back safely and with the resources of the Miami P.D. in this room, she had to believe they could do it. Why should Shannon risk her life to meet a woman who'd already shown not just an ability to kill but an affinity for murder?

Because A.J.'s phone call to Shannon proved she had no intention of making a trade with Michael. And Shannon knew that A.J. wouldn't hesitate to kill Michael's sister, just as she knew that losing Rachel would kill something inside of him. She'd seen the look on his face when he'd learned that A.J. had kidnapped his sister—the pain and fear and helplessness.

He'd quickly shut down his emotions, forcing them aside to concentrate on what needed to be done. But she recognized that his apparent detachment was only a coping mechanism to get through this period of uncertainty.

She also knew that the sense of responsibility he still carried over Brent's death was nothing compared to the guilt that would eat at him if something happened to his sister.

If Shannon didn't show up to meet A.J. as planned, Rachel would be killed. It was a risk she couldn't take. Not when she had the opportunity to prevent it.

Taking a deep breath to bolster her flagging courage, Shannon went to Michael, touching his arm to get his attention.

"I'm feeling pretty useless here," she told him. "I'm going to slip into the other room to take a shower."

He frowned. "Now?"

She shrugged. "I just need a few minutes to think without all these people around."

He linked their hands together. "You know I don't like the idea of you being out of my sight for even a minute."

Despite everything that was going on with his sister right now, there was genuine concern for her in his voice. Because he did care about her. And although she hated knowing he would be hurt by her deception, there really was no other way.

Her throat tightened, and she leaned her head against his chest, breathing in his familiar scent. "I'd prefer to shower without all these people hanging around outside the bathroom."

"Okay," he agreed with obvious reluctance. Then he touched his lips to hers. "Be quick."

She started to turn away, but the possibility that this might be the last time she ever saw him was more than she could bear. This time *she* kissed *him,* trying to tell him what was in her heart without the words that were stuck in her throat.

When she drew back, there were tears on her cheeks. "I'm so sorry that your sister got dragged into this."

He gently brushed the moisture away. "It isn't your fault, Shannon."

"Isn't it?"

"No. And Rachel is going to be fine. I'm not going to let anything happen to her."

She nodded and made her way to the bathroom, conscious of his eyes tracking her progress through the open door that connected the two rooms until Officer Flaherty addressed him, drawing his attention away.

She turned on the shower, twisting the tap to adjust the water temperature. As if it mattered whether the water was hot or cold when she had no intention of stepping under the spray. It was merely a diversion so that she could slip out of the hotel to meet with A.J. And then…

She felt her stomach heave, fought against the wave of nausea. There was no point in speculating about what would happen after that.

She wished there was a way she could take Michael's gun to her meeting. She knew he'd locked it inside the safe, but she didn't know the combination he'd programmed, and, even if she did, she couldn't risk going back into the other room. Odd that she'd felt so uncomfortable the first time he'd put the gun in her hands, and now she was desperate for the reassurance of its power. It would be easier to face A.J. with a weapon.

She glanced around the bathroom, looking desperately for something—anything—that might be useful.

Hairspray? If she got close enough to A.J., she might be able to spray it in her face, temporarily blinding her. But the shape of the trial-size can made it difficult to hide.

Nail clippers? Mouthwash? She gave up, forced to admit she would have nothing but her wits to take into this final showdown with A.J. Still, she wasn't going to back down.

She took a deep breath and counted to ten, slowly. Peeking through a crack in the door, she found the room empty, Michael obviously was still occupied next door. She locked the bathroom door then slipped out, pulling it closed behind her.

Her heart was pounding so hard against her ribs it hurt. How long would Michael wait before checking on her? How much time did she have before he'd notice she was gone?

Shannon could only hope it would be long enough to get out of the hotel and flag down a taxi.

She still didn't have any identification or money, except for the ten dollars she'd slipped out of his wallet earlier. Hopefully, that would be enough to get her to the waterfront.

She didn't worry about return fare.

Chapter 15

It didn't seem to matter to Garcia or the rest of the Miami P.D. that it was Mike's sister who'd been abducted. As soon as he'd called them in, they'd taken over. At first he'd been annoyed; now he was only grateful.

It was impossible for him to think about the situation clearly. He could only trust that they had the experience and expertise to find Rachel and bring her back unharmed while he concentrated on keeping Shannon safe.

He eyed the connecting door between the two rooms, waiting for Shannon to walk through it again. He knew she was concerned about Rachel and he'd expected that she'd want to be here, to know what plans were being made to get his sister back.

He glanced at the clock again, frowned.

A.J. had said she would call back in half an hour, and that time had passed nearly fifteen minutes ago.

And what the hell was taking Shannon so long?

He stood up and strode through to the other room. The shower was still running.

He pounded on the bathroom door. "Shannon?"

There was no response.

"Shannon!"

He pounded again, then tried the handle. It was locked.

He broke the door down.

The warehouse was an abandoned structure of crumbling blocks and boarded-up windows with Clam Digger Foods spelled out on the side of the building in what had probably once been dark-red paint but had long since faded to pink. Shannon walked around to the back and found a sliding wood door with a rusty metal latch and an oversize padlock, unlocked.

She hesitated, her heart thudding heavily in her chest.

This was it—the point of no return. As soon as she walked into this building, she would be completely at A.J.'s mercy.

Panic, sudden and violent, surged through her veins. She took an instinctive step in retreat.

She closed her eyes and forced herself to breathe.

The odds that she could beat A.J. at this game might be slim, but she wasn't going to give up without trying.

She pushed the heavy wooden door only far enough to slip through the narrow opening.

It took a moment for her eyes to adjust to the dim interior. There were a few windows that weren't boarded up, but they were too crusted with dirt to allow much light into the dank, airless building.

"I wasn't sure you'd come," A.J. said.

Shannon started, and turned to see a young attractive woman leaning back against the wall. In the sleeveless floral-print sundress and high-heeled sandals she wore, she didn't look different from most other women in Miami. Certainly there was nothing about her that suggested she was a cold-blooded killer.

Shannon glanced around the barren room, noted the single wooden chair set up in the middle of the room. There was no sign of Michael's sister, nothing else but dust and cobwebs. "Where's Rachel?"

"She's at a secure location not too far from here."

"Is she okay?"

"Sedated, but otherwise unharmed."

Shannon wanted to be relieved, but she didn't trust this woman. "How do I know you're telling me the truth?"

"You don't," A.J. said evenly. "You're just going to have to trust that I've lived up to my end of the bargain, as you've lived up to yours." Her lips curved in a cold, cruel smile. "Or maybe that's a poor choice of words, under the circumstances."

Shannon held her breath as A.J. unzipped the purse slung over her shoulder, waiting for the gun. She exhaled softly, silently, when she saw it was a cell phone instead.

A.J. dialed, a neatly manicured nail punching in a series of numbers, and Shannon let her mind wander.

Maybe she could stall long enough that Michael would somehow figure out where she'd gone and rescue her. She discarded the thought immediately. Knowing what A.J. was capable of, she didn't want Michael anywhere near her.

"Your sister is in Room 310 at the Red Carpet Motel," A.J. said without preamble when the call was answered.

Shannon couldn't hear what Michael's response was on the other end, but A.J. smiled again.

"You lost another woman?" Her voice was filled with mock sympathy. "You really should be more careful, Michael."

Fury replaced Shannon's fear.

She'd come here because she wanted to spare Michael the pain and regret of having to choose between his sister and his assignment. She wasn't going to let A.J., with a few careless words, make him feel responsible for a choice Shannon had deliberately taken away from him. Impulsively she launched herself at A.J., knocking the woman to the ground.

The element of surprise was on her side but it was, Shannon quickly realized, the only advantage she would have. A.J. was faster and stronger, obviously trained in combat and completely merciless. Although Shannon managed to land a couple of blows, substantiated by the outraged curses A.J. spewed in her direction, their positions were quickly reversed.

Even so, she derived a small measure of satisfaction in seeing the red welts on A.J.'s face and the slight swelling of a cheekbone that was already starting to discolor. Until A.J. grabbed a handful of her hair and wrenched her head back so hard she actually saw stars.

Then she smashed Shannon's head against the concrete floor and everything went black.

Mike had never known such helplessness as when he'd burst into Shannon's bathroom and found it empty.

Even when Brent had been killed, he'd known immediately what to do. He'd been on a mission, understood the procedure and followed the protocol. And if ever one course of action failed, there was always a contingency plan. It was all about anticipating the variables and being prepared for them.

But in all of the careful plans he'd made with Garcia and Flaherty, there had been one consistent expectation: that Shannon would stay put. In the hotel, with him, where he knew she would be safe.

Now she was gone.

The situation was eerily similar to what had happened on another day, in another hotel.

"Do you think A.J. got in here somehow?" Flaherty asked.

"No." Mike reached into the empty shower stall and turned off the water. The sting of the cold spray was nothing compared to the icy fear that penetrated the depths of his soul. Because this was where the scenario changed. Unlike the first time, when she'd been abducted by Peart, Shannon had walked out of this room of her own free will. Without a single word.

Of course, he knew why she hadn't said anything—because there was no way in hell he'd have let her go. And he knew why she'd gone—to find A.J. But he didn't know why Shannon would confront a woman who wanted her dead.

"You think she's gone to meet A.J.," Garcia guessed.

Mike nodded.

"But how would she have known how to contact her?"

It was something he'd wondered himself. "A.J. must have contacted Shannon."

You're underestimating her, Shannon had said.

He'd ignored her warning, but Shannon hadn't made the same mistake. She'd anticipated the call and been here to receive it. She'd told him she was going to call her mother, and he'd believed her.

"Dammit." He slammed his fist into the wall and didn't even wince at the pain that shot up to his elbow from the point of impact.

He pushed aside the anger and frustration. He needed to clear his mind and refocus his thoughts. He knew that Shannon had gone to meet A.J., but where?

"I'll go talk to the doorman at the front," one of the police officers volunteered. "Maybe he saw her leave, whether she took a cab or went on foot, what direction she was heading."

Mike nodded. "If she didn't leave through the main entrance, we can find that out, too. All of the exterior doors—even the service areas—are monitored with security cameras. We need to find out which exit she took and whether or not she was alone."

He sat behind the desk, grabbed a pen to make a list…

He stared at the notepad in front of him.

Shannon would have sat at this desk to answer the call—maybe she'd taken notes during the conversation. He ran his fingers over the top page and felt the subtle indentations. "Does anyone have a pencil?"

Garcia handed him one without question.

Mike rubbed the lead gently over the top page of the message pad. The imprint was faint, but mostly legible.

"What's the Clam Digger?"

"It's an old warehouse on Walkerton Street, down by the waterfront," Flaherty said. "It's scheduled for demolition next week."

Could it be so easy?

He almost laughed at the absurdity of the question. Easy would have been finding Shannon still in the shower. Figuring out the possible location of her meeting with A.J. didn't make an impossible situation easy. He only prayed the knowledge made it possible—because Shannon's life depended on it.

"That's where Shannon's gone to meet A.J.," he said.

"Wake up."

Shannon heard the voice as if from a distance, impatient and demanding, and it made her head hurt. She forced her eyelids open, wincing at the pain.

"Finally. I was beginning to think I'd killed you."

She licked her lips, winced again at the coppery taste of blood. She was seated in the wooden chair she'd noticed earlier, her hands tied behind her back in an unnatural and uncomfortable position. "Isn't that your plan?"

"Not like that," A.J. said. "It would be too easy—you fight like a girl."

"I am a girl."

"And one willing to fight for her man. I have to say I admire that."

"Thanks." Shannon wondered how she managed sarcasm

when her head was in danger of splitting open and her life was counting down to its last moments.

"And yet I can't help wondering why you bothered," A.J. continued. "I'm sure you're not naive enough to think Michael would ever want a future with a woman like you."

"I have no illusions," Shannon agreed. "I was just in it for the sex."

A.J. chuckled. "I like your spirit," she said. "That's why I didn't want to let you die without knowing how."

"Does it matter?"

"I don't like to leave loose ends." She picked up her purse from the floor, slipped the strap over her shoulder. "I spent a lot of time considering how to kill you. And as much as I'd like to pump a couple of bullets into your gut and watch the life drain out of your body—as the life drained out of my brother's along with his blood—I decided that was too quick. Instead, I've come up with a plan that will both prolong your suffering and ensure my escape."

"You really think you're going to get away with this?"

A.J. smiled. "The cops have been after me for years. They've never been able to pin any charges on me."

"But now they know who you are."

"That won't make any difference if they can't find me."

Shannon knew there was no point in trying to reason with an obviously crazy woman. "Are you going back to Righaria?"

Surprise flickered briefly in A.J.'s cold eyes. "Did Michael tell you about that?"

"Yeah. He didn't tell me you were responsible for the attack on his camp, though. I managed to figure that one out on my own."

"I'd like to take responsibility," A.J. admitted. "But I only passed along the relevant information to certain interested parties."

"Why?"

"Because it was an easy way to cement relations with my local contacts."

"Were you planning to take over your brother's business even then?"

"I never wanted to take it over," A.J. denied. "Not while Zane was alive. I just wanted to work *with* him, by his side. But my brother was very traditional in a lot of respects, including his determination to shield me from the more unsavory aspects of his business."

"Unsavory?" Shannon echoed in disbelief. "Is that how you would describe drugs and prostitution? Torture and murder?"

"That's how Zane would describe them," A.J. said evenly.

"And you sold Michael out to impress your brother?"

"It was a prudent business decision."

Shannon felt her stomach churn. "He loved you."

A.J. merely shrugged. "It's a common mistake men make—thinking that women are weak. The truth is, women are *their* weakness."

"I'm sure your brother would be proud to hear you say that."

Icy blue eyes narrowed. "My brother would have been proud of everything I've done."

"Then why didn't you ever tell him that you were A.J.?"

"Because he couldn't accept that I was capable of the things he needed A.J. to do. For example, blowing up this building with you in it."

As A.J. crouched down to flick the switch on the timer attached to her chair, Shannon remembered Garcia mentioning that explosives were one of A.J.'s trademarks. The clock started counting down from thirty minutes.

Was it really going to end like this—without even saying goodbye to Michael? Without seeing her sister married? Without making peace with her mother?

Of course it was.

From the moment she'd agreed to this meeting, she'd

known it might. But she'd dared to dream that she might somehow triumph over adversity, to believe that she could succeed against A.J. when so many others had failed. In retrospect, she acknowledged the futility of the hope she'd carried in here. And yet, if she was given the choice again, she wouldn't hesitate to make the same decision.

For Michael. Because she loved him.

"There are additional charges already set around the perimeter of the building," A.J. explained. "All set to go off simultaneously. When the dust has settled, not even dental records will be able to identify your remains."

Shannon had to bite down hard to stop herself from pleading for her life. She knew nothing she said would change A.J.'s plan, and begging would only increase the other woman's satisfaction over her demise.

"Oh, and just in case you get any ideas about trying to escape, you should know that there is a balance switch under your chair. If you attempt to get up or turn around, if you so much as shift your weight, the switch will be triggered and the bomb will detonate immediately.

"As further insurance, I have a remote." She held up the device for Shannon to see. "If anyone comes near the building before my boat is out of sight, I'll press this button."

A.J. glanced at the digital display on the timer. "You have twenty-seven minutes to contemplate your life before the beginning of the end."

Then, without so much as a glance over her shoulder, she walked out of the building.

The door slid shut behind her, blocking out the thin sliver of light that had streamed through the narrow opening and leaving Shannon in darkness.

Garcia had been barking orders at his men, establishing teams to dispatch to the motel and the warehouse, when Mike raced out of the hotel room. While in the military, he'd learned the importance of teamwork, and he'd respected the chain of command. But he wasn't in the army anymore, Garcia had no authority over him, and Mike didn't intend to wait a single minute longer to get to Shannon.

He had his gun in hand when he slipped around to the back of the old warehouse and saw Lisa securing the lock on the door. Irritation flickered briefly in her eyes before she regained her composure and smiled at him, seemingly oblivious to the weapon trained on her heart.

"You're efficient," she said approvingly. "I expected to be long gone before you got here. Of course, I also thought you'd be more concerned about your sister than your lover."

"I've covered all the bases."

"You sent someone else to the motel." She sighed, shaking her head. "I'm afraid that's going to blow the little surprise I had waiting for you."

It was the gleam in her eye as much as the triumph in her voice that gave her away, and he felt his blood turn to ice. "You rigged the motel with explosives."

"I never wanted to kill your sister."

With his weapon still in one hand, Mike dug his cell phone out of his pocket with the other. He had to contact Garcia, to warn him before someone went charging into Rachel's room unprepared.

"It was really just a simple device," she continued, "easy enough for someone who had demolitions training in the army to identify and neutralize."

The phone was ringing, but Garcia wasn't answering. Dammit.

"It looks like you made the wrong choice, Michael. Again."

He tamped down on the emotions, forced his mind to clear. Officer Flaherty was going to the Red Carpet Motel. She was an experienced cop with good instincts, and she knew about A.J.'s penchant for explosive devices. Mike had to believe that she wouldn't take any action without first evaluating the situation. He needed to trust that the cops could take care of Rachel so that he could concentrate his attention on Shannon.

"Why did you target Shannon? And Rachel? Is it because of me?"

She smiled again. "The male ego never ceases to amaze me. As if I haven't had more important things to do than plot an elaborate scheme of vengeance against a man who didn't mean anything more to me than a distraction from boredom."

"Good to know," he said. "Now I won't feel any remorse about you spending the rest of your life in a cell."

"Are you arresting me, Michael?"

"I'll leave the technicalities to Detective Garcia. He's on his way."

She glanced at the watch on her wrist, frowned. "I hope he won't be too long. There isn't much time left before the building blows—and your girlfriend along with it."

He fought against the emotions that threatened to overwhelm him. He needed to be cool, rational. It was the only chance he had.

"Unlock the door, Lisa."

"I'm afraid I don't have the key."

His eyes narrowed. "How much time?"

She glanced at her watch. "About fifteen minutes now— give or take. Less if I press this little button."

He felt a bead of sweat slide down his spine as he eyed the remote in her hand. "If you set off the explosives, we'll all die."

"It beats going to prison, and if those are my only choices…" Her words trailed off deliberately.

"What do you want, Lisa?"

"That's my ride at the dock. If you let me go, I'll leave you with this and the remote possibility—" she smiled at her own joke "—that you can save her before the building falls down on both of you."

He didn't hesitate. "Give it to me."

"Not yet." She held it out of reach. "Not until I'm in the boat."

He was tempted just to pull the trigger. He knew she wouldn't be quick to press the button—she didn't really want to die. She wanted to escape, to walk away from the havoc she'd wreaked and rebuild the headquarters of her organization somewhere else. But he wasn't willing to gamble Shannon's life on it.

"It's decision time, Michael."

"Fine." He grabbed her arm, held the muzzle of the gun to her back as he walked with her to the dock where her transport was waiting.

She started to climb into the boat, hesitating when he refused to let go of her arm.

"The remote," he reminded her.

"How do I know you won't shoot me as soon as I hand it over?"

"Because as tempted as I am right now, I would never stoop to committing cold-blooded murder."

She nodded and handed him the remote. Then she stepped onto the boat, moving immediately to the bridge to start the engine.

Despite his assurance to her, he couldn't deny that he wanted to pull the trigger. He wanted A.J. to pay for everything she'd done—to Shannon and Rachel, to Brent and to his own soul. He didn't doubt that she deserved to die, but if he killed her now— if he took her life simply to satisfy his thirst for vengeance—it would be murder and he wouldn't be any better than she was.

He turned away from the boat.

The only thing that mattered now was getting to Shannon.

There were five minutes and twenty-two seconds left on the timer when Shannon heard the first thump against one of the boarded-up windows. Four minutes and fifty-nine seconds when she heard the wood splinter. Four minutes and seventeen seconds when Michael climbed through the opening.

Her heart leaped with hope…then plummeted.

She'd been praying that he would find her. That he would somehow, miraculously, track her down and save her.

But she'd given up that hope when A.J. had started the clock ticking. It was even more dangerous for him to be here now, with less than four minutes on the clock. She hadn't gone to all this trouble to save his life only for him to die beside her.

But he was oblivious to the threat, racing across the room toward her.

If A.J. knew he was here—

She swallowed around the tightness in her throat, fought to hold back the tears that burned her eyes. "You have to leave, Michael. Please." Her voice was weak, unsteady. "There are remote-controlled explosives around the room."

"I've got the remote."

She exhaled a shaky breath, but she knew the danger hadn't been completely averted. "There's still the timer, and everything's set to blow in—" she glanced again at the clock. "Two and a half minutes."

He dropped to his knees beside her. "Two and a half minutes is more time than I'd hoped for."

She didn't understand what he was saying. Time for what—to say a final good-bye?

"Please, Michael." She couldn't look at him, didn't want him to see the tears that filled her eyes. Instead, she stared at the clock, at the seconds that ticked away to the end of her life. "I want you to leave the building. Now."

"I'm not going anywhere without you."

"You can't save me," she said. "A.J. made sure of that. She put a second detonator—a balance switch—under my chair."

His gaze was steady and sure as he said, "Trust me."

She managed a watery smile. "You know I hate when you say that."

"Yeah," he agreed. "But explanations will have to wait until I get you out of here."

Then he ducked his head beneath the chair.

One minute and seventeen seconds.

She swallowed. "Do you have any idea what you're doing?"

"I wouldn't be risking both of our lives here if I didn't."

One minute and eight seconds.

"I was something of a demolitions expert with the rangers," he told her. "I had extensive training in the building and disarming of bombs."

"Now you're talking to me about your career?" She didn't know whether to laugh or cry at the absurdity of the situation.

"It wasn't relevant before."

Fifty-six seconds.

"You left the army a long time ago."

"Some things you never forget," he said. "Like riding a bike—or sex."

Forty-nine seconds.

She closed her eyes, unable to continue watching the seconds tick away. "I can't believe you're making jokes at a time like this."

She felt his hand on her knee and opened her eyes to see he was sitting up again, a ball of something resembling putty in his hand.

"C4?" she asked.

He nodded, already turning his attention to the knotted rope that bound her ankles together.

"What about the other bombs?" she asked, noting that the timer continued to count down.

Thirty-two seconds.

He freed her wrists from their restraints. "It looks like

they're hardwired to the same timer. I'm not going to have time to disarm them."

She slipped out of the chair and into his arms. He held her tight against his chest for just a second.

Shannon's gaze slid to the timer.

Twenty-six seconds.

"Those other bombs are going to detonate on schedule," he told her. "So I'd suggest we get out of here. Now."

She didn't need to be told twice.

They'd pushed through the opening in the boards and were racing away from the building when time ran out.

Chapter 16

The blast hurtled him through the air.

Mike felt the whoosh of air escape from his lungs as he slammed down onto the concrete, the force of the impact like being hit by a wrecking ball. His ears were ringing, and every muscle and bone in his body ached, but he ignored the pain and pushed himself to his knees.

"Shannon." He tried to shout, but succeeded only in croaking her name.

She didn't respond.

The only sound he heard over the ringing in his ears was the crackle of the fire as greedy flames consumed the warehouse.

He felt something dripping into his eyes, wiped it away. He didn't realize it was blood. He wasn't thinking about anything but Shannon.

Through sheer force of will, he managed to stagger to his feet. He turned around and finally spotted her.

She was lying only a few feet away, still and silent.

He stumbled over to her, dropped to the ground beside her.

He'd never known such a deep and primitive fear as he felt in that moment, when he saw the crimson stain on the concrete. He turned her gently to examine the wound at the back of her head, the angry gash that continued to spill her blood.

He felt his throat tighten as he lifted a shaky hand to check her pulse. It was weak but steady.

"Hold on, Shannon. Please, hold on."

He could barely speak around the tightness of his throat. But there was so much he needed to say, so many things to tell her. All he managed was a whispered, "I'm sorry."

He was sorry for so many things. For not realizing sooner that she'd left the hotel. For letting Lisa drag out their confrontation. For not disabling the igniter fast enough. For failing, in so many ways, to protect her and keep her safe.

He hadn't let himself feel the fear when he'd gone into the warehouse. He hadn't let himself think about the fact that whether Shannon lived or died depended on how he handled the situation. He hadn't let himself watch the seconds tick away on the clock as he'd disabled the bomb with steady hands. He hadn't considered the possibility of failure. He'd ruthlessly controlled all of his emotions.

He couldn't control his emotions now. With every second that passed, his guilt weighed heavier and the fear sliced deeper. Too many endless, agonizing seconds passed before he heard the sound of sirens in the distance.

The fire trucks arrived first, then the police and finally the EMTs. Mike rode in the ambulance with Shannon to the hospital, but once they were there, she was whisked away to an exam room and he was firmly steered to the waiting area.

So now he waited…and worried.

"Michael?"

He glanced up to see his sister standing in the entrance to the waiting room. Detective Garcia had already been and gone, reassuring him that Rachel had been rescued from the motel without incident.

Her presence here now confirmed it. Except for the paleness of her skin and the dark circles under her eyes, she looked unaffected by her ordeal. At least he could be grateful for that. He started to cross the room toward her.

She stepped back, shaking her head. "If you touch me right now, I'm going to have a meltdown," she warned. "And you know how I hate to cry in front of witnesses."

"Tough." He took her in his arms. "I just need to know you're okay."

As predicted, her eyes filled with tears, but she nodded. "I am okay. Angry with myself more than anything."

"Why?"

"Because A.J. got the jump on me by pretending to be a lost tourist in need of directions. She even had a series of maps spread over the passenger seat. When I got close enough to look—trying to be helpful—she jabbed me with the needle."

"I should have warned you," Mike said softly. "I'm sorry."

"Did you know she would come after me?"

"Of course not."

"Then don't be stupid."

He smiled. "That might have been more effective if you weren't blubbering."

"I don't blubber," she said indignantly.

He wiped the tears from her face. "Cry-baby."

"Rat."

It was an old, familiar routine, and it reassured him that she really was going to be okay.

"Detective Garcia said you were on your way back to the hotel."

She nodded. "I have to get back soon, but I wanted to find out how Shannon was doing first."

"I don't know," he admitted. "No one will tell me anything."

"I think that's about to change," she said.

He looked up as a tall, thin woman in wire-rimmed glasses and a lab coat stepped into the room. Dr. Elisabeth Finch, according to her name tag. "Mr. Courtland?"

He nodded. "Is Shannon okay?"

"It took seven stitches to close the gash in her head, and she has some nasty cuts and bruises, but that seems to be the worst of it. Amazingly enough, nothing's broken and there don't seem to be any internal injuries."

He exhaled a shaky breath.

"Is she conscious?" Rachel asked.

The doctor shook her head. "Not yet. But that's not unusual. We fully expect her to wake up, we just don't know when that will be."

"Can I see her?" Mike asked.

The doctor frowned as she looked him over. "As soon as you let me take a look at your injuries."

She was walking through a fog, her steps slow and uncertain, her arms stretched out ahead of her, reaching for something she didn't see, couldn't reach. Disjointed images swirled through her mind like unconnected pieces of a jigsaw puzzle.

A warehouse. An island. A boat.

Drugs. Guns. Bombs.

Swimming. Running. Falling.

Lisa. Peart. Michael.

She opened her mouth to speak, but no sound came out. She licked her lips, tried again. "Michael?"

The raspy voice that croaked his name didn't sound familiar, but the warm touch of the hand that covered hers was instantly recognizable.

"I'm here."

Tension she'd been unaware of slowly seeped from her limbs. Her eyelids were heavy, but she managed to ease them open, then blinked slowly.

The fog dissipated into blinding whiteness.

"What—where—"

She sipped gratefully through the straw that was held to her lips, the cool water easing some of the dryness.

"You're in the hospital," Michael explained.

The images fell into place. "The warehouse."

"You remember."

She turned her head to look at him and winced at the pain that reverberated through her head. "Is there a reason I shouldn't?"

"You have a concussion." He leaned over to press his lips gently to her temple. "The force of the explosion…let's just say, I'm glad you're finally awake."

"How long was I unconscious?"

"Forever."

She frowned.

"Okay—a couple of hours," he admitted. "But it seemed like forever."

"You look as if you need medical attention as much as I do," she said, noting the myriad of cuts and scrapes on his arms, the dried blood on his cheek.

"I've been checked out." He indicated the butterfly bandage on his brow. "The rest are just superficial wounds."

"Macho idiot."

He grinned. "Now I know for sure you're okay."

"Not ready for a swim in the Atlantic or willing to battle snakes, but other than that…" She managed a smile.

"Ready for some company?"

"Company?"

He didn't have a chance to answer before the door was pushed open and Rachel peeked in. "Is she awake yet?"

She smiled, relieved by this firsthand evidence that Michael's sister was unscathed despite her altercation with A.J. "Yes, I'm awake."

Rachel came into the room. "I just wanted to make sure you were okay."

"I am," Shannon said, gratefully accepting the pain she felt as proof that she was alive. "How about you?"

"Ready to get back to work."

"Do you ever give yourself a break?" Michael asked his sister.

"Not when there are two hundred guests coming in for an environmental law conference," she said.

"Don't you have a staff to handle check-in?" Shannon asked.

"Of course. But I like to be around in case any problems arise."

"She's another Type-A personality," Michael said.

Shannon smiled at Rachel. "Then I guess I'll see you back at the hotel later."

"I'll look forward to it." Michael's sister hugged her gently. "Maybe I'll even get Dominic to make peanut butter and jelly sandwiches."

"Does anything ever slow her down?" Shannon asked after Rachel had gone.

"I don't think so." He shifted his chair closer to her bed. "Detective Garcia was here earlier."

She turned her head too quickly, closed her eyes against the throbbing pain. "Any news on A.J.?"

"Not yet." Michael brushed her hair away from her forehead, stroked his fingers gently down her cheek. "But he did find your purse and your suitcase."

"Where?"

"In the trunk of Peart's car at the marina."

"Oh. Well. That's good." She cleared her throat, trying to affect a nonchalance she didn't feel. "Having my identification and credit cards back will make it easier to book a flight."

His hand dropped away. "I didn't realize you were still planning to go back right away."

Did he sound disappointed? Did he want her to stay?

Shannon wasn't sure if she was reading his signals correctly or if she was hearing what she wanted to hear. From the beginning, they'd both known she would be going back to Chicago when the situation with A.J. was resolved. There wasn't any reason to change those plans now. But she couldn't help asking, "There isn't any reason for me to stay, is there?"

She held her breath, waiting for his answer.

Before he could respond, there was another knock on the door, and then Natalie and Dylan came in.

Shannon stared at her visitors, torn between the pleasure of seeing her sister and disappointment that Michael hadn't answered her question. "What are you doing here?"

"Checking up on my big sister," Natalie said lightly.

"But—why aren't you in Fairweather? And how did you get here so fast?"

"After talking to you the other day, Natalie wasn't convinced that everything was fine," Dylan explained. "So we decided to come down and see for ourselves."

"Well, everything *is* fine," she said.

"Yeah, that's why you're in the hospital," her sister countered.

"It's a concussion—not sixty-three stitches." She looked pointedly at her sister's arm, still in a sling.

"It's a concussion and seven stitches," Michael interjected. "Plus the nine stitches that were already in your foot."

"I'm *fine,*" Shannon said again. "Or I will be as soon as I can get out of here."

"Why don't you guys go find the doctor?" Natalie suggested.

"Trying to get rid of us?" Dylan asked.

"Yes," his fiancée said, unapologetically.

He grinned and brushed his lips over hers before moving toward the door.

Michael hesitated.

"A.J.'s long gone," Shannon reminded him. "I'm sure I'll be safe if you leave me alone with my sister for a few minutes."

"Okay," he finally agreed. "But I won't go far."

Shannon felt the sense of loss all the way down to her toes as she watched him walk out of the room. She knew he would be back, but she also knew that their time together was almost over.

A.J. was gone and, therefore, so was the threat to Shannon's life. As grateful as she was for that, she wasn't as anxious as she thought she'd be to leave Florida. Because she didn't want to say goodbye to Michael.

"Well," Natalie said.

Shannon turned her attention away from the door to focus on her sister. "Well?" she echoed.

"I'd guess there's been some, uh, progress in your relationship with Michael since we last spoke."

"Some," she agreed casually, conscious of the flush in her cheeks. Then, in a blatant and desperate attempt to change the topic, she asked, "Where's Jack?"

"Don't think you're going to distract me so easily," Natalie warned.

"I just can't believe, after everything that's happened in the past few weeks, he isn't here with you."

"He's safe," her sister said confidently. "Under FBI protection."

"What?"

Natalie grinned. "Dylan's sister is watching him."

"Dylan's sister is with the FBI?"

"*All three* of Dylan's sisters are with the FBI."

"That's got to be a little intimidating."

Natalie nodded. "At least I won't have to worry about anyone stealing the silver from the wedding reception—not with all the badges that will be in attendance."

"Speaking of the wedding," she said. "Have you set a date yet?"

"Three weeks from tomorrow."

Shannon gaped at her.

"And before you ask—no, I'm not pregnant. We just decided—Dylan, Jack and I—that we didn't want to wait any longer to become a real family. And we wanted to make sure we had the wedding before you left for Paris."

She didn't want to think about France or the fact that her new job didn't fill her with the same excitement it had only a week earlier.

"*If* you're still planning on going to Paris," Natalie said, somehow following her sister's unspoken thoughts.

"My plans haven't changed."

"Oh." Natalie's smile couldn't mask her obvious disappointment.

"But I wouldn't miss my little sister's wedding for anything," Shannon promised her.

"Will you be bringing Michael to the wedding?"

She shook her head. "No."

"Why not?"

Because as tempting as it was to think they could have a relationship, it wasn't realistic. They'd been thrown together by the threat to Shannon's life. Now that the threat was gone, there was nothing to keep them together and a whole bunch of factors pushing them apart. Not the least of which was the three thousand miles between Pennsylvania and Paris.

But she didn't share any of those thoughts with her sister, saying instead, "For starters, you just told me when the wedding is. He could already have plans for that day."

"Even if he did, I'm sure he'd change them," Natalie said.

"It's obvious to me—even after only two minutes in the room with both of you—that he cares about you."

"He feels responsible for me, because he was hired to protect me."

"He feels a lot more than that," her sister insisted.

"Whatever he feels—whatever I feel—it could never work."

"Why not?"

"Because he's a Courtland."

Natalie shook her head. "It's his name, not his identity. And you're not shallow enough to judge him on the basis of his wealth just because Doug made you feel like you couldn't fit into that world."

"Maybe I am."

Her sister's eyes narrowed. "Or maybe your feelings for him are a lot deeper than you want to admit."

"And maybe you need to accept that not everything in life leads to a happily-ever-after," she chided her sister.

Natalie pouted. "I just want you to be happy."

"I'll be happy when I get out of here."

Shannon couldn't sleep.

After spending only a few nights in Michael's bed, she was finding it next to impossible to sleep without him.

She knew he wasn't far away. He'd only gone down to the police station to check in with Detective Garcia and get an update on the search for A.J., but she wished he was here.

Tomorrow she would be on her way back to Chicago.

She'd anguished over her decision to leave, but in the end she'd decided she should go. She'd intended to discuss her plans with Michael, and she'd been willing to be persuaded to spend another couple of days—even another week—with him.

But when they'd gone back to his room after dinner in the hotel dining room with Natalie and Dylan, Michael had turned around and walked out again. Abruptly and inexplicably.

So Shannon had booked her flight, deciding there was no point in delaying the inevitable. But she wanted this one last night with Michael. Another night of memories to take with her when she was gone.

At last she heard the soft click of the door opening and then closing again.

He didn't switch on any of the lights, probably assuming she was sleeping. She listened to the comforting sounds of his presence, deeply attuned to his movements—the clink of glass on wood, the splash of liquid into the glass, the deep swallow, the long exhale.

"Did they find A.J.?" she asked softly.

The clink of glass on wood again, silent footsteps, then the dip of the mattress as he sat beside her, and the gloriously welcome feel of his fingers brushing over her cheek.

"You should be sleeping." His voice was tight, strained.

"I was waiting for you."

"I posted security outside the door so you wouldn't need to worry," he reminded her.

"I wasn't worried." She sat up to wrap her arms around him. "Just waiting."

"Oh."

She let her head rest on his shoulder. "Are you coming to bed?"

"Yeah." But he moved out of her embrace and returned to the other side of the room again to down the rest of his whiskey. "They arrested A.J."

She exhaled slowly and climbed out from under the covers. "I was afraid they wouldn't find her. That I'd never know for certain it was over."

"It's finally over," he told her.

But she heard the undercurrents of anger and frustration in his voice.

"You were right." He picked up his glass again, frowned

to find it was empty. "That whole unlikely scenario about A.J. choosing to seek revenge through you because of me."

The anger and frustration suddenly made sense. "You saw her?"

"Yeah. And she admitted that she couldn't ignore the irony of my being with you."

"That doesn't make it your fault, Michael."

"She wanted revenge on your sister—she probably wouldn't even have considered you a worthy target if I hadn't been there." He slammed the glass down so hard she was surprised it didn't shatter. "You were almost killed. Rachel was almost killed. Because of me."

"We were almost killed because of A.J. We're alive because of you."

He remained silent, unconvinced.

"Your sister sent up a bottle of champagne," she told him. "With a note that said 'Get over it.'"

His chuckle was strained. "That sounds like Rachel."

"It sounds like pretty good advice to me." She lifted herself on her toes, ignoring the twinge of the stitches pulling in her foot, and pressed her lips to his.

He resisted, for about two seconds. Then, with a shuddering sigh that reverberated through the length of his body, he wrapped his arms around her, pulling her tight against him and devouring her mouth with his own.

As his tongue plunged deep into her mouth, she tasted the heady tang of the whiskey he'd drunk and the even more intoxicating flavor of his desire. His hands were hard, his fingers gripping her hips. She felt the press of his erection low against her belly, grinding into her, and the answering flood of heat through her veins.

It was only now, experiencing this fierce and almost violent need, that she realized he'd been holding back all the other times they'd made love.

Not that she'd had any complaints. In fact, she'd marveled at the contrast of torturously gentle caresses and endlessly slow kisses from a man of such physical strength and take-charge personality. She'd never felt so completely loved, so thoroughly cherished, as she did with him.

And she'd never guessed at the depth of passion he'd kept under tight control until it was unleashed.

It was both staggering and empowering to be wanted with such intensity, equally startling to realize that she could want as much. It was a whole new—and wholly arousing—experience.

Until, as quickly as he'd lost control, he pulled it back again.

His hands gentled and his mouth eased from hers. Exhaling a long, unsteady breath, he stepped away. "You said something about champagne."

Emotions welled up inside her. Disappointment. Frustration. Anger. Need.

He'd given her just a teasing glimpse, a tantalizing taste, of something that was so much more than what they'd already shared, and then he'd taken it away. Because he didn't think she could handle it.

Yes, she could read the reason as clearly as the desire that still smoldered in his gaze. And while understanding tempered her anger, it fueled her frustration. He'd been making decisions for her for too long now.

"Dammit, Michael. I'm not fragile."

"I think you've proven that more than once over the past several days."

"Then stop treating me as if I'm going to break."

She closed the distance he'd put between them, then took his hand and brought it to her breast. "I want you to touch me."

His eyes were dark, dangerous. "You don't know what you're asking."

"I know exactly what I'm asking." She started to undo his shirt, wanting—no needing—to feel the heat of his skin against hers. "I'm asking you to make love with me, this time with no holding back."

She'd only managed the first three buttons when his hands stilled her movements.

"I can't. I don't want to hurt you, Shannon."

She heard the strain in his voice, knew that his rigid control was costing him.

Her own throat tightened. Had anyone ever considered her needs before their own? Had anyone ever taken so much care with her?

"You won't hurt me." She made the statement with absolute trust and complete confidence. "So long as you don't turn away, you won't hurt me."

He'd been terrified for her.

It was something Mike would admit only to himself, only now.

When he'd realized she was no longer in her hotel room, that she'd gone to meet A.J., he'd thought he was going to lose her. He'd forced his mind clear of emotion and focused his thoughts on doing what needed to be done.

Now, more than twelve hours later, A.J. was in prison and Shannon had been released from the hospital. But he couldn't forget that he'd almost lost her today. If any one of a dozen variables had gone wrong, she would have died. If he'd been mistaken about her being at the warehouse. If he hadn't got there in time to get the remote detonator from A.J. If he hadn't neutralized the balance switch.

She was finally safe, but there was still a lot of unresolved fear and frustration churning through his system. He was sure he'd never experienced such violent emotions as he had today, and he knew he wasn't in control of them yet. If he touched her now, if he took what she was offering…

He couldn't.

Despite her assurance, she couldn't possibly understand what she was asking of him. She didn't know what he was capable of right now.

Shannon was watching him, waiting for his response.

"You're really starting to annoy me, Michael."

There was a hint of steel beneath the softly spoken words that set off warning bells in his mind. But he was still unprepared for her next move, was stunned when she took hold of the two sides of his shirt and tore it open.

The sound of popping buttons and rending fabric tore at the last of his restraint. The touch of her hands, searching and eager on his bare skin, obliterated all reason. Need—primal and unstoppable—took over.

He crushed his mouth down on hers, hot and hungry.

She didn't hesitate to respond, meeting his demands with her own.

His hands slid over the silk nightshirt she wore, then under it. He filled his palms with her breasts, his thumbs stroking over the peaked nipples. He swallowed her moan.

She already had her hands inside his pants, reaching for him. He felt the coolness of her fingers wrap around his heated arousal and nearly lost it.

He broke the kiss only long enough to whisk off her nightshirt and shed the rest of his own clothes.

Then their mouths fused again and they fell together, a tangle of needs both indescribable and undeniable.

She rolled on top of him to straddle his body, then lowered herself to take him deep inside her. His vision hazed. He gripped her hips, a desperate and futile attempt to restrain her movements, establish some control.

But control had already slipped away, leaving only a desperate and greedy need. He thrust upward as she glided down, their bodies no longer their own but two parts of a whole locked together in a frenzied race to the final peak. Faster and faster, until he felt the tightening of her muscles around him. The rhythmic spasms of her release were more than he could stand, and he leaped over the edge with her.

They were still on the floor.

Shannon was still on top, nestled against the hard length of Michael's body. She was thoroughly satisfied and completely spent.

"I think there's a bed over there somewhere." She lifted a hand to gesture vaguely in the darkness.

"We'll find it later."

She smiled at the lazy contentment in his voice.

A heartbeat passed, then two, then he asked, "Should I apologize for ravishing you on the floor?"

"Only if you want to annoy me."

She felt the vibration of his chuckle beneath her cheek.

"Okay, what if I thank you for letting me ravish you on the floor?"

"Better," she said. "Although I'm not really clear on who ravished whom."

"Good point."

She sighed blissfully as his fingertips traced a slow path down her spine. He had the most incredible hands. And the most amazing body. A body that even now was beginning to show signs of renewed life. Definite signs of life.

She felt the stirring of arousal deep in her own belly and pressed her lips to the side of his neck. "Do you want to ravish or be ravished this time?"

He chuckled again. "I think this time we'll try something a little different."

"Oh?" She lifted her head to look at him, definitely intrigued by his suggestion.

In a movement so quick she wasn't sure how it happened, she was in his arms and he was carrying her toward the bed.

"What are you doing?"

"I think I've already shown you how much I want you and need you. This time—" he kissed her softly "—I'm going to show you how much I love you."

The words weren't new. He'd said them to her before. But this time, with her body warming from the heat of his touch and her mind fogged by his kisses, her heart came perilously close to believing.

Damn him, she thought furiously. She didn't want the complication of emotions—his or her own. She was perfectly content with the reality of her life.

Or at least she had been, until he'd come along.

But now, in his arms…suddenly she wanted everything he was offering. And more.

Chapter 17

Mike awoke again with the uncomfortable feeling that something wasn't quite right. Not really alarm, but a niggling sense of unease. This time, however, he knew what the problem was as soon as he opened his eyes.

Shannon was hovering by the desk, pen in hand, worrying her bottom lip with her teeth. She was fully dressed, and a quick survey of the room revealed her suitcase by the door.

"Should I be grateful you were at least going to leave a note?"

She started guiltily. "I, uh, didn't want to wake you."

"Why not?"

"Because it was late when you came in last night and—"

"And later still before either of us got to sleep," he reminded her.

Their lovemaking the previous night had been unlike anything he'd ever experienced. It wasn't just the joining together of their bodies, but the forging of an emotional connection between them. A connection that had obviously scared the hell out of her.

"That's why I didn't want to wake you. I knew you'd be tired and—"

"I am tired," he interrupted. "And pissed off."

She winced.

"Where are you going?"

"To the airport. I've got a two-o'clock flight to Chicago."

He peered at the bedside clock. It wasn't even 8:00 a.m.

"I was going to stop by my mom's on the way," she said, answering his unspoken question.

"You made these plans last night?"

She nodded.

"And you didn't bother to tell me."

"Because I was hoping to avoid exactly this kind of confrontation."

"You'd rather run away than face your feelings."

She sighed. "My life has been complete chaos for the past week. How can I even know what my feelings are?"

"By listening to your heart."

He was disappointed, although not surprised, when she shook her head. Emotions were too messy and unpredictable for her. Shannon the scientist wanted more empirical data, hard proof.

But he'd already put his heart on the line—there wasn't anything more he could say or do. And he sure as hell wasn't going to beg. If she was determined to go back to Chicago, he wasn't going to stand in her way.

"I'll take you to the airport," he said shortly.

She shook her head. "That's not necessary—"

"I'll take you," he said again, sliding out of bed and heading into the bathroom. "Give me ten minutes to shower and dress and we can go."

She was going to have to introduce him to her mother.

She was thirty-three years old and she was nervous about taking a man to meet her mother.

She would keep it brief, Shannon decided. A quick hello and goodbye, drop off the gift, and head to the airport.

Except it wasn't her mother but Deborah's new husband who answered the door.

"Hi." She forced a smile, decidedly uncomfortable facing a stranger who was now her stepfather.

"Shannon." Ray's smile was quick and easy as he reached for her hand to draw her into the house. "Your mother will be so pleased to see you."

Before she could protest that they couldn't stay, he called over his shoulder, "Deb, your daughter's here. With a friend."

"Um, this is Michael," she said, deciding that *friend* was as appropriate a description as anything else. "Michael, this is Ray Sutherland."

The two men shook hands.

Then Ray said to Shannon, "Deb's been so worried—we both have."

She shifted guiltily. "I should have called, but I didn't think you'd have heard about what happened and I didn't want to worry Mom."

"Natalie and Dylan stopped by last night," he said. "They told us."

Which only made Shannon feel even guiltier.

Then her mother came into the room, her eyes bright with tears. She wrapped her arms around her daughter's shoulders. "We were going to come by the hotel to see you today, but this is even better."

Shannon felt her own throat grow tight as she returned the hug. "Congratulations on your marriage."

Deborah laughed and released her. "Of all the things that have happened in the past week…" She shook her head and turned to Michael. "I'm guessing you're the private investigator who saved my daughter's life."

Shannon caught the slight grimace, knew he wasn't comfortable having been cast in the role of the hero. But he offered his hand to her mother, anyway.

"Michael Courtland," he said.

"Of Courtland Hotels?" Deborah asked immediately.

Michael was less successful in masking the grimace this time. "Yes," he admitted.

"Please, come in to the dining room," Ray invited. "We were just about to sit down to a late breakfast."

"We're actually on our way to the airport," Shannon said.

"You're going back to Chicago already?" The disappointment in her mother's voice was obvious, causing Shannon another twinge of guilt.

"She has a two-o'clock flight," Michael said.

"Then you have time for breakfast," she insisted.

And so it happened that Shannon ended up seated across from Michael at an antique table in Ray's formal dining room, nibbling on flaky pastries and drinking mimosas made with freshly squeezed orange juice.

She'd expected it would be awkward, but after those initial introductions had been made, it wasn't. Instead, she found herself drawn into conversation with her mother's new husband. Even more surprising, she found herself taking an immediate liking to the man, so much so that she was genuinely sorry when Michael said, "It's almost noon."

She glanced at the clock, surprised to find that the time had passed so quickly.

"We should go if you don't want to miss your flight." It was a question as much as a statement.

She pushed her chair away from the table. "I don't."

"You're welcome to come back and visit anytime," Ray told her. "We have plenty of room."

She smiled and thanked him, impulsively hugging him goodbye. Then she went through the same routine with her mother, and finally she and Michael were back in his car, on their way to the airport.

Unlike the scene in the dining room, this *was* awkward— the silence between them tense and unnatural.

"I didn't realize you'd bought them a wedding gift," Michael said at last.

Shannon shrugged. "It seemed the appropriate thing to do. I didn't expect my mother would get all misty-eyed over a crepe pan."

"It wasn't the pan. It was the fact you'd remembered her telling you that Ray makes her crepes for Sunday-morning breakfast in bed."

"Yeah, it's become a tradition in the whole six weeks they've been together." But her response lacked the sarcasm she'd intended, because she'd seen how attuned her mom and Ray were to each other.

"I think their relationship proves that time is irrelevant when it comes to love," he said pointedly.

She shrugged again.

"You didn't like your new stepfather?"

"I did," she admitted. "And I think he'll be good for her."

"You sound surprised."

"When she first told me she was getting married—for the fifth time—I didn't know what to think."

He turned into the airport parking lot. "I think she deserves credit for having the courage to open up her heart again."

"Courage?" she said doubtfully.

"I thought you had the same fortitude, the way you seemed to confront obstacles head-on. Escaping from Peart's yacht, facing him from the wrong end of an automatic, your show-down with A.J."

He found a vacant spot and steered into it.

"I was furious with you for that. For putting your life in danger. For not trusting me to handle the situation."

"It wasn't a matter of trust."

"Yeah. I finally figured that out."

She opened her door, stepped out of the car.

He met her at the back of the vehicle. "Although I have to admit I was still stumped as to your reasoning until I had my little chat with A.J. last night."

"I need my suitcase," she said pointedly.

"In a minute." He leaned back against the trunk, folded his arms over his chest. "You went to meet A.J. because she threatened me. And the only reason I could think of for you to risk your life to save mine is that you love me."

She refused to respond to the challenge in his tone. Instead, she glanced at her watch—a ten-dollar purchase from the discount pharmacy across from the hotel. "I still have to check in and get through security."

He stared at her for a long moment, then finally turned to unlock the trunk. She exhaled a silent breath as she slung her carry-on over her shoulder.

"I'm not going to chase you, Shannon. And I'm not going to beg. If you don't have the guts to give us a chance, then you're not the woman I thought you were."

She picked up her suitcase. She didn't hesitate. If she did, she knew that all of her resolve would crumble. "I have to go."

His gaze was cool and guarded as he took a step back. "Goodbye, Shannon."

"Goodbye, Michael."

She held the tears in check throughout the journey back to Chicago. It was only when she was finally at her apartment, inside the familiarity of her own world, that she let herself cry.

She cried tears of relief and regret, but mostly she cried because she knew Michael was right. She was a coward. She loved him, more than she would have thought possible, but she was too afraid to let him know. Too afraid to give him the chance to break her heart.

Only now could she acknowledge that by walking away she'd broken it all by herself.

She was being watched.

Shannon fussed with the train of Natalie's dress, straightened her veil and tried to shake the feeling that prickled the hairs at the back of her neck.

It was the same feeling she'd had on the beach in Florida a few weeks earlier, a feeling she'd disregarded as paranoia. Only later had she found out that her fear was valid, that Michael had been watching her for Dylan. And Peart had been watching Michael watching her.

But Peart was dead, A.J. was in jail, and Michael…

Her heart gave a little sigh of longing.

A sigh she hadn't realized she'd let escape until Natalie turned around. "Is everything okay, Shan?"

She forced a smile. "Everything is just about perfect. My little sister is married to the man she loves—a man who loves both her and her son. Mom and her new husband are here to celebrate the occasion, and I'm actually starting to think that Ray might be the right man for her."

"I didn't think you believed in 'the right man' theory," Natalie said.

Shannon shrugged and picked up her glass of champagne. "It's hard to remain a skeptic when I can see how happy she is—how happy you are."

"What about you?"

"I'm fine." She forced another smile, hoping that if she said it often enough, she'd start to believe it.

"Have you seen Michael since you left Florida?"

Trust Natalie to zoom right in on the topic she least wanted to discuss.

Shannon shook her head, keeping the smile firmly in place. No, she hadn't seen him or heard from him. It had been three weeks—which was three times longer than they'd actually been together—and she couldn't stop thinking about him. And she was frustrated by this inability to get over her infatuation.

Because she knew now that what she felt for Michael was nothing more than infatuation. She'd overreacted to an emotionally charged situation and mistakenly interpreted her feelings. Logically she knew it couldn't be love.

And yet, after three weeks, he continued to interfere with her thoughts and haunt her dreams. Her heart continued to ache. Logical or not, she was beginning to suspect that her feelings for him went a lot deeper than she wanted to admit.

"You're in love with him, aren't you?" Natalie asked gently. Then, as if anticipating her sister's response, she continued, "You can deny it. You can even move across the ocean and pretend it doesn't exist, but you can't change what's in your heart."

"Why is it that everyone thinks they know my feelings better than I do?"

Natalie lifted a perfectly arched brow. "Everyone?"

"You. Mom. Michael." Shannon swallowed another mouthful of champagne.

"He knows you're in love with him?"

She set the half-empty glass down. "He *thinks* I'm in love with him."

"Is that why you were in such a hurry to leave Miami?"

"I left because I had a plane to catch."

"And it would have been completely impulsive and irrational to have changed those plans," Natalie guessed.

"What's the point in making plans if you don't intend to follow through with them?" Shannon countered reasonably.

"I had a plan when I moved to Fairweather," Natalie admitted. "To build a career and make a home for my son. I didn't want anything else, least of all the complications of a relationship.

"Then I met Dylan. I tried to deny the attraction between us. I was determined, for once in my life, to be like you—rational and reasonable and responsible."

She smiled at the memory. "My determination was no match for the chemistry. And although it hasn't been all champagne and roses, there's no denying that he's the best thing that ever happened to me."

The heartfelt emotion in her sister's voice brought tears to Shannon's own eyes. Or maybe it was the mention of champagne and roses and the memories of the first night she'd spent at the Courtland Hotel with Michael.

"It scared me, at first," Natalie continued. "The way I felt about Dylan. I knew that if I gave him my heart, I would be giving him the power to break it. I didn't know I would also be giving him the power to heal it."

Shannon blinked away the moisture in her eyes as the lights dimmed and the band launched into the opening notes of the first song. She saw Dylan moving toward them, the love he felt for his bride shining clearly in his eyes, and her heart gave another little sigh. "If I never said it before, I'm really glad you left Chicago."

Natalie's smile was brilliant as she accepted her husband's outstretched hand. "Me, too."

Shannon watched them walk hand in hand to the dance floor. Both her sister and brother-in-law had taken circuitous routes to get to this point, both had valid reasons for being wary of making such a commitment. Natalie had been a twenty-four-year-old law student when she got pregnant by a man who'd failed to tell her that he already had a family, and Dylan's first wife had been pregnant with their child when she was brutally murdered. Yet somehow, despite the obstacles in their paths, Natalie and Dylan had found their way to each other, and found a way to carve a new path together.

It takes courage to open up your heart despite having had it broken before.

Did she have that kind of courage? Was she willing to risk her heart again?

She'd walked away from the man she loved rather than admit her feelings because she was afraid to let herself be vulnerable, afraid that he might hurt her. Instead of taking a chance, she'd packed her suitcases and bought a plane ticket to France. As if a job in Paris might somehow compensate for everything that was missing from her life. As if seeing the Eiffel Tower could make her forget about Michael.

She knew now that nothing would make her forget, and not even moving to Paris would stop her from loving him.

She waited until the song was finished then intercepted the newlyweds on the dance floor. "I'm sorry," she apologized. "But I have to go."

"Go?" Dylan queried.

Natalie's brows drew together. "Now?"

"Yes," she responded to both of their questions.

"But—oh." Whatever her sister saw in Shannon's eyes must have revealed her intentions, because Natalie abandoned her protest and smiled. "Go."

"I am sorry, but—"

"No," Natalie interrupted. "No apologies. Just be happy."

Shannon managed a tremulous smile. "I think maybe I will be."

She lifted the long skirt of her taffeta gown and hurried toward the doors, her heart pounding a frantic rhythm against her ribs.

Oh God—she was doing it again. Acting on impulse, not stopping to think of the consequences. But she'd spent the past few weeks thinking, and nothing had changed.

She burst through the French doors and onto the patio, skidding to a halt on the flagstones.

He was there.

Michael.

Leaning against the stone wall that marked the perimeter of the patio, a flute of champagne in his hand.

"In a hurry to catch another plane?" he asked.

"No. I, um…" She clamped her jaw shut as her brain scrambled to find the words. Any words. "I was on my way to find you."

"Why?"

She couldn't read anything in his tone or his body language. He sounded casual, completely relaxed, while everything inside her was twisting into intricate knots.

"Because I, um, realized there was something I forgot to tell you."

Finally he set down his glass and moved toward her. Some of her tension started to ease as he took her hands in his, linking their fingers together.

She took a deep breath and finally said, "I love you."

He started to speak, but she didn't give him a chance to respond.

"And," she hurried on, knowing that if she didn't put all of her feelings on the line right now, her courage might falter, "I owe you an apology."

"An apology?" He lifted a brow.

She took a deep breath. "I said I trusted you, but I didn't. Not completely.

"I trusted you with my life, unconditionally, but not with my heart. Loving you, being loved by you, required a leap of faith I just wasn't ready to take.

"Part of that stems from the failure of my first marriage," she admitted. "I'd put my heart on the line once before and I was terrified to do so again.

"Not because you're anything like Doug," she said quickly. Although she might have worried about that at first, she'd spent enough time with Michael to know it wasn't true. The only similarities between her ex-husband and this man were superficial. "But because I love you so much more than I ever loved him.

"When I fell in love with him, I was young and more than a little naive. Easily dazzled by his charm and sophistication, too trusting to see through his empty promises.

"What I feel for you is so much sharper and deeper. It's a need that goes straight through my soul."

She tipped her head to look up at him, hoping she could somehow make him understand. "Loving someone that much is a terrifying feeling."

His lips curved slowly. "I know."

He did know, she realized, because he loved her the same way. And, as her bruised and battered heart began to heal, she knew her sister was right.

"Are you going to let me off the hook that easily?" she asked softly.

He tugged her closer, letting go of her hands to loop his arms around her waist. "I don't think the last few weeks have been easy for either of us."

"I can't begin to tell you how miserable I've been since I said goodbye to you."

His lips feathered over her temple. "Do you want to know how I've spent my time since I left you at the airport in Miami?"

"How?"

"Trying to talk myself out of being in love with a woman who obviously wasn't my type."

She pulled back. "That's hardly flattering."

"I was annoyed with you for walking away so easily and taking my heart with you. So I tried to convince myself that I was better off without you, that a relationship between us never could have worked out, anyway.

"And I realized you really weren't my type." He smiled again. "Which is probably why you are exactly the right woman for me."

"Is there supposed to be some kind of logic in there somewhere?" she asked.

"None of the other women I'd dated ever made me feel a fraction of the passion you've brought to my life," he explained. "And I don't just mean physical passion, I mean passion for life and for living. You stand up to me, you challenge me, and you inspire me."

He slid his hands up her back, drawing her close again, closer. "I don't want to lose that. I don't want to lose *you*."

Then finally he lowered his head and kissed her. Softly, slowly, but with a devastating thoroughness and depth of emotion that made her tremble.

"I've missed you, Shannon."

"I missed you, too," she admitted. "I missed you before I even got on that plane. But I was determined to walk away, determined to stick with the plans I'd made for my life."

"And now?" he asked.

She felt the nerves jumping in her belly, but she was determined to put it all on the line. Not just her love, but her hopes and her dreams for a future with Michael.

"I still want to go to Paris," she said.

"I could live in Paris."

She was surprised by his quick response, more surprised to realize it was obviously something he'd already considered. "You'd move to France?"

"I'd move anywhere to be with you," he told her.

She didn't doubt that he meant it, and she was awed by the depth of love that would allow him to make such an offer. A depth of love equaled only by that in her own heart.

"I said I want to *go* to Paris, not *move* to Paris. I was thinking we could spend our honeymoon there."

"Honeymoon?"

"The romantic getaway that usually follows a wedding," she explained.

He lifted a brow. "Are you proposing to me?"

"Yes, I am. Should I get down on one knee?"

"No, I don't want you on your knee. I want you beside me—for the rest of our lives."

She smiled. "Is that a yes?"

"That is very definitely a yes."

And he sealed the promise with a kiss.

* * * * *

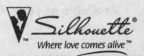

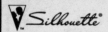

INTIMATE MOMENTS™

Don't miss this exciting and
emotional journey from

Michelle
Celmer

OUT OF SIGHT

#1398

Available December 2005

After a treacherous life in a crime family,
divorce counselor Abigale Sullivan finally
found a place to call home in the bucolic
wilds of Colorado. Her dream world came
screeching to a halt when FBI special agent
Will Bishop came after her and demanded
she testify against a brutal criminal. Now
she had a choice to make: flee again, or
risk her life for the man she loved.

Available at your favorite retail outlet.

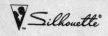

INTIMATE MOMENTS™

New York Times
bestselling author

MAGGIE SHAYNE

brings you

Feels Like Home

the latest installment in
The Oklahoma All-Girl Brands.

When Jimmy Corona returns to Big Falls, Oklahoma,
shy Kara Brand shakes with memories of a youthful crush.
He targets her as the perfect wife for him and stepmother
for his ailing son. But Jimmy's past life as a Chicago cop
brings danger in his wake. It's a race against the clock
as Jimmy tries to save his family in time to tell Kara how
much he's grown to love her, and how much he wants
to stay in this place that truly feels like home.

Available this December at your favorite retail outlet.

COMING NEXT MONTH

#1395 FEELS LIKE HOME—Maggie Shayne
The Oklahoma All-Girl Brands

When Chicago cop Jimmy Corona returned to his small hometown, all he wanted was to find a mother to care for his son while he took down a perp. Shy Kara Brand, who'd once had a youthful crush on him, was the obvious choice. But danger soon followed Jimmy to Big Falls, and only Kara stood between his little boy and certain death....

#1396 MOST WANTED WOMAN—Maggie Price
Line of Duty

Police sergeant Josh McCall came to Sundown, Oklahoma, for some R & R and fell for an alluring bartender with a dark past and an irresistible face. Josh was determined to uncover Regan Ford's secrets despite the distrust he saw in her eyes. Would persistence and energy win this troubled woman's heart…or endanger both their lives?

#1397 SECRETS OF THE WOLF—Karen Whiddon
The Pack

Brie Beswich came to Leaning Tree for answers about her mother's tragic death. But all she found was more questions and hints of an earth-shaking secret. The small town's handsome sheriff seemed to know more than he was saying. As danger loomed, could Brie trust this mysterious man and the passion that threatened to consume them both?

#1398 OUT OF SIGHT—Michelle Celmer

After a treacherous life in a crime family, divorce counselor Abbi Sullivan finally found a place to call home in the bucolic wilds of Colorado. Her dream world came screeching to a halt when FBI special agent Will Bishop came after her and demanded she testify against a brutal criminal. Now she had a choice to make: flee again, or risk her life for the man she loved.

SIMCNM1105